THESE BOOTS WERE MADE FOR STRUTTING

These Boots Were Made For
STRUTTING

Lisa Cach
Gemma Halliday
Melanie Jackson

LOVE SPELL NEW YORK CITY

LOVE SPELL®

May 2008

Published by

Dorchester Publishing Co., Inc.
200 Madison Avenue
New York, NY 10016

ISBN 10: 0-505-52758-8
ISBN 13: 978-0-505-52758-5

Visit us on the web at www.dorchesterpub.com.

These Boots Were Made For
STRUTTING

TABLE OF CONTENTS

LISA CACH

A Rose by
Any Other Name

*To Melanie, who taught me
the beauty of shoes.*

CHAPTER ONE

Kelsey hid behind a goat and spied on her employee.

Plump, fifty-six-year-old Bridget was being dusted with kisses by her husband. He pressed lips to her eyelids as if he were worshipping an idol, both giving and receiving blessings with his touch. He pressed his brow to hers, the two of them joined gazes, and the soft murmurs of their devotion drifted up the weedy slope to Kelsey.

Kelsey sniffled. It was the same routine every morning, corny and excessive, and enough to make her sick with yearning for the same thing in her own life.

The goat, Little Bastard, said, "Nay."

Kelsey wiped her nose on the back of her sleeve. "I can *too* have that," she whispered. "Someday. If someone as weird as me exists, then there's got to be an equally weird guy out there for me."

"Nay."

"Shut up. Stupid goat."

Little Bastard narrowed his yellow eyes and abruptly moved away. Kelsey lost her balance and plopped onto her butt amidst the thorny brambles, her yelp drawing the eyes of Bridget *et homme*.

3

Bridget's husband waved uncertainly. Bridget said something to him, and after one more doubting look up the slope to Kelsey, he got back into his ancient, bumper-stickered Volvo and putt-putted off to work. Bridget waved until he was out of sight.

"I *will* find someone," Kelsey whispered.

Little Bastard, whose tether had stopped him from completing his offended exit, stared at Kelsey over his shoulder.

"I will! He'll be awkward and geeky, just like me. And shy." She painted a mental portrait of her dream mate: pale, unmuscled, a look of concern in his eyes. She saw him in an old T-shirt, camping shorts, and Teva sandals, carrying a canvas grocery bag. They'd go to a farmers' market, and then cook their squash and chard in the kitchen they'd built together out of recycled materials. And when the meal was over and the wine had been drunk—just one glass each, because they liked it for the taste, not the effect—they would slowly undress each other in the moonlight and he would trace his shaking fingertips over her breasts . . .

Little Bastard bleated a firm pronouncement of his low opinion of her chances.

Kelsey stared into the caprine eyes. "He's out there, and I'll find him."

The goat shook his head, ears flapping, and turned his attention to the consumption of blackberry vines, every line of his goaty body declaring he was done with her.

Kelsey tore her overalls loose from the thorns and

trotted down the slope to Bridget, who was donning work gloves and a sun hat. "Hi," she said, and found herself unable to say more. Bridget had worked for her for five weeks now, and this was the start of their second landscaping project together, but Kelsey was still shy with her, the mere act of speaking to an unfamiliar human scattering the thoughts in her head and filling her with the certainty that, even if by happy chance a word did manage to emerge from her lips, it would be the wrong one.

It didn't help that Kelsey was the twenty-seven-year-old boss of a woman who had grown children.

"What a lovely location!" Bridget said. "I didn't know this little neighborhood even existed, and so close to the city. You could walk to a dozen restaurants from here, but it feels like you're on the edge of the wilderness."

"The property backs onto a park." Kelsey pointed up the hill. "Just over the ridge."

Bridget smiled gently, like a mother humoring a child. "I'm sure it does. Well, that does explain the quiet, doesn't it? But what a strange house to build in the midst of it all!"

Kelsey turned around and looked at the 1930s Art Deco home at the bottom of the slope. It was a long, boxy building in white stucco, with a flat roof. Large windows looked out from the back of the house toward the slope, which had to have been a depressing view for many years, given the wild overgrowth. "The previous owner died here. He was an old man. He lived alone."

"Oh dear, how very sad."

"He built it for his wife. She died before him. Many years before."

"Oh . . ." Bridget pursed her lips in concern, then forced a sunny smile. "But the new owners want a garden! It will be good to bring life to this place. Have the new owners moved in?"

Kelsey nodded. "It's a man. Jack Lovgren."

"Single?"

Kelsey shrugged.

"Young? Old?"

Kelsey shrugged again.

"Didn't you meet with him, go over your landscape design, all that?"

She shook her head. "Everything was e-mail and fax. He travels a lot, for work."

Bridget glanced toward the nearest windows, bare of curtains. The dim shapes of packing boxes and a couch could be seen. In a lowered voice she asked, "Is he home?"

"I don't think so." Kelsey privately wondered why the man was bothering with a house and extravagant landscaping when he was home so seldom. Why not buy a condo in a Seattle highrise, downtown, where he wouldn't have to do any maintenance? He must have more money than sense.

"Then I won't disturb him if I take a peek." Bridget trotted over to the window and pressed her face to the glass, hands cupped round her eyes. "Yes, definitely a bachelor. Why do single men always buy black leather couches? There's some sort of gong hanging on a wood stand. A few cardboard boxes. Nothing much else. Hmm."

"What?"

Bridget came away from the window. "He doesn't look like a man with roots. He'll sell this place within the year."

"You can tell that from looking at his stuff?"

The older woman slowly nodded. "When you get to be my age, you develop a sense about people. It takes only a few clues to know who you're dealing with."

Embarrassment fluttered in Kelsey's chest, and she looked away. What must Bridget understand about *her*? "We should get to work clearing the ground. You go up by Isis and dig out any roots. I'll clear the beds along the house." Isis was another of Kelsey's goats; there were six of them at work on the property, chomping weeds and brush.

"Tell me what we're going to do to this yard," Bridget insisted, not moving. "What does our rootless mystery man want? No, let me guess: a big patio with room for a barbecue, a pergola over a hot tub that he'll use three times, and a bit of lawn on which his future neglected dog can relieve itself." The woman giggled.

Kelsey cracked a smile. Bridget shared her loathing for run-of-the-mill suburban backyards, with their bark dust flower beds and random bits of badly pruned shrubbery. "He wants a Northwest version of a Japanese garden, with a waterfall and pond."

"Really?" Hands on hips, Bridget looked again at the house. "Huh! I wouldn't have thought it. Maybe he saw a photo in a magazine somewhere, next to an ad for barbecues."

"He said in an e-mail he likes visiting Japanese gardens. In Japan."

Bridget sniffed, unwilling to accept defeat. "He must be older than I thought." Her expression brightened. "Or maybe he's gay!"

A little while later, after they got to work, Kelsey grunted under her breath as she wrapped her gloved hands around some ivy. The noonday sun beat down. Sweat trickled between her breasts, smashed flat under her athletic bra. "I'll kill you! Just see if I won't! Suffer, you damned life-sucking, rat-harboring fiend! Die! Die!"

With a muscle-wrenching heave, she yanked the ivy from the ground. Dirt flew into her face, and with it beetles, spiders, and glossy white slug eggs. Kelsey spit grit from her lips and wiped her face on the long sleeve of her SPF forty-five shirt. At least her big orange-tinted prescription goggles had kept the mess out of her eyes.

She squinted along the length of the flower bed against the house. Ivy didn't give up easily. A single fragment of root left in the ground would sprout anew. It was the Hydra of gardening.

She tightened her knee pads and got down on all fours, swearing and muttering as she dug and yanked, squishing the odd cutworm or beetle larva as she worked her way down the bed. Snails she tossed into a covered bucket she dragged along with her. There was a strange satisfaction to the destruction she wrought, her gardening wrath acting as a purging fire upon the earth. The beds beneath her hands and trowel became rich, crumbly brown dirt, virgin soil upon which she would later work her creative magic.

It beat an office job. She was no good at working with people. But plants? She and plants understood each other. Unfortunately, landscaping was not the best career choice for a fair-skinned redhead with a family history of skin cancer. It meant covering every inch of skin, which made for hot work even on a gentle spring day like this.

"Oh, you evil devil," she muttered, as a particularly stubborn length of ivy clung to the ground. "You don't think you're going to get away from *me*, do you? Well, you've got another think coming . . ."

Inside his house, behind a window left ajar for air and a blackout curtain pulled tight against the light, Jack Lovgren thrashed in his bedsheets. Half-asleep and jet-lagged, he struggled to make sense of the female voice muttering murderous obscenities. He was in Japan, his dreaming brain told him. The voice was an angry *oba-san*, one of those fearsome older Japanese women who pushed their way through life. She was mad at him for wearing his shoes on the *tatami*, the woven mats that made up the floors of traditional Japanese houses, and now she was chasing him down the street, swinging a broom.

"You slimy piece of—"

Was she swearing at him in *English*?

Jack peeled open a raw eyeball. He wasn't in the middle of a narrow Tokyo street. He was somewhere dark and unfamiliar, and the cursing voice was coming from behind a backlit curtain.

He stumbled from his bed, angry at the disruption. He'd barely slept for three days, and now that he was finally enjoying some hard-earned rest, some witch started ranting in his ear. "For God's sake, woman, will you shut up?" he yelled and, grabbing the edge of the curtain, yanked it open.

Retina-searing sunlight hit his wincing eyes, and he shut them fully. The witch's cursing was cut off by a shriek that vibrated his eardrums.

"Shut up! For the love of God, shut up!"

The shrieking abruptly stopped.

Jack carefully opened his eyes a slit. On the other side of the window, kneeling in a flower bed with her dirty face three feet from his hips, was a woman in a French legionnaire's hat and enormous orange-tinted goggles. The buggy eyes behind the goggles were fixed firmly to his crotch.

His *naked* crotch.

"Shit!" He grabbed the curtain and pulled it over his privates. "Who the hell are you? What the hell's going on?"

"Are you okay?" a distant female voice called, followed by what he could have sworn was bleating. He squinted up the slope. Was that a goat?

"F-fine!" the goggled woman called over her shoulder. "I'm fine!"

"Who. Are. You?" Jack demanded. And why was there a goat? Was he still asleep? He must be asleep. Why was he dreaming about a goat?

"K-kelsey Safire."

"Who?" he asked, even as the name rang a distant bell. He should know who that was, shouldn't he? He looked out at the half-denuded slope, not recognizing it. Where was he? Not Japan, obviously. He turned and looked at the room.

That was his bed frame and sheet set. His clock was on the bedside table. His lamp.

The fog of sleep finally cleared. "Shit. This is my house."

The gaping woman in front of him was the landscaper he'd hired based on a coworker's recommendation. He'd been so busy, he'd approved her plans and fees with barely a thought, and then scratched her existence from his mind.

"Er. Sorry," he said. "Will you excuse me?"

She nodded, and he yanked the curtains shut.

Great! Just great. What a fabulous first impression, Jack.

He dug his last pair of clean underwear out of his suitcase and pulled them on. He tore open a cardboard box and dumped it on the floor, pawing through the clothes until he found jeans and a T-shirt.

Way to set up a positive working relationship. You gave her something to talk about at her next barbecue, didn't you?

Pants on and personal jewels safely stowed behind two layers of clothing, he paused and blew out a breath. An image popped to mind: Kelsey's eyes, huge behind her tinted goggles, fixed on his crotch. He chuckled.

Forget the stories she would tell her friends: He couldn't wait to tell his own.

He went back to the window and listened from behind the closed curtain. The volume of her voice was down, but she was at it again, muttering curses and threatening dismemberment. He twitched the edge of the curtain aside and peered out. She was digging like a terrier after a rabbit, and looked ready to take a vine between her teeth and shake it to death. When it came free of the ground she flipped it over in front of her and plucked three snails off its leaves, then dragged a bucket closer and dropped them in, one by one, *thunk thunk thunk*. She stared into the bucket, grinning.

"Yesss, eat up, my pretties!" she cackled. "Eat! Eat!"

An odd duck, this one. He should probably go out and talk to her. Introduce himself. Make sure she wasn't freaked out or anything by his yelling at her and waving his morning wood in her face. The last thing he wanted was to go through the bother of hiring a new landscaper.

She didn't *look* freaked out. He shrugged and let the curtain drop. He'd make some coffee first.

Ten minutes later he had a cup in his hand and was congratulating himself for having had the foresight to unpack the machine and coffee canister before taking off on his trip. A box of semistale Cheerios and three cans of chili were the only food in the house, though. The chili had been with him since the late nineties, toted from home to home like a talisman against hunger. He hated canned chili, and hoped never to eat it. Today wasn't going to be the day he broke down, either. He could more easily survive without breakfast than without his morning caffeine.

He glanced at the clock on the microwave. Make that afternoon caffeine.

Through the window he saw Kelsey go by, pushing a wheelbarrow heaped with greenery. She looked busy. He'd talk to her after he checked his messages.

Kelsey worked with fervor, powered by embarrassment and anxiety. At any moment Jack Lovgren would emerge from his house and say something to her, and she would have no idea how to respond. His penis loomed above her in her mind's eye, bold and thick and staring her down with its narrow eye. It was a pink-skinned cobra, freezing her with its gaze. One wrong move and it would . . .

It would . . .

She didn't know what she thought it would do. What *could* it have done? It couldn't even have poked her in the eye, not with her goggles on. She imagined the end of it, pressed against her goggle lens like a lamprey, futilely sucking with its open mouth.

Still, there'd been something deeply threatening about that bobbing bludgeon, not least because the man behind it had been yelling at her.

The encounter had left her with only a vague impression of Lovgren's face. She had a fair memory of his lightly haired, well-defined chest, and narrow hips. His package, however, glowed in her brain like an image on a high-definition plasma screen.

What was the proper response to having a penis waved in one's face? she wondered. Pretend nothing had happened? Make a joke? She was no good at jokes. Any minute now he'd come out and say something apologetic, she'd fumble for words, he'd think she was offended, she'd be unable to explain that no, it was her, she was incapable of normal social interaction, and discomfort and awkwardness would follow them forever after.

She'd better think of a joke, something light and witty. Or maybe naughty and knowing? She patted her cheeks and shook her head, anticipating the disaster to follow.

As the afternoon wore on and Jack did not emerge, Kelsey's tension pulled ever tighter. After much deep thinking, she'd come up with what she was pretty sure was a funny joke. She'd worked it over in her mind, refined it, practiced it on Little Bastard, and now she wanted to use it. But every passing minute brought the possibility that she'd forget some crucial element of the joke before she could unfurl it for Lovgren and ease the tension.

She finished clearing the flower bed and went to help Bridget and the goats on the slope. She could see Lovgren in his kitchen, sitting on a bar stool at the island, working on his laptop. Nothing about his posture said he was sparing a thought for her or what had occurred.

Pique pinched at her, small at first, then growing as the hours passed. Was the event so inconsequential— was *she* so inconsequential—that there was no need for so much as a word between them?

Apparently. She was the hired help, after all. A manual laborer.

Kelsey paused in her work to stare at Lovgren,

now on the phone, gesturing as he paced and talked. Manual laborer or no, if she looked like her sister, Holly, she bet that he'd have been outside hours ago, chatting and making nice.

Kelsey knew she was invisible to men. Always had been, always would be.

"He is a good-looking man, I'll give him that," Bridget said, following Kelsey's gaze with her own. "If you like that type."

"I don't," Kelsey said reflexively, although it was like saying she didn't like blancmange. She'd never tried it.

"I knew he wouldn't appeal to you. He looks high-strung, doesn't he?"

In his kitchen, Jack took the phone away from his ear and mock strangled it, his face twisted in frustration.

"Yes."

"One of those aggressive, acquisitive types. They're well and good for a certain type of woman, but I think you'd want someone a little more sensitive."

Kelsey wrinkled her brow. A sensitive guy? Geeky, yes. Sensitive? She didn't want a girly man, weeping at imagined affronts. She wanted a guy on whose shoulder *she* would do the crying. She shrugged. "Maybe." Jack had the phone back to his ear and his face tilted toward the ceiling as if asking for divine intervention.

"My husband Derald works with someone I think might be right for you."

Kelsey tore her gaze away from Jack.

Bridget's gloved hands were clasped together, her

eyes dancing with excitement. "I wasn't going to say anything until I heard from Derald—he's going to talk to Mark about you today."

"Mark?"

"He teaches at the community college, biology and botany. Perfect for you!"

It seemed scant criteria for perfect. "How old is he?"

"A little older than you, I think. Thirty-two, thirty-three. He's mature enough that he's ready to settle down."

"Is he cute?"

"I think he's quite attractive, in his own way. He's a little overweight and losing some hair, but aside from that he looks a bit like George Clooney."

"He doesn't sound like Clooney."

"Oh, but he looks like him. Sort of. Minus some hair."

Kelsey tried to imagine a stout, balding Clooney. She'd never liked the actor, so a pudgy version failed to thrill. But on the other hand she'd never dated handsome men: They had all been in the lower to middle class of physical attractiveness, just as she considered herself to be. Holly insisted she could be a knockout if she made an effort, but all Holly's attempts at makeovers had been failures, Kelsey's natural oddity shining through any pretty veneer, making her look like a walking Picasso.

Her mind filled again with the image of Jack's toned torso and his rampant manhood. She wished she could just once know what it felt like to touch a body that looked like that—one that was muscled and vibrant, and didn't yet have a pillowing of middle-aged fat over it.

Kelsey sighed at the impossibility of such a dream. "Does Mark have kids?"

"No kids, never married. And he owns his own home. He likes board games, home improvement projects, he writes the newsletter for his neighborhood association, he's a gourmet cook . . ."

Mark sounded exactly like the type of mate she'd been hoping for, and it would be worth her while to find out how cuddly and warm a plump, balding, community college George Clooney could be. He sounded perfect for her, just like Bridget said.

She watched Jack stuff his hand into a Cheerios box and eat the dry contents as he sat down again in front of his computer. The man couldn't even take the time to use a bowl! Bridget was right in her assessment: Jack seemed to be an aggressive, rootless man, and beyond his delicious body Kelsey had seen nothing to attract her.

What did she care about a gorgeous body?

Nothing. Nothing at all.

Really.

CHAPTER TWO

The sound of a car in the driveway made Jack look up from his computer. A glance out the window showed the sunlight slanting in from the west, telling him the day was drawing to a close.

"Shit!" He scrambled off the stool and over to the window, looking for Kelsey. The yard was empty except for the goats, which were munching on brush. He dashed through the house and out the front door, hoping that he could still catch her.

An older man stood in the driveway, swaying slightly as he held a digital camera at arm's length and tried to compose his shot. His target was Kelsey, standing stiffly with her arms at her sides, a tight-lipped smile on her face. The middle-aged woman Jack had seen working in the yard was stage directing. "Come on, let me see a big smile," the woman cajoled. "Let me see that pretty smile!"

Kelsey bared her teeth.

The photographer made a noise under his breath. "A little more relaxed, sweetheart," the woman said. "You look ready to eat someone. Are you sure you won't take off your hat and goggles, and let us see your face? Mark will want to see those pretty eyes of yours."

Kelsey's smile fell.

The woman sighed and the man took the picture. They looked at the results on the camera screen and both shrugged. "At least you look thin," the woman said. "That's all men really want to know about a blind date."

"Hi," Jack said. All three jumped. Kelsey shrank into herself as he approached, shoulders hunching and neck drawing in like a turtle's. "I'm Jack Lovgren," he said, extending his hand to the older woman. The couple introduced themselves while Kelsey edged away.

Bridget leaned close to him and whispered, "She's very shy."

Apparently so. Shy girls, however, were easy to win over as long as you weren't too forward with them. A bit of patience, a few quiet words, and they were yours. Waving a weenie in their faces didn't help, he imagined, but still, with gentleness, restraint—

Kelsey turned her head with the smoothness of an automaton and met his eyes. "Your penis scared me," she said in a flat voice. "I'll probably have to check under my bed when I get home to make sure it's not going to creep out in the middle of the night and get me." She grinned, waiting.

Bridget sucked in a breath. Derald's mouth dropped open.

Jack blinked, confused. "Er, I promise to keep it at home with me. I won't let it loose again."

She sidled closer and nudged him with her elbow.

"I wouldn't want to have to tether it like Little Bastard," she said.

What?

The young woman giggled. "It wouldn't like being tied to the hillside and made to eat blackberries. That's not its natural diet."

Bridget made a worried sound in her throat. "Kelsey . . ."

But the younger woman didn't stop. She laughed. "And nettles!" She brought the fingers of one hand together and made biting motions toward Jack's face. "Poison oak! It wouldn't like eating poison oak!"

"Er, no, it wouldn't," he said, flinching away. What the hell was going on here? What was with this chick?

The woman's hand froze midbite and she stared into his eyes, her own distorted by her tinted goggles. "You don't think this is funny?"

"Funny?"

"My joke. To lighten the mood."

Surprise quickly turned to pity, and Jack cringed with embarrassment on her behalf. The poor awkward girl! She was like a nerdy middle school kid trying to be witty, but doomed to failure from the first word out of her mouth. "Oh, yes, I see. Bravo! Very clever!" He tried to sound convincing.

"Oh God . . ." The young woman moaned, and smacked herself on the forehead of her legionnaire's hat. "Stupid, stupid, stupid!" She crossed her arms over her head. "I'm *such* a dork. I knew I shouldn't have tried a joke. I knew it!" She shook her head, arms covering her face.

"No, no, it was funny. My penis is like a monster

under the bed—yes, I see it. And it's a mean bastard that must be punished, right? Bad penis! Bad! Bad bastard penis!" He pinched his fingertips together and made biting motions at his crotch. He tried to smile reassuringly.

Kelsey peeked out from under her arm, her mouth pulled down in an unhappy frown. "Little Bastard is a goat."

"Ah. That makes it all much more clear."

Kelsey groaned, then turned away from them all and ran back to the yard.

"Kelsey?" Bridget called after her, taking a step as if to follow, then hesitating.

"She's a loon," her husband said, as if finding proof of what he'd long suspected. "A verifiable loon. I *told* you we shouldn't set her up with Mark. The guy deserves a normal girlfriend."

"She *is* normal," Bridget said crossly. "And deserves a good man. I don't know what got into her."

"Bridget, she has a penis fixation."

Jack cleared his throat, feeling bad about Kelsey's distress. "Er, it's my penis that's on her mind. I'll have to take credit for the fixation."

Bridget snorted. "That's rather a high opinion you have of yourself."

"No! I mean I gave her an eyeful of it earlier today. Apparently it was more than she could handle."

Bridget scowled at him. "What kind of pervert are you?"

"It was an accident! I opened the curtains and she was right there! I thought she was an angry old Japanese woman!"

"And that's *better*?"

He grimaced. "One of those *oba-sans* would have whacked it with a stick!"

Derald and Bridget frowned at him. "I don't know what type of kinky sexual practices they get up to in Japan," Derald said slowly, "but I don't think you should be springing them on young women you don't know. All this S and M—type talk, it makes me uncomfortable leaving my wife here to work."

Bridget patted Derald's arm. "I can take care of myself, darling. I have a fresh pair of pruning shears, and I know how to use them."

"I'm not going to touch or harm anyone, I swear it!" Jack said.

"I'll have my eye on you," Derald warned, tapping the corner of said oculus with a fingertip. "And I'm checking the sex offender website when I get home. I don't want to find your name on it."

Jack threw up his hands. He was surrounded by lunatics. "It was a pleasure meeting you," he said, nodded to them, and went to find Kelsey.

He found her sitting on the slope with a goat in her lap, scratching it behind the ears and murmuring. She glanced up as he approached, then returned her gaze to the top of the goat's head.

He stopped a safe distance away, visions of cartoon billy goats butting people in the rear springing to mind. He wasn't exactly afraid of animals, but neither had he been in close proximity to anything other than dogs and cats. The goat was watching him out of yellow eyes with eerie, horizontal pupils.

Eesh. No wonder they were associated with Satan worshippers.

Jack moved his attention from the goat to Kelsey—or rather, to what he could see of her. She was a rangy girl, all long limbs and hard angles. There were no soft curves that he could see. She had a square, dirty jaw and pale, chapped lips, and the end of her nose looked unremarkable except for a smear of white zinc oxide. Her hat and goggles would be perfect for a bank robber.

As she whispered unintelligible words to the goat, he belatedly recalled what his coworker had said when recommending Kelsey Safire as a landscaper: "She's a bit unusual in her methods and comes across as an organic nutcase, but if you want high-quality unique work, I can't say enough about her. Just don't expect a crew of twenty to come in with gas-powered machinery and transform your yard inside a week. Be patient with her. She's worth it."

He'd thought it an odd recommendation at the time, but it made much more sense now.

"Kelsey," he said.

She continued scratching the goat.

"Kelsey?"

Her gaze flicked up in acknowledgment before returning to the goat.

"I'm sorry we got off to such a bad start. How about we forget any of it ever happened and start over?"

She nodded, the motion barely perceptible.

"Great. Hello! You must be Kelsey Safire, the landscaper I've heard so much about. I'm Jack Lovgren, and am thoroughly delighted to make your acquaintance."

He stuck out his hand, low enough that she could see it over the goat's head.

He waited, hand hovering, until finally she put her gloved one in his and they shook. A smile curled gently along her chapped lips, and she peeked up at him.

He released her hand and squatted down on his haunches. He nodded at the goat. "Does it bite?"

"It depends."

"On what?"

"Whether she wants to."

"How do I know?"

"She tells you," Kelsey said. "You just have to know how to read her."

"I think that's true for people, too," he said softly, and was rewarded by her wide-open eyes meeting his. What color were they? He suddenly wished he could see. "Can you take those goggles off?"

She shook her head. "I can't see without them. They're prescription."

"Ah." He could think of no plausible reason to insist. "So, what's the story on the goats?" he asked, rising. "Are they yours?"

She eased the goat off her lap and stood. "Yes, although I think of them as coworkers."

He laughed. "I sometimes think of *my* coworkers as goats."

She didn't laugh, blinking at him instead as if wondering why he'd taken a cheap shot at his coworkers. "Goats are easy and organic, and they clear the land without destroying it," she said. "They're like machines for turning weeds into fertilizer. And you can milk them."

He looked at the goat standing nearby, its two teats distended and smudged with manure, and decided not to touch that topic. "You don't use poisons on the blackberries?"

"Don't need to."

Which reminded him. "How are you going to kill those snails in the bucket? Drown them?"

"Oh, no. Come see." She led him down to the bucket and pried off the lid. Inside, at least a hundred of the slimy buggers, large and small, slid over each other and the greenery tossed in with them. It looked like a snail orgy.

"You're not going to set them free, are you?" he asked, repulsed.

"No. I'm going to eat them!"

His gorge rose. "Not really?"

"Oh yes. These here are *Helix aspersa*, which is not your tastiest snail, but they're still quite edible, especially if you use a lot of herbs and butter."

Jack swallowed back his nausea. "Why eat them? Why not just kill them?"

She smiled, revealing perfect white teeth. "Because it satisfies my desire for revenge. Eat my garden, and I'll eat you."

"Oh."

"Garden snails aren't native to the region, you know. They're only here because someone back in the 1800s introduced them, assuming people would pay heaps for the delicacy. But they didn't." She snapped the lid back on the bucket. "They're a lot of work to prepare: You have to get the slime off, and that means soaking them in salt water, which makes for a big vat of mucous-y froth. Clams are far easier, so when people here want chewy mollusks, that's where they go."

"I guess so," he murmured, feeling faint. At least the topic had made her come out of her shell, so to speak. She was positively animated on the subject of snail consumption.

"When I cook my next batch, do you want to try them? I mean, these are technically your snails. I suppose I should have asked if I could have them."

"No, no, you go right ahead. Take all you want. I'm not much of a gourmet."

"I saw that."

"Huh?"

"I saw you eating cereal out of the box."

Jack shifted, uncomfortable with the thought of being watched all day like a fish in a bowl. "It was convenient."

"Can't you cook?"

He couldn't resist playing with her. "Sure I can. I know how to reheat Chinese takeout." Actually, he could do more than that, or at least he used to be able to, before he got so busy. He couldn't remember the last time he'd made a full meal for himself.

She shook her head, obviously pained.

"I'm not home enough to cook much, or make it worthwhile to stock a pantry," he temporized.

She tilted her head to the side, looking at him.

"If you're not home much, why do you want the garden?"

"Because I don't find it relaxing to look out the windows at a bunch of blackberries. I want order at home. Peace."

She nodded. "A refuge."

"Yes! I want to sit and look at the garden, and let the rest of the world disappear. I want it to quiet the mind, like those Japanese temple gardens are supposed to."

"I think you must have a lot of static in your head."

He laughed. "I could wish for something as innocuous as static. It's more like a thousand voices reminding me of everything I need to get done."

"If a quiet mind is what you want, you'll have your own part to play in this garden."

She sounded as certain as a Zen monk, and he found himself hanging on her words, awaiting her wisdom. "How so?"

She picked up her bucket of snails and started to walk away. "Step one: Turn off your phone."

"Sorry, can't do that."

She shrugged, but didn't turn.

He watched her go, a half smile on his face. She was a strange one, all right: all oversensitive shyness on the surface, and unfiltered, babbling honesty underneath. She was, of course, a social train wreck. Her physical appearance was no help, either: She was as androgynous as a stick, and with less sex appeal. Heaven help the guy Bridget and Derald were setting up with her.

He went back into his house and, with the lights

off, watched as Kelsey gathered her flock of goats and herded them down to her truck. In the low slanting light of late afternoon there was something timeless about her movements, and about the animals surrounding her with the yellow light limning their forms. For a moment, the rest of the world disappeared.

Then his phone rang.

CHAPTER THREE

"Whatcha doing?" Holly asked, coming into Kelsey's room.

Kelsey glared at the contents of her closet. "Looking for something decent to wear. All I see are jeans, T-shirts, and a few ugly old dresses I've only worn to funerals."

"Wait a minute! Let me catch my breath here." Holly fanned herself. "Are you telling me that you might, possibly, perhaps be interested in buying new clothes?"

"I don't know. If I have to. I guess."

"Hallelujah! My prayers have been answered!" Her sister dropped to her knees and clasped her hands together, her glossy dark brown hair and perfect oval face making her look like a Madonna. "Thank you, Lord. Oh, thank you."

"It's not that exciting," Kelsey grumbled.

Holly was two years older, and had long felt it her duty to bring her gangly younger sister into the heavenly light that was Fashion. She sold luxury cars for a living, but even her hardest sell couldn't get Kelsey into a dressing room.

"What's brought you to this revelation?" Holly

asked, getting to her feet and moving past Kelsey to dig in the closet. The sisters lived together in the bungalow they'd bought three years earlier with a small inheritance from their grandparents. A third girl, Holly's friend Erica, rented a room in the attic.

"I knew you'd ask me that."

Holly's turquoise green eyes met Kelsey's own, the remarkable color the only obvious similarity between them. "A man?" she guessed.

Kelsey scowled.

"It is! It's a man! Who is he? Where did you meet him? He asked you out? Of course he asked you out, you're looking for something to wear!"

"No, no one's asked me out. And I haven't met him yet. I'm getting set up on a blind date," Kelsey said, which was not a lie in fact, if a lie in her heart. It was Jack she'd been thinking of while going through her closet, not Mark; Jack, whose face she could now clearly picture, his lean, narrow features stalking her like a wolf in her imagination. She wasn't a fool: She knew she'd made a bad impression with her penis-under-the-bed joke and blathering about snails. She knew she hadn't a hope in the world with Jack Lovgren, and she wasn't sure she wanted one, either. She just had a crush on him, and it was a delicious, private passion that could only be nurtured in solitude.

"So, what's the story?" Holly asked. "Are you going out, or not?"

"Bridget is trying to set me up with a guy who teaches biology."

"Wow! That actually sounds promising."

"It does, doesn't it?" Kelsey rattled off the rest of Bridget's specs on Mark.

"He sounds perfect for you. Cooking, botany, board games . . . I've got a good feeling about this."

Kelsey shrugged. "If we ever meet." She explained about the photo.

"*Pish*. Don't worry about that. If anything, you were smart to keep the hat and goggles on. Can you imagine what your hair must have looked like? And those goggles leave a big red dent on your face when you take them off. I don't know why you can't just wear your contacts and sunglasses."

"The sunglasses might fall off."

"Newsflash, sweetie. You put them back on." Holly shut the door to the closet. "There's no point looking through that. C'mon, we're going shopping!"

"Right now?" Kelsey cried, as her sister grabbed her arm and dragged her from the room. "Isn't it too late?"

"The Internet is always open!"

Three hours and a quart of ice cream later, Kelsey's wardrobe hadn't grown by so much as a stocking. "We must have looked at five hundred dresses," Holly complained, her eyes bloodshot and her mouse hand cradled against her belly with a pack of ice, suffering from carpal tunnel. "How can you think they're all horrible? How?"

"Some of them looked okay. It's just that the ones I like are not the ones I think would look good on me."

"You don't think *any* of them would look good on you!"

"Not really."

Holly groaned and pushed away from the desk. "Sunday we're going shopping downtown. You will try things on, see that you look great, and buy them."

"I'd rather buy something online," Kelsey said faintly, imagining department stores with entire floors full of clothing to be tried on in dressing rooms with three-way mirrors and overattentive clerks.

"Then *buy* something. For God's sake, Kelsey, just buy something. It can't be worse than what's in your closet."

"Everything's so expensive, I don't want to make a mistake—"

"That's why they have return policies."

"But it's such a bother to—"

Holly put up her hand, stopping her. "It's always no with you. You say no to new clothes, no to makeup, no to cutting or coloring your hair, no to almost every guy, no to invitations. You say no to fun. No, no, no. No more no, Kelsey! I don't want to hear it. It's past time you said yes to something other than a new garden project. Either buy something online, or we go downtown on Sunday." She stood. "I'm going to bed."

Kelsey spun round in her desk chair as Holly walked away. "Don't go! You have to help me choose!"

"You don't listen to what I say, and I'm tired."

"I'll listen! I'll say yes!"

"I'm going to bed."

"Holly!"

"Good night."

Kelsey whimpered and looked back at the computer screen. It was two o'clock in the morning and she was alone with the vast shopping jungle that was the Internet. Her guide had abandoned her. Bad taste and unflattering silhouettes lurked on every site, and one wrong click could bring box-loads of sartorial evil to her front porch, delivered by UPS. That's what she'd get for saying yes.

Half the problem was that she had no idea what she was looking for. What she wanted was for the perfect garment to announce itself on the page, with labels saying it was designed expressly for five foot six sandy redheads with sinewy, square-shouldered bodies and 34B chests, and if she bought this garment a tornado of fairy dust would sweep out of the delivery box and transform her into a Disney princess. If a dress clearly said that to her, then she'd say yes in a heartbeat.

She clicked through clothes she and Holly had already looked at, at Saks, Nordstrom, Neiman Marcus, Anthropologie, MaxStudio, Trashy Diva . . . There were so many pretty dresses, and so few clues as to how they'd look on her. She *wanted* to say yes; she just didn't know how.

Her eyelids heavy, Kelsey took off her glasses and shoved the keyboard aside, then laid her head on her folded arms. She closed her eyes and imagined herself transformed.

Jack would see her in her new clothes and stagger from the shock. "You? You were the one working in my garden? How could I have been so blind? All this time, I didn't know there was a goddess right outside my window."

She would leave Jack brokenhearted and go to Mark, because men like Jack were never as sweet as they acted. Jack's type had charm to spare, but it rarely came from their heart. They smiled and joked and made gallant gestures, but beneath it all was the urge to make other people like them so that they could get ahead. Life was easier and people did things for you when you were charming.

Mark, she hoped, would be gifted with the charm that came from being interested in other people. He would see the goddess in her no matter what she wore, or what a dork she was.

She needed goddess clothes, she suddenly realized. Why hadn't she thought to search for that before? her half-dreaming mind asked. She sat up, a new energy reviving her, and put on her glasses. *Clothes for a redheaded goddess,* she typed into the search engine.

Several thousand hits came up. She skimmed down the list. Blog, blog, redhead pride site, blog, redheads in art, blog, discussion forum, forum, blog . . . And then, at the bottom of the second page:

Shoes for a redhead.

She clicked on it.

Celtic harp music plucked from the speakers. A curtain of red hair swayed on the screen, then parted, pulled up and to the sides like theater curtains, revealing an empty chair shaped like a giant leopard-print high-heeled shoe. A message scrolled atop the screen and then disappeared:

Welcome to Hiheelia, heavenly seat of Shoestra, Goddess of Shoes.

Kelsey moved her mouse over the screen, looking for something to click.

Do you wish to summon the goddess?

"Yes!" Kelsey said.

Put your finger on the shoe.

Kelsey rolled her eyes. Like that would do anything.

Do you want to summon the goddess or not?

Kelsey tensed. How did it know? She checked the webcam mounted to the computer. It was off.

They must assume no one did it on the first prompt.

Last chance.

"I'm not doing it," Kelsey muttered. "You're faking."

Thank you for visiting Hiheelia.

The leopard-print shoe started to fade. Panicked, Kelsey quickly stuck her finger onto it.

Bells tinkled and flower petals fell from the top of

the screen. The lighting softened and gas footlights flared in an arc across the bottom of the screen. Nude animated nymphs in gold high-heeled shoes cavorted out from behind the curtain on the right, two of them blowing on trumpets and two more unfurling a length of blue silk. They scampered around the shoe and then exited the opposite side.

Kelsey gaped at the screen. Was this a porn site?

Moments ticked by, the last of the flower petals settling to the floor. The footlights flickered, the faint sound of gas jet flames fluttering through the speakers.

Far-off high-heeled footsteps sounded, approaching with each sharp step. Kelsey leaned in close to the screen, as if pressing her face to it would let her see off to the side of the stage.

K-thk, K-thk, K-thk, the unseen feet said, then paused.

Please don't fog the goddess with your breath.

Embarrassed, Kelsey sat back. She glanced around the room, making sure no one else had seen her faux pas.

The footsteps resumed.

Thank you.

"No problem," she mumbled.

I shouldn't think so.

"Lay off her, will ya?" a tart female voice said, and from the right of the stage emerged a blond bombshell in a tight 1940s gray skirt suit, a saucy black hat angled on her head over her side-parted hair. She strode to the shoe chair on black patent peep-toe heels fully five inches tall. Black seams ran up the backs of her stockings.

"Okay, who's the funny one who dug this out of the donation pile?" the blonde demanded, pointing at the leopard-print shoe.

There was giggling offstage.

I don't know, Goddess.

"I'm gonna make you all wear sensible shoes with arch support for this!"

Moans and cries of distress.

The blonde turned to Kelsey, meeting her eyes through the computer screen. "Sorry about that. In case you haven't put it together by now, I'm Shoestra, the Goddess of Shoes," she said, and sat down primly on the leopard-print shoe throne. She crossed her Barbie doll legs and clasped her hands over her knee. "And you are?"

"Kelsey," Kelsey said, and again glanced over her shoulder. She didn't want Holly or Erica to catch her talking to the computer. Was she hallucinating?

"Kelsey, yes. A redhead in need of shoes, and of a little more than that, too, if I'm not mistaken."

Kelsey nodded. "Clothes."

Shoestra waved that suggestion away. "Deeper in your soul than that."

"Confidence?"

"Even more fundamental than that."

"A new personality?" Kelsey ventured.

"Keep digging."

Kelsey tried, but her "self" seemed too shallow to hold much more in the way of discoveries. She shrugged. "I've got nothing."

"That's right!" Shoestra bounded out of the chair and pointed a crimson-nailed finger at her. Her scolding face looked like a perky young Ginger Rogers. "And do you know why that is?"

Kelsey shook her head.

"It's because your womanly powers are like this," she said, and held up a tightly clenched fist. "They're wrapped up tight in a bud, waiting for the chance to bloom. They want to effloresce; they want to spread their petals like a rose and fill you with their intoxicating scent. The 'nothing' inside you is the empty space where the blooming rose of feminine power should be."

Yes, yes, it made sense! It explained so much! It—

It was a little loopy, wasn't it? She'd never felt any bud of womanly powers striving to be set free. "Why didn't my bud ever blossom?"

Shoestra shrugged. "Congenital defect? It happens sometimes. But you're in luck, because here in Hiheelia we have a cure for your type of problem." Shoestra smiled, eyes twinkling as if she were about to spread the Good Word to a heathen. "Shoes!"

Kelsey sighed. Shopping! Of course. What else was a shoe website about except commerce? She was embarrassed she'd let herself get sucked in. "Shoes aren't going to solve my problems," she said, reaching for the mouse. She'd go back to the normal clothes websites and buy the first thing she saw—quickly, before she hallucinated any further.

"Wait!"

Kelsey's finger hovered over the mouse. "What?"

Shoestra came up to the edge of the stage, her animated face luminous with concern. "This isn't just a shoe store. Think of your visit here as your first step to becoming who you want to be. Close your eyes, Kelsey, and envision who that woman is. Come on, close your eyes."

"Fine." Kelsey crossed her arms and closed her eyes.

"Who do you want to be?"

"I don't know."

"Yes, you do. There's a redheaded goddess inside you, waiting to break free."

"I don't know where she is," Kelsey complained. "I don't know how to set her free. Help me!"

"Are you sure you want my help?"

"Yes!"

"It'll cost $189, plus shipping."

"Okay! Yes! Anything, yes!"

Click here.

"Kelsey, sweetie, have you been here all night?" Holly asked, shaking her awake.

"Hunh?" Kelsey raised her face from her arms, crossed in front of her on the desk. She fumbled for her horn-rimmed glasses and slid them on, wincing as her neck cramped. "What time is it?"

"Seven." Holly reached over to Kelsey's wallet, a Visa card sitting on top. "Did you buy something after I went to bed?"

Kelsey yawned. "I don't think so." The sum $189 appeared in her mind, unconnected to anything else. "Did I?"

She woke the computer. Her browser was closed, but her open e-mail retrieved a message, announcing its arrival with a cheerful chirrup. It was from Hiheelia.com, and the subject line read: Your order has shipped!

"Oh crap." Kelsey opened the e-mail and read the cheerful fluff about hoping she was satisfied with her order, but there was no hint of what, exactly, she *had* ordered.

"What's Hiheelia? I've never heard of it. Oh God, it's not Hawaiian clothes, is it? Muumuus and board shorts?"

"It's a really weird shoe store. Let me show you." Faint memories were coming back, of a curtain of red hair and an animated Ginger Rogers sitting on a giant leopard-print shoe.

Kelsey brought up Hiheelia.com and grunted in surprise.

There was no curtain of hair. No big shoe. There was text about Hiheelia and Shoestra, about giving women just what they needed and wanted, but no naked nymphs or talking goddess. The site came across as a shoe store with an overly creative marketing style.

"Kind of corny," Holly said, looking over her shoulder. "So what'd you buy?"

"I don't remember," Kelsey mumbled.

"Let's look. You'll remember when you see it." Holly grabbed the mouse and clicked the "Go Shopping!" link.

An error message came up.

Holly clicked the back button, but instead of getting the home page, they got a message that the site was experiencing technical difficulties, and to please return later. "I hope that doesn't mean that they have your credit card number and have taken off for the Cayman Islands."

Kelsey groaned and put her face in her hands. "It's always going to be a disaster when I shop; it's like I'm missing the gene for it. I think it may be a congenital defect." A vision of a rosebud blooming suddenly filled her mind and she dropped her hands, her gaze focusing inward as she tried to catch from whence the image came.

"What is it?" Holly asked.

Kelsey shook her head, an odd and unfamiliar feeling washing over her. "I don't know. But I think I'll wait and see if a package arrives from Hiheelia before I call the credit card company. I think there might something interesting on its way."

CHAPTER FOUR

"Thank God it's Friday," Kelsey grumbled as she backed her truck and goat trailer up the driveway of her house.

It had been a week of bitter disappointment. Bridget had given Kelsey's e-mail address to Mark, but so far there was no sign he would ask her out. Jack had taken off on another trip, so there was no chance of glimpsing him undressed. Little Bastard broke loose and ate one of Jack's neighbors' flower gardens, then attacked another neighbor's Pomeranian. Granted, the dog had been making a nerve-shredding amount of noise over the week and Kelsey had fantasized about violence herself, but now she might be saddled with the little beast's vet bill.

And worst of all, every day when she came home she was greeted with an empty front porch, no box from any shoe store to be seen. The fear of identity theft and her credit card being used to buy daiquiris on a beach somewhere was a constant, quiet worry. The site still showed no signs of coming back online.

She took care of the goats and her snail farm, did

a bit of maintenance on her composting worm bins, fed the chickens and gathered eggs, picked a few hardy herbs from her garden, and went in the basement door to the house. She stripped by the washing machine and started a load, then took a shower in the basement bathroom. Afterward she donned the thin robe that waited for her on its nail at the bottom of the stairs.

She heard the doorbell when she was halfway up the stairs and dashed to the top, dumping the eggs and herbs in the kitchen, then running across the living room. Through the sheer curtains she could see the shadow of someone moving away, and she yanked open the door. "Wait!"

A college-age boy holding a box turned around, his eyes running over her body. "Sure!"

Kelsey looked down and realized her dripping hair had dampened a spot over one nipple, turning the fabric transparent, and her robe was half-open. She pulled it closed, crossing an arm over her breast. "Is that package for me?"

"I think so. It was delivered to my mom's house by mistake. She lives down the street," he said, pointing.

Kelsey reached for the box.

The boy moved it out of her reach, grinning. "How about as thanks for delivering the box, you let me take you out tonight?"

The demand was too unexpected to process. Her? Him? "I'm at least five years older than you!"

"So? I'd rather be with someone with a little more experience."

"Experience with *what*?"

His grin widened.

"Are you going to give me my box or not?" she demanded.

"Are you going to go out with me?" He raised the box all the way above his head.

Kelsey narrowed her eyes. She'd never had patience with this junior high form of mating ritual. "You better give that to me."

He winked.

She punched him in the gut. The box dropped and she caught it, and was dashing up the porch stairs before he caught his breath.

"Is that a 'no'?" he wheezed from his crouch.

"Get off my property!" she yelled, and slammed and locked the door behind her.

She leaned against the door, panting and cradling the box against her chest, wondering what had gotten into that boy. Guys never came on to her like that.

She lowered the box in her arms. *Hiheelia.com* was written on the side in bold black print. She flipped it over to find the return address, but it had been damaged during shipping, the skin of the cardboard peeled off where the address should have been.

She took the box into the kitchen and cut open the packing tape with a knife. Underneath the packing straw was a shoe box, an envelope attached on top. She plucked off the envelope and opened it. Inside was a note card with gold-and-pink edging. In black script was a message:

A Rose by Any Other Name

To Kelsey Safire, the redheaded goddess
May she be everblooming

"And drought tolerant and disease resistant," she muttered. Everblooming was a gardening term. Shrugging, she set the note aside and took the lid off the shoe box.

She stared at the contents. There was no way she would have ordered those.

She went to the fridge and pulled out a half-drunk bottle of wine and poured herself a glass, then edged back to the table and peered again into the box. The shoes hadn't changed. In a bed of silver tissue nestled a pair of high-heeled sandals, the straps made of pale green leather cut in the silhouette of a thorny stem. Down the vamp of each shoe was an inch-wide strip of small red silk roses.

She muttered a curse under her breath. $189, gone! Wasted on a pair of shoes she would never wear. It made no sense.

She picked up one of the shoes to check the size. Yup, an eight. Compared to her usual work boots, the sandal was light as a feather. It seemed so . . . *feminine*.

Hardly knowing she was doing it, she sat down and tried on the shoes. The long thin straps at the ankle seemed to wrap themselves around her lower leg of their own accord, crisscrossing to beneath her calf.

She held her feet out in front of her. They looked sexy. She carefully stood, and grew three and a half inches in the process, sending the familiar view of the kitchen off-kilter. She felt tall and willowy.

Giggling to herself, she walked across the room. The shoes were a perfect fit. She put a hand on her hip and did a model catwalk stomp through the house, pausing only to pick up her glass of wine before repeating the circuit. On the third lap she flipped on the radio.

When Holly and Erica came home half an hour later, Kelsey was singing along in front of the television as she tried to copy Beyoncé's music video moves. Holly's jaw dropped open when Kelsey got her skinny butt to shimmy in ways it had never moved before.

"Hi!" Kelsey called over the music. "Can we go out dancing tonight? I want to go dancing!"

Holly found the remote and muted the TV. "Kelsey, what's going on?"

"Nothing! I got some new shoes. Look!" She held up a foot. "They want to go dancing."

"The shoes do?"

"Yeah! Erica, can you fix my hair? I think maybe I need to liven up the color. I'm thinking red, red, red! Fire engine red!"

"Is she on something?" Erica whispered to Holly.

"I got new shoes!" Kelsey said again, standing still now and pointing to her feet. "I'm on new shoes!"

"Yeah, we see them," Holly said. She picked up the empty wineglass on top of the TV. "How much did you drink?"

Kelsey shrugged. "Do you have anything I could wear tonight?"

Holly and Erica exchanged glances.

"I could be back in fifteen minutes with the dye," Erica, a hairdresser by trade, said in a low voice. "We've been wanting to do a makeover on her for ages. I say we take the opportunity and run with it. Who cares if she's drunk?"

"I'm not drunk. I'm efflorescing!"

Holly dug in her purse and handed Erica a wad of cash. "Get the dye."

CHAPTER FIVE

"I can't believe I let you talk me into this," Jack said.

"It's one of his last nights of freedom," his old friend Richard said. "On Sunday my baby brother is delivering himself into the clutches of one Marielle Huntington, may God help him. She's a 'short leasher.' He'll never have another night out with the boys."

Ahead of them on the sidewalk, their arms around each other's shoulders, three younger men staggered forward together, hooting and howling and staring too long at groups of women. It was approaching one o'clock in the morning, and the nightclubs were hitting their stride.

"I'm getting old, man," Jack said. "I wish I were home in bed." Four short hours ago he'd gotten off a fourteen-hour flight from Kuala Lumpur, and he was beat.

"Look at all the hotties!" Richard said, the sweep of his arm taking in a group of drunk, muffin-topped women huddling together, sucking on ciga-rettes. "One of these beauties could be yours tonight!"

"My lust knows no bounds."

"Suffer through one more club, and then I absolve you. You'll be free to go."

"One more."

Their group—twelve in all—joined the slowly moving line outside a basement nightclub, the thump of overamplified music banging out onto the street.

"Can I tell you again how glad I am I moved out of downtown?" Jack said, slipping in earplugs to bring the decibel level down a notch.

"Yeah, yeah, but you're never going to meet anyone living in that neighborhood. It's no place for a single guy."

They reached the front of the line and worked their way into the club. The rest of the group was already absorbed into the dancing mob. Jack pointed at the stairs to the balcony, where there were civilized things like tables and cocktail waitresses. Richard followed.

"I never met anyone downtown, either. It's quiet in my neighborhood. I like it. No one plays loud music."

"You *are* turning into an old man. Next you're going to be yelling at kids to get out of your yard."

"Damn right," Jack said, snagging a table at the rail and sitting down. "I don't want them messing with the goats."

"With the what?"

But Jack didn't hear him. His attention had been snagged by a woman on the dance floor below, her mane of glossy red hair bobbing and swinging with her movements. Her skin was as white as the moon, and glowed in contrast to the backless, short black dress she wore. Half a dozen men were gyrating around her, vying for her attention, but she was lost in her own world. Arms above her head, she swayed and undulated with her eyes closed, her lips slightly parted. It almost looked as if she were having sex.

Then her eyes opened and locked with his, the twenty feet between them too little to keep the power of her gaze from pinning him in place. Her mouth moved, and for one insane moment he thought he'd read his name on her lips.

"Jack! Jack!" Richard shook his arm.

"What?!" he demanded, angry at the interruption. He turned and saw the waitress standing beside their table.

"What do you want to drink?" Richard asked.

"I don't care. Anything. Gin and tonic." He looked back to the dance floor, and she was gone. A cry of frustration rose in his throat and he stood, leaning over the rail, trying to spot her.

"What's the matter with you?" Richard demanded after the waitress left. "Jack? Jack!"

"Where'd she go?" he asked, hanging as far as he could over the rail. He stood straight and scanned the rest of the balcony. "She can't have disappeared!"

"Who are you talking about?"

"Didn't you see her? The knockout redhead on the dance floor."

"It doesn't look like your long flight is bothering you now," Richard said dryly. He pulled on the hem of Jack's sport coat. "Christ, man, sit down. She probably ran off because you're acting like a deranged stalker."

Jack eased back into his seat, eyes still scanning the club. "I think I just saw my future wife."

"Oh, for crying out loud. Wake up, Jackie boy! I think you fell asleep with your eyes open. You're dreaming."

"You're right." An involuntary laugh rose in his throat. "Maybe I have lost it. I don't even want to get married yet."

Richard was staring at something over Jack's shoulder, his eyes round as poker chips. "Ho-ly crap, you were *not* kidding."

The hairs rose on the back of Jack's neck and he slowly turned. The redhead was walking toward him, trailed by two pretty women as handmaidens. The club went silent around him and all he heard was the ringing of silver bells in his ears and the racing of his own heartbeat. He popped the earplugs out and shoved them in a pocket.

The redhead stopped in front of him. "Hi."

Jack and Richard both stumbled to their feet, Jack's chair falling over behind him. He scrambled to right it, feeling like a klutz, fearing that any chance he had with her was already slipping away. "Hi," he said, struggling to find words to follow. He gestured at their vacated seats, and grabbed a temporarily empty seat from another table, sliding it into place.

"Thank you," she said, and the trio of eye candy sat down.

Jack and Richard stole more chairs and crowded into place between the women. Jack introduced himself and Richard, the redhead's piercing blue-green eyes on him the whole time, gently laughing at some secret joke.

"I'm . . . Rosa," she said, offering her hand. It was surprisingly rough and strong. "Rosa Rugosa. This is my . . . cousin, Holly, and our friend Erica."

Jack was vaguely aware that the handmaidens looked confused and uncomfortable, but Richard would take care of them. The waitress returned with his and Richard's drinks, and took new orders for the women. Rosa asked for a gin gimlet.

Gin gimlet, gin gimlet. He had to remember that.

"I saw you dancing," he said to Rosa, feeling like an idiot even as he said it. Of course she knew he'd seen her. Her proximity was fogging his rational thought: His arm was up against hers, their faces only a foot apart. He could see dewdrops of sweat on her skin, and the places where her hair had stuck to her forehead and neck. She was breathing heavily, still recovering from her exertions on the dance floor.

He barely controlled the urge to lick the sweat off her.

"Do you want to get out of here and go get something to eat?" he asked, and immediately cursed himself. Too forward, too fast! Dammit, where was his self-control?

"Sure."

"Great!" They got up, and he surreptitiously handed some cash to Richard to cover the drinks.

"Wait a minute," the brunette handmaiden said,

grabbing Rosa's arm as they went past. "Where are you going?"

"It's okay," Rosa said. "Don't worry."

The brunette—he'd forgotten her name and that of the blonde—got up and pulled Rosa aside, whispering furiously to her.

"I'm not a psycho," he offered to the remaining handmaiden. "Really."

"Rosa is more naïve than she looks. We don't want to see her get herself into trouble."

"He's not much trouble," Richard said. "He wants to marry your friend."

The blonde raised a brow. "You *really* don't know her," she said, the words heavy with unspoken meaning.

"What's that supposed to mean?" Jack bristled.

"It means you don't know her," Richard said, then he leaned close to the blonde. "So what gives? What's the story?"

She tightened her lips and shook her head.

The confab between cousins ended and Rosa rejoined him, sliding her hand into the crook of his arm. Her touch sent an electric jolt down his torso and straight to his loins. "Jack, would you please show my cousin your driver's license?" Rosa asked.

He'd show her his bank statements and give her the password to his debit card if it meant she'd let Rosa leave with him. He dug out his wallet and handed her the card. She copied down the information on a piece of paper from her purse and then looked up under her brows at him, like a suspicious policewoman. "Is this information current?"

"Uh, no. I just bought a house, you see, and I haven't had time . . ." He trailed off. "Here, let me write down the new address." He took the paper and wrote, then handed it back.

Rosa whispered something in the brunette's ear. She nodded, not looking happy about it. "You call me if you need *anything*," she said. "I don't care what time it is."

And then finally, miracle of miracles, he had Rosa on his arm and they stepped out of the club and into the cool, open air.

CHAPTER SIX

The happy, hazy glow of unreality through which Kelsey had been viewing the evening slipped a bit as she and Jack walked up the street from the nightclub. The night air was cold on her damp skin, its chill slapping her into consciousness and reminding her that in the real world, there were consequences to her actions. She shivered.

Jack shrugged out of his jacket and draped it over her shoulders, then put his arm around her, enveloping her in instant warmth. Chill reality slid back into hiding and she snuggled against his side, luxuriating in the contact and the attention. No guy had ever done the borrowed-coat thing for her before.

This is what it's like to be one of the beautiful, careless people, she thought. *I like it.*

Since putting on her new shoes, her fears and inhibitions had gone into hiding. She didn't care what she said, didn't care what people thought of her, didn't care if she made a fool of herself. The only emotion that motivated her was desire: to be beautiful, to dance, to be in the company of a handsome man. She'd lost the power to say no to herself, and it was glorious.

"I think we have enough time to get to Dick's Drive-in before they close," Jack said.

"All right." Agreement came easily to her while she wore the shoes. Everything came easily: dancing, beauty, conversation. Men.

She peeked up at Jack. His face was stark in the harsh amber glow of the streetlights, his encircling arm moving her along as if afraid she might bolt and escape him.

Holly's concern was beginning to make a vague sort of sense. What did she truly know about Jack? Not enough to make going off alone and half-drunk with him in the middle of the night a good idea. She wasn't afraid, but cold logic told her that this was not smart.

Kelsey tried to stop, but her feet disobeyed her and kept on walking. There wasn't so much as a hesitation in her forward movement.

Uh-oh.

She looked down at her feet, prancing swiftly up the sidewalk in the high heels. They looked like they knew where they wanted to go, logic be damned.

And wasn't that really where she wanted to go? To hell with caution, that's what tonight was about. To hell with hesitation and doubt, self-censorship and stifled desires.

They reached his car; it was low, sporty, and silver. He opened the door for her and she slid into the passenger seat, careful to keep her thighs together as the skirt rode up her legs.

"What do you do for a living?" Kelsey asked as he

got in the driver's seat and started the car. The question rolled easily off her tongue without her usual worries about offending someone or making a fool of herself.

"I'm a project manager for global event marketing for the video game division of a software company," he said, pulling out onto the street.

"What does that mean?"

"It's marketing, basically. We plan events to gain publicity for our games, and also look for ways to partner our games to other events."

"Do you travel a lot?"

"Too much."

"You don't enjoy it?" she asked, surprised. "I would love to be able to travel."

"Everyone thinks it sounds glamorous to travel for work, but after the novelty wears off it's a slog. You're away from friends and family and you're working fourteen-hour days in unfamiliar cities. You don't know where to eat, you don't even know where to buy toothpaste, and your body can't figure out what time it is. The constant change in environment is exhausting."

"Sounds miserable," Kelsey said. Holding up her end of a conversation with a man was a lot easier than she'd known. All she had to do was ask him questions about himself.

"Maybe I oversold the negatives," he said, looking over at her with a grin. "It's not *that* bad. I can handle it better than the people who have spouses and kids at home, and I do make an effort to explore and talk to the locals. I always have to leave a place before I'm ready, though—before I feel like I've gotten more than a taste of it. Not even a taste—more like the whiff of food you sometimes get outside a restaurant, when you're hungry but on your way to someplace else. My job has left me with an enormous appetite for places I don't have time to go back and see."

"Rush, rush, rush."

"Yeah," he said, changing lanes and turning into the parking lot of Dick's Drive-in. He parked and they got out of the car, walking together to one of the windows. A dozen other club-goers were hanging around, waiting for food or wolfing down burgers. Dick's was a longstanding fixture in the late-night food map for Seattleites, the '50s era architecture giving it a retro-chic air.

"I think you might be the type to thrive on busyness," she said. They stood close together, her arm brushing his.

"Maybe."

She smiled at him.

"I can't go a hundred miles an hour all the time, though. I'm trying to find space for the important things in life."

She didn't even have to talk! Smiles and attention were all he needed. Why hadn't she figured this out about men sooner?

They ordered and moved aside, standing with the other couples waiting on fries and milk shakes. A jostling tumult erupted amongst a group of loud young men, but it seemed to be happening on the other side of a glass wall. She felt protected from the other patrons, shielded as she was by Jack's body. She saw his gaze go to the rowdy guys, and he shifted his position to put himself more squarely between her and them.

"What *are* the important things in your life?" she asked, pulling the edges of his jacket close around her.

"I'm still trying to figure that out." He met her eyes. "The only thing I know for sure is that I want someone to share it with."

Her heart went *ker-thunk* in her chest and she felt heat in her cheeks. He reached over and traced his fingertips down the side of her face, down her neck, and then slid his warm hand under her hair, along the back of her neck. With gentle pressure he pulled her toward him.

Her stomach dropped and her limbs went weak. She let him tilt back her head, her lips parting. As his face lowered to hers she closed her eyes, dissolving into the sensation of touch. She was exquisitely aware of the cold air on her legs, the silken liner of his jacket on her arms, and the heat of his hand on her neck and of his body a few inches from hers. His lips brushed over her mouth once, then again, and then she felt the full pressure of his kiss. He slid his other hand inside the jacket and around her waist, pulling her up against him.

Kelsey lost all strength in her legs. She clutched at his shoulders for support and felt the hardness of his thigh against her sex as she sagged against him. She pressed herself against it, hunger rousing in her.

He deepened the kiss, and beneath the jacket she

felt his hand slide down to squeeze her buttock. She moaned into his mouth, and he lifted her off the ground, pressed like wallpaper to his body.

"Get a room, will ya?" someone said loudly. "Kee-rist!"

"Two shakes!" the girl at the food window called. It was their order. "Two shakes. Two vanilla shakes?"

She felt Jack's chuckle in his chest as he lowered her back to the ground and released her. "The gods have spoken," he said.

She barely processed his words, standing stunned and mussed while he retrieved their milk shakes from the window. There were no thoughts in her head; she was lost in sensation, her body throbbing with aroused passions.

Jack stuck her milk shake in her hand and with an arm around her shoulders led her back to the car. "Let's go to my place," he said.

She nodded. Inside the car she stuck the un-tasted milk shake into the cup holder, then leaned back in the seat and like a dumb animal stared at Jack. He caught her gaze, and when she knew he was looking at her she slowly slid her hand up her bare thigh and closed her eyes. A small part of the normal Kelsey watched her actions and was horri-fied. The rest of her purred with satisfaction when she heard Jack's helpless moan and felt his lips come down hard against her own, and his hand slip inside the loose neckline of her dress. He mas-saged her naked breast as if his palm were starving for the feel of it. He paused only long enough to fumble for the seat-back release and dropped her to a reclined position. "Sorry," he mumbled against her mouth, then plunged his tongue inside.

His hand left her breast and found a place to rest on her knee, his fingertips stroking the sensitive skin at its side. Kelsey's shod feet began to slide away from each other on the car floor, taking her legs with them. With a distant sense of shock she felt her thighs part in invitation to his hand.

He did not decline. His palm slid slowly along the inside of her thigh, moving inexorably north toward her sex. Kelsey writhed under his touch, her body desperate for more of it even as a small voice of reason told her she would regret this when all was said and done.

Jack's fingertips found the damp, thin layer of panty over her sex, and brushed lightly across it. Her body came alive with shooting stars of sensation and she raised her hips against his hand. He played his fingers over the center of her sex, then traced the edges of her panties, fingertips running underneath the edge of the elastic.

Kelsey's feet hit the sides of the footwell until her left foot found its way past the center console and waggled into the free space on the driver's side. The milk shake got squished, cold ice cream dribbling over her ankle. Wider! The shoes were demanding of her. Open wider!

Jack's tongue slowly thrust against hers as his palm covered her sex, rubbing gently. A cry of desire squeezed from Kelsey's throat, and in answer Jack nudged aside the crotch of her panties and pressed a fingertip against her entrance. She was wet and swollen, and when she thrust against his hand she felt him slide inside her without hindrance.

It was not enough. She wrapped her arms around his neck, pulling him closer with her powerful landscaper's muscles, her strong body arching toward him.

"Rosa, oh God, Rosa," he murmured against her mouth. "I've got to get you home." He released her, tugging down her skirt as he sat back. He righted the squished milk shake cup. "Put on your seat belt," he said, and started the car. Rubber squealed as they pulled out onto the street.

By the time Kelsey was upright again and had regained some faint semblance of composure, they were halfway to his house. Her whole body ached with desire. The intensity was greater than anything she'd experienced outside of the dreams that woke her with the rippling waves of orgasm.

"I don't normally do this," Jack said, taking a hard left and tearing down a residential street. "I don't pick up women in clubs and take them home."

"It's been two years since I've had sex," Kelsey said. "I'm *really* ready."

"Two years? Jesus, how could you keep guys off you for that long?"

"You're the first who's tried." She remembered the college boy with the box. "Except for the guy I punched."

Jack cast her a surprised look.

She shrugged. "It was effective."

They pulled into his driveway, the garage door opening in front of them. He led her through the door into the kitchen. "Can I get you anything? A glass of water?"

She shook her head.

He took her hand and pulled her into the living room. "Do you want the grand tour?"

"No."

"Thank God."

He rushed her down the hall to his bedroom, then stopped her inside the doorway. "I'm sorry, that's not inviting, is it?" he said, looking at the bed-sheets in a tangle, the blanket half on the floor.

In answer, Kelsey crawled onto the mattress and shoved the rumpled bedding onto the floor. She lay sideways on the tight bottom sheet. "Now it is."

"God yes." A pained look crossed his face. "Oh shit."

"What?"

"I haven't unpacked yet. The condoms are in a box somewhere."

She laughed. "I'll go wash the ice cream off my leg while you search."

"I know right where they should be," he said, ripping into cardboard.

She went to the bathroom down the hall, running the faucet until the water poured hot over her wrists. She stepped out of her panties and used a wet cloth to clean herself, her eyes closing as the wet heat soaked into her hungry flesh. She rinsed and rewet the cloth, sitting on the edge of the tub as she wiped at the sticky white film on her leg. It had soaked the green strap of her shoe, and she undid it to get at the underside.

As the strap fell away from her skin, she suddenly asked herself what the hell she was doing in Jack Lovgren's bathroom, preparing herself for sex?

Kelsey stopped, washcloth poised above her ankle. Had she really let him put his finger inside her, in the parking lot of Dick's Drive-in?

"Found them!" Jack hollered from his bedroom.

Kelsey looked warily at her shoes. The roses down the vamp looked larger than she remembered, their blooms fuller.

She gingerly picked up the end of the loose strap and draped it back over her leg. A tingle ran through her body and her whole soul whispered, *Yesss! Do it!*

She made herself knock the strap off her leg and a hint of reason instantly returned, bringing with it doubt and caution, and a rising wave of embarrassment.

"Rosa?" Jack called.

Kelsey raised her head and caught sight of herself in the mirror behind the sink. Her newly bright red hair fell in a sultry cascade of waves around her face and over her shoulders. Abundant dark bronze eye shadow masked her eyes, setting off the blue-green color. Her lips were swollen and pink from kissing, her cheeks flushed.

She looked the best she ever had, but she knew she was no unique beauty. Made up as she was, she had the average prettiness that most women achieved with a little effort. There was no reason Jack should have been so drawn to her.

Her hand again on the green strap, she wrapped it round her leg and watched her face transform. Her chin rose, her eyes became seductive, her tongue darted out to lick her lips. She leaned closer to the mirror and watched the pupils of her eyes dilate, growing large and black. Bedroom eyes. Women used to put drops of belladonna in their eyes for the same effect.

"Rosa?" Jack said again, this time from outside the door.

"Be right there."

"Okay." His footsteps retreated.

She undid the strap again and stared at the shoes on her feet. *"Shoes aren't just something you walk on,"* she heard a tart, 1940s voice say in her head. *"They're a way to get where you're going."*

But where was that?

CHAPTER SEVEN

"That's what you're wearing?" Holly asked.

Kelsey smoothed the flowered skirt of her maroon dress. "What's wrong with it?"

"It's kind of matronly. And why is your hair in a bun, and why don't you have your contacts in? The lenses on those glasses make your eyes look tiny. Is this Mark guy some sort of ultrareligious conservative?"

"No." Kelsey checked herself over in the full-length mirror on the bathroom door. The dress was sleeveless with a V-neck in front and back, and reached almost to her ankles. On her feet were a sensible pair of black Naturalizer flats. "I think I look okay. I look like me."

"Kelsey! You're dressed like you're going to teach kindergarten, not go out on a date. At least put on some makeup."

"I'm wearing mascara and lip gloss."

"You know, there can be a happy medium between party diva and Mennonite, especially if you don't down a bottle of wine before going out."

Kelsey knew it wasn't the wine that had turned her into a Lindsay Lohan wannabe, letting loose like the world was coming to an end. It was those devilish shoes, her own personal kryptonite. They were sitting now in a locked metal box in the back of her closet.

"I don't think Mark would want a party girl."

"Now you're shaping yourself to be what you think a man wants? Great recipe for happiness, Kelsey."

"Let me figure this out on my own, okay?"

Holly held up her hands in surrender. "Fine!"

"You should be glad I'm going on a date," Kelsey grumbled.

"I am! And I hope you have a nice time, and that he's as nice as he's come across in his e-mails. His looks aren't anything on that guy you picked up at the club, but . . ."

"Please don't go there," Kelsey said, pained.

"Look, Kelsey, I don't think you did anything wrong by changing your mind and running out of there. I'm sure he was disappointed, but he'll get over it. He'd probably be delighted to hear from you if you called him. I still have all his contact information."

She shook her head. It had been three weeks since the Jack fiasco, too late to make amends. She'd left a piece of toilet paper with "Sorry!" scrawled across it on his bathroom vanity. Barefoot and carrying her shoes, she'd run down his driveway and hid in the neighbor's bushes, hoping the foul little Pomeranian wouldn't be let out, and called Holly for a ride.

It had been a coward's retreat, but it had been the only way she could think to save herself from her own animal instincts. Even with the shoes off there had been part of her that wanted to throw herself on Jack's bed and demand that he have his way with her, *Yes yes yes!*

Yes, she was a woman with rampant sexual hungers.

No, she was not a woman who slept with men she barely knew. Morals, feminism, and culture aside, she didn't think it was a behavior that was good for either her mind or body, and she would stick to that no matter what any damn shoe goddess told her.

Every night since, she'd dreamt of Jack's hands on her in the car, only in her dreams the encounter didn't end with only his hand between her legs. In waking hours she remembered him looking at her and saying that he wanted to find someone with whom to share his life.

Of course, it was impossible that such a pairing could work. She'd have to keep the Hiheelia shoes on twenty-four hours a day to keep up the Rosa façade. Jack's words were spoken out of a momentary lust, anyway. He'd grow tired of a nymphet who only wanted sex and to hang, big-eyed, on every word he spoke.

Wouldn't he?

At any rate, she'd surely grow tired of playing that role. Her natural self might be weird and awkward, but she liked harvesting snails and hanging out with goats and digging in the earth. She liked creating gardens, and couldn't see how the Kelsey with dirt under her nails and a composting fetish could find a satisfying existence within Rosa.

Jack adored Rosa. He didn't look twice at Kelsey. *And never the twain shall meet.*

The doorbell rang.

"Prince Charming!" Holly said. "Yippie!"

"Maybe he has a brother for you," Kelsey said, going past her sister to get the door.

"God, I hope not."

Kelsey paused to compose herself, then opened the front door.

A bald hobbit with a bouquet of flowers smiled up at her. "Hi!"

"Hi!"

"You're taller than you looked in your picture," Mark said.

"And you're, uh . . ." *Shorter, much shorter.* "Much *cuter* than in yours!"

He laughed. "Didn't Bridget tell you I'm only five foot four?"

Kelsey shook her head.

"I make up for it in girth," he said, patting his barrel chest. "These are for you." He handed her the flowers: a cheap bunch of Peruvian lilies from a supermarket, a small produce sticker still affixed to the cellophane. She'd once spent an entire day ripping out a bed of the invasive plants for a client.

"Thank you." Kelsey took them, then didn't know what to do with them. Was she supposed to take them with her? Make Mark wait while she put them in a vase? What she wanted to do was compost the monsters. She turned around, looking helplessly to Holly.

"I'll take care of those for you," Holly said, taking

them. "I'm Kelsey's sister, Holly," she said, holding out her hand to Mark.

"It's a pleasure to meet you."

The three of them stood in awkward silence for a moment, then Mark bounced on the balls of his feet and clapped his hands together. "Well, shall we go?"

Kelsey grabbed her shawl, and while Mark was looking the other way, Holly gave her a thumbs-up.

Kelsey raised a brow. *Really?*

He's sweet, Holly mouthed.

They bustled out to Mark's Prius, Mark leaving her to open her door herself. She chided herself for noticing. Mark probably believed utterly in the equality of the sexes.

Would he want to split the check, too?

"So, Bridget says you're building quite a waterfall on your present job. I want to put a small one in my backyard. What type of material do you use?"

She told him, and answered the rest of his waterfall questions all the way downtown. His queries were so detailed that she began to wonder if he'd asked her out for free landscaping advice.

More likely he had asked her out to get Bridget to stop nagging him to do it. Kelsey was discovering that Bridget had a way of picking at a topic until she got what she wanted. Ergo, the short introductory e-mail from Mark a week ago, and after a brief back-and-forth here they were.

They found a parking spot on the street and walked to the restaurant, Cascadia. It had a reputation as one of the better restaurants in town and was popular with people dining on expense accounts. Holly had once seen Bill Gates Sr. eating there.

The restaurant was crowded, but after a short wait they were shown to their table, weaving amongst the other diners on their way. As they passed a table of men, a voice pierced through the hubbub, making Kelsey start. She gaped at the back of the male head two feet from her. She didn't need to see his face to know that it was Jack.

She stumbled forward, hurrying after the hostess and hoping their table was far, far away.

The distance was ten feet.

She sneaked a peek back at Jack's table. They still had their menus. *Shoot!* They were going to be there all night. She'd been keeping her distance from Jack at his house, afraid that he might somehow make the connection between her and Rosa. The sight of him in his kitchen every morning also filled her with shame—not for what she'd done in his car, but for running off without explanation. Her cowardice had been unspeakably rude.

"You can have the better seat," Mark said, gesturing to the bench seat along the wall. If she sat there she'd be staring right at Jack, and she might be in trouble if their eyes met. Her bun and the big glasses were a good disguise for Rosa, but the unusual eye color she and Holly shared made an impression on people. "I'll sit here," she said, and grabbed the outer chair.

"Are you sure? You won't be able to people-watch."

"There's too much going on. I'd rather concentrate on you."

"Well, I can't argue with that, can I?" He slid into the bench seat.

Kelsey was left to scoot her chair in and out herself. It wasn't that she *wanted* him to mess around with her chair, she told herself, but the gesture would be romantic. She would bet her worm bins that it was something Jack did with every woman he took out.

She mentally slapped her hand. *Stop it, Kelsey! Mark's a nice guy; don't sabotage this before it even begins.*

She draped her shawl over the back of her chair and resolved to give Mark a fair chance, even as her ears pricked for every murmur of Jack's voice behind her. A wicked part of her hoped that he *would* notice her.

And if he did, would it be Rosa he thought he saw, or Kelsey?

It was shortly after the arrival of the entrees that Jack noticed the redhead sitting with her back to him at a nearby table. His colleague across the way had excused himself to make a phone call, leaving a clear view from Jack's seat to the long alabaster neck and coiled red hair of the woman.

"Rosa," Jack said under his breath.

"What was that? Rosebud?" Todd asked. He was a business guest from Toronto. "Ro-o-o-sebud," he repeated, echoing Orson Welles.

Jack smiled and shook his head. "No snow sleds here."

"Not much hockey, either."

"Can't argue with a Canadian on that one." His gaze went back to the redhead. Could it be her? Skin like glowing moonlight was rare even in Seattle, where most people looked like a carp's underbelly by the end of winter. It was rare to wear pale well.

The redhead said something to her grinning toad of a companion, her long, sculpted arms briefly rising above her head in illustration.

Jack saw Rosa on the dance floor, slender, shapely arms swaying above her head.

It *was* her!

He had half risen from his seat when she turned her head slightly, and he caught sight of the heavy horn-rimmed glasses she wore. He eased back into his seat.

"Do you know her?" Todd asked, following his gaze.

Jack shook his head. "She reminds me of someone."

"She must have been some someone. You're staring a hole in the back of that girl's head."

Jack breathed a laugh. "Yeah, she was someone, all right."

Their colleague returned from his phone call and sat down, blocking Jack's view but not his thoughts. His night with Rosa had been haunting him for weeks now.

He'd gone over their time together in his house again and again, looking for where he'd gone wrong, for what he'd done that had made her bolt. Was it his pigsty of a room?

Possible, but she hadn't seemed to care.

His overeagerness for sex?

She'd been equally eager.

Did he pester her too much while she was in the bathroom? Did his house smell bad? Did he smell bad?

Maybe she had a boyfriend, and had second thoughts about cheating on him. Richard said that Rosa's friend had told him he couldn't know whom he was getting involved with. Maybe she was mentally ill, or maybe she got off on messing with guys' heads.

It was the not knowing that was killing him, and making it impossible to forget her. "Sorry," was all her note had said. *Thanks for the thought, but I'd rather you told me why.*

He'd gone to the club the next night and stayed until three, hoping she'd appear. He'd Googled *Rosa Rugosa* in as many variations—Rosalie, Roseanne, Rosamund—as he could come up with, but kept hitting sites about rose bushes. He didn't care about friggin' rose bushes.

In the rare dark moments when he was honest with himself, he admitted that part of the reason he was obsessed with her was that she'd dumped him. He wasn't used to getting dumped.

Richard said he'd been boobstruck. It was like being starstruck, only earthier in nature. Richard hadn't missed an opportunity to razz him about how far out of his mouth his tongue had been hanging, or of his certainty that he'd found his future wife. "Quickest marriage and divorce on record," Richard taunted. "You beat Britney!"

He couldn't explain why he had been so overcome by Rosa's beauty. Richard admitted she was a looker, but he hadn't been felled by her the same way Jack had.

No, of course you weren't, Jack thought. *She was put on this earth for me.*

Boobstruck was right.

As the meal wore on and his dining companion shifted in his seat, the redhead came back into view. Her bun had started to slide down the back of her head, and one long wisp of hair had already lain itself against the perfect whiteness of her neck. He imagined his lips there, against the soft skin, and could almost smell her. The hairstyle and glasses might not fit what little he knew of Rosa, but there was still something familiar about the woman.

The angle of her shoulders, the way she carried her head . . . He'd heard that one could recognize a person from their shape and posture long before one was close enough to see their face.

The woman stood and headed toward the restrooms. Jack excused himself from his companions and did the same. She was wearing an ugly sack of a dress: It was so big on her, she looked like a stick swishing around under a wet towel. Even so, there was a set to her shoulders and a lope to her gait that rang bells of familiarity so strongly that he almost knew who she was. Images flashed beneath the sur-

face of his mind. He saw sunlight, the outdoors . . .
He almost had it.

As if sensing him trailing her, the redhead cast
a glance over her shoulder and visibly tensed when
she saw him. She hurried down the hall to the
ladies' room and disappeared inside.

She'd recognized him! He knew he knew her!

Or maybe all she'd recognized was that a strange
man was following her to the ladies' room.

He loitered in the hall, avoiding the eyes of other
restroom patrons, and waited for her to emerge.

The door cracked open an inch and he came to
attention, but then it shut again. He stared at it, willing it to open.

A short, middle-aged woman came out. Jack
scowled, and she dashed away.

After another minute, the door again opened a
crack, and again he popped to the alert.

It shut.

It dawned on him that she was checking whether
the coast was clear. He pressed himself up against
the wall on the handle side of the door. She'd have
to put her face all the way outside the door frame to
be able to see him.

A man leaving the men's room gave him an as-
sessing look. Jack put a hand on his gut and mimed
vomiting, pointing at the ladies' room door. "My
wife," he whispered.

"She didn't have the duck, did she?" the man
asked in alarm.

Jack shook his head. "Salmon."

The man shook his head and hurried away.

It occurred to Jack that he might not be acting in a completely rational manner.

The door creaked open once again, then after a moment creaked wider and her head and one foot emerged. She checked out the other end of the hall, then turned her face in his direction.

He had a quick impression of huge thick glasses and a mouth opened in a shriek and then she darted back inside, but not before his hand shot out and grabbed her forearm. A tiny rational voice inside him screamed that he was not supposed to grab women, but the rest of him had to know who she was. The need overrode all social conditioning.

It couldn't override her, though. She threw her weight to the side and he went with her, his head meeting the door frame with a crack.

"Ow! God dammit!"

He shot his arm around her shoulders and pulled her close, where she couldn't do any harm.

Mistake number two.

She wrapped her own arms around his hips and hoisted him off the ground. Before he could overcome his shock and react, they were halfway into the hall and she was trying to toss him aside like a bag of rotten potatoes. All he had to do to prevent it, though, was hold on to her shoulders.

They swayed together, her grunting against his chest and trying to shake loose his hold on her shoulders so she could toss him. Him holding her and letting his toes drag on the carpet.

"Kelsey!" a man yelped.

She dropped Jack.

"Kelsey?!" Jack said. The sense of familiarity made perfect sense now: Every morning he watched her out in his yard. Even with her hat and goggles on there was enough revealed in her movements to give him a sense of recognition now, in a different context. Although, how he could ever have confused her with Rosa, even for an instant, was beyond him.

"Are you okay?" the toadlike man asked, keeping a safe distance at the end of the hall.

Kelsey nodded, her face tilted downward, hidden from Jack. "It's fine, Mark. I know him." She made shooing motions to her date. "I'll be out shortly."

"You sure you're okay?"

She nodded, and he reluctantly left.

Jack narrowed his eyes at the retreating man. What type of guy left his date in a back hall with a man with whom she'd been struggling?

Kelsey started to inch away from him, sliding sideways like he wouldn't notice.

"Kelsey! Jeez, I'm sorry."

"It's okay," she mumbled.

"No, it's not! I'm so sorry; I didn't realize it was you."

"Was there someone else you were going to attack?" she asked dryly, her face still averted.

"Christ, I'm so sorry." He grabbed two handfuls of hair, feeling like a loon. He'd *manhandled* a woman he didn't recognize, in a public place! He was one lucky fool that it turned out to be Kelsey, and not a complete stranger. "I can't really explain it; I've been trying to find this amazing woman I met, and she has hair the same color as yours."

"It's from a bottle, Jack. It's not unique."

"Oh. I wouldn't have known." Damn. An unhappy thought struck him: Maybe Rosa's brilliant eyes had been from colored contacts. They'd been unnaturally vivid, after all. "I saw the red hair and knew there was something familiar about you, and here we are. Can you forgive me?"

"Sure. No harm done." She still wouldn't make eye contact.

"I've never done anything like this before. You must have a terrible impression of me. First I flash you, now this."

"It's okay."

"It's not. Did I hurt you? How's your arm?" He wished she'd look at him. With her eyes averted he felt that she hadn't forgiven him.

"You startled me, is all." A smile curled on her lips. "I gave as good as I got. A girl gets strong, moving dirt and rocks all day."

He rubbed the bump forming on his head. "You aren't kidding. Kelsey, I am so sorry. Please put it down to temporary insanity. I do *not* abuse women. Are we friends?" He put out his hand.

She shook it, firm and quick, as if afraid to touch him. "Friends. And Jack?"

"Yeah?"

"Can I come by tomorrow and go over the garden design with you?"

"Tomorrow's Saturday. You work weekends?"

"I need your undivided attention, and I don't think I'll get that on a weekday."

"How did you get to know me so well?" After he saw another trace of a smile on her lips, he said, "Yes, come over whenever you wish."

She nodded. "Noon, then. I'd better get back to my date now." She hurried away, white shoulders held straight.

Jack gave her a moment for distance, then returned to his table.

"Thought you'd fallen in," Todd said as he sat down. "I overheard there's a problem with the salmon." He looked pointedly at the half of a fillet still on Jack's plate.

Jack put his hand on his stomach and made a face, shaking his head.

Todd pursed his lips. "Oooh. Sorry, man."

Jack shrugged, but his attention was once more on Kelsey. The obvious question he'd forgotten to ask her was staring him in the face: She must have recognized him on the way to the restroom. Why, then, did she hide from him?

Tomorrow he'd have to find out.

CHAPTER EIGHT

Vanity, vanity, evil wicked vanity, Kelsey scolded herself as she pulled into Jack's driveway at noon sharp. The man was bonkers over Rosa, and Kelsey wanted to hear all about it.

She didn't know where the inspiration to invite herself over for a "design consultation" had come from, but she'd blurted it out and been silently gleeful when he'd approved.

She didn't hold his bathroom stalking of her against him: He was suffering the lingering effects of those evil shoes. But as Jack had groveled in the hall outside the restroom, appalled at his behavior, she'd realized she had the moral advantage over him. Any questions she asked about his redheaded mystery woman would be answered, and she wanted more time to enjoy his lovelorn complaints than could be provided in a few stolen moments away from her dinner date.

It was wicked of her, she knew it. Wicked and vain.

Kelsey checked her reflection in the visor mirror. Her hair was in a tight French braid and she had on her glasses. More importantly, she was also wearing a nonprescription pair of black contact lenses she'd bought for Halloween a couple years earlier, when she'd dressed as a vampire. They looked a little unnatural, and in very bright light her pupils contracted so much that her blue-green irises showed in the centers of the lenses, but he probably wouldn't notice: her Coke-bottle glasses made her eyes look puny like a rat's.

She gathered her things off the passenger seat and walked up the path to the front door. In normal circumstances, she insisted on total design freedom from clients once she'd gotten a sense of the type of garden they wanted; in her experience, homeowner input was either bad or a pain in the ass to incorporate. She was willing to suffer that possible consequence in exchange for hearing Jack talk about Rosa.

He answered the door in a blue T-shirt and wellworn jeans, his feet bare. His hair was wet, and as dark as beaver fur. She wanted to rub her bare skin against it.

"You're punctual," Jack said in greeting, opening the door wide for her to come in.

She caught a waft of damp, clean man as she passed by him and closed her eyes to inhale. Her lower belly responded, coming to life with remembrances of his hands on her.

He led the way to the kitchen. "The island is the best work surface in the house. I hope that's okay?"

She set down her materials and thrust a small paper bag at him.

"What's this?" he asked, taking it.

"Neufchâtel and zucchini bread."

"Neufchâtel?"

"A peace offering."

"Okay, but what *is* Neufchâtel?"

"Oh. It's like cream cheese."

He opened the bag, peering inside. "You made the bread?"

"And the cheese."

He lifted out the plastic Glad container full of white cheese. "You're kidding."

"Ha ha." She tried to laugh, although it was a joke she'd heard a hundred times.

"You *are* kidding."

"What? No. I thought *you* were. You know, a pun: kid-ing. As in 'kid.' "

Understanding swept over his face and his mouth pulled down in disgust before he could control his expression. "This is goat's milk?"

"Of course," she said, hurt.

"But—that's not sanitary, is it?"

"People have been making their own goat cheese for thousands of years. It's good cheese." She felt tears welling in her eyes and sniffed them back, horrified.

"Are you crying?"

"No!"

"God *dammit!*" he said, dropping her gifts onto the island. "Why do I do the wrong thing every time I see you?" He glared at her as if it were her fault.

A tear dribbled down Kelsey's cheek and she wiped it away with the back of her hand.

Jack's face turned red and he yanked open a drawer and took out a knife. He tore open the wrapping on the zucchini bread and popped the lid off the Neufchâtel, and a moment later he had a slice of bread loaded with soft cheese. He looked at her and took a bite. And chewed.

His face relaxed in wonder. "Mother of God," he murmured through the food. "This is good."

"Thank you," Kelsey said softly.

"No, I mean this is really good. You could sell this." He stuffed half the piece of bread in his mouth, his eyes wide with wonder.

She smiled and shook her head. "It's for my family and friends."

He put his arm around her shoulders and gave her a squeeze, then kissed the top of her head. "Thanks. You're a sweetheart."

It was the type of hug and kiss you gave to a sister. As casual a bit of attention as it was, she would have reveled in it if not for what she'd experienced as Rosa. Rosa had set new standards, and being given a crumb from the cake of sensual assault she'd had from Jack before only angered her. She was the same woman; how could one version of herself be desired so much, and the other so little?

She bit back her bitterness. She would *steal* her cake from him, bite by bite.

Kelsey spread out her landscape plans on the island. "So, let's talk garden."

Jack groaned in frustration and pushed the drawings aside. "I can't visualize what any of this is going to look like in real life." He gestured at the books on Japanese gardens that Kelsey had brought, overflowing with beautiful photographs. "Too many choices! I know what I want to feel when I'm in it, but I don't know how to get from *here*," he said, pointing at his heart, "to *there*." He pointed at the slope out the window. "That's why I hired you."

"I'm trying to make sure you get exactly what you want," she said, her small black eyes patient as a monk's behind her thick glasses. He wouldn't have guessed her eyes were black: They'd looked lighter in her orange-tinted goggles.

"I know. I'm sorry. I'm just not good with this type of visualization."

"Would it make it easier to walk through a real Japanese garden with me?"

"Yeah."

She slid off her bar stool. "Let's go to Kubota Garden."

"Where?"

"It's a Japanese garden, and the best-kept secret in Seattle."

"Yeah, sure, let's go." It would be a relief to get away from the stacks of designs and diagrams and the Latin lists of plant names. The past hour and a half hadn't clarified for him what his yard was going to look like when Kelsey was done, but it *had* increased his respect for what she did. Besides being a physical Wonder Woman, she had a master's degree in landscape architecture, an encyclopedic knowledge of plants, a civil engineer's comprehension of waterfalls, pumps, and ponds, and an ability to visualize in 3-D that disproved all the studies that claimed women were spatially challenged. A formidable, creative brain resided behind those five-pound glasses and quirky personality.

She'd been running such circles around him, he hadn't found space to squeeze in the question of why she'd run *from* him, at the restaurant. A peaceful walk in a park would provide that opportunity.

A rainsquall had come through while they studied the garden plans, but the sun was back out and the spring-green leaves of the trees looked fresh and renewed. Kelsey drove them in her battered old truck, and he rolled down the passenger window and stuck out his elbow, enjoying the breeze and cool, damp air, and the rare luxury of having nothing demanded of him. She turned on the radio—the same station he usually listened to—and he relaxed in the worn old seat of the truck and watched the road go by. Neither of them spoke on the drive, and somehow he knew that was fine with her.

He was sorry to arrive at the park and have it end. There were only three other cars in the lot, though, putting truth to Kelsey's statement about the place being a secret.

"This garden was built over a span of fifty years by Fujitaro Kubota, a Japanese emigrant," Kelsey explained as they walked through the entry gate. "He had a landscaping business and used this land as a display garden and nursery. After he died it was made into a public park." Kelsey stopped by a tall hedge with a window-sized hole cut into it at head height. "Look through here."

He did. The land dropped away on the other side

of the hedge, into a valley that combined the best of native Northwest vegetation with the art of the Japanese garden. Dark Douglas fir trees rimmed the valley and covered the hills in the distance, with only occasional pieces of the twenty-first century showing through in the white of a distant house or the pole of a cell tower. He knew, though, that a busy street was less than three blocks away. The garden was an impossible well of tranquility amidst the fractured noise of the city. "No way," he breathed.

She laughed and led the way down the path. "I know it's not as impressive as some of the gardens you've seen in Japan, but what I love about this one is that it was one man's dream, one man's passion. His vision. His creation."

"You'd like to do something like this, wouldn't you?" Jack asked, seeing the joy in her face as they walked the paths. She'd put her legionnaire's hat on when they got out of the car, and he found himself wanting to toss the ugly thing behind a bush. She wouldn't be half-bad looking if she let her hair down and smiled like this more often.

"I get to do this with each job I take, to some degree. It's like playing God: I get to create a world exactly as I see fit."

"As long as the client approves."

She cast a sly look at him over her shoulder. "I make them think it's their idea."

He laughed. They explored the park for a while, Kelsey explaining the design philosophies that made some areas successful and others less so. She was fluent and uninhibited when discussing land-scape design, and nothing like the borderline freak who'd made the awkward penis joke that first day. He was finding to his surprise that he liked her.

"That guy you were out with last night, was he the one Bridget set you up with?" he asked, feeling bad now for the uncharitable thoughts he'd once had about the poor sod who'd be stuck going out with her.

"Yes, Mark. It was our first date."

He winced. "I screwed that up for you, didn't I?"

She shrugged one shoulder. "Not really. I lied through my teeth. I said you were an old family friend with whom I used to wrestle, and that you were a big enough jerk to still think it was funny as an adult. He seemed to buy it."

He'd noticed the toad giving him patronizing looks through the remainder of the meal. "Do I look like I could be that big an asshole?"

"You think the truth was better?"

"Touché, *ma chère*. Is there going to be a second date?"

"I don't know yet."

"He'd be a fool not to ask you."

She glanced at him, but said nothing.

"When you saw me following you to the rest-rooms, why did you run?"

She scowled. "I didn't run."

"Not *technically*, but you did hide. You didn't want me to see you."

"So?"

"I'm just curious."

"I . . . I was embarrassed. It was a blind date, you're a client—I don't know! I was surprised to see you, and I got flustered."

He nodded, thinking he understood. "The collision of private life and work life."

She nodded quickly. "Yes."

"Well, I hope it works out for you with the guy. If that's what you want."

She cocked her head. "Do you think I *shouldn't* want it?"

"He seemed quick to abandon you to the ruffian by the ladies' room."

"We were in a public place, with people constantly coming and going," she said defensively. "You couldn't have hurt me. There was no danger."

Walking alone with her in a secluded park was not the time to point out what harm a man could do to a woman in the space of a few minutes. "I'm just saying, a bit of bravado has its place now and then."

"Can I ask *you* a question?" Kelsey asked.

"Sure."

"Who's the 'amazing' redhead you were looking for?"

He let out a breath. "I don't know. A dream? I'd wonder if I'd imagined the whole thing if my friend Richard hadn't met her, too."

"You only met her once?"

"A few weeks ago, at a club." He gave her a bowdlerized version of the story.

"So what's so special about her, other than being beautiful?"

"Heck if I know. I don't think we ever *do* know why we fall for one person and not another."

"Sometimes it's pretty clear. I think looks have a lot to do with it."

He shook his head. "There were other beautiful women at the club. Hell, I've met hundreds of beautiful women. But there was something about her, something about her smile, and the look in her eyes. And the way she moved—it was like her whole body was saying *yes!* to everything that is joyful in life."

Kelsey plucked a leaf off a shrub and shredded it. "Maybe she *was* just a dream. You can't say yes to everything good in life, all the time. You'd never get anything done. You'd never *become* anyone."

"But wouldn't it be beautiful if you *could* live that way?"

Kelsey looked up at him with her small black eyes. "Maybe, once in a while." A smile crept shyly onto her lips. "I might enjoy it."

The moment stretched between them, pulled by a glimmering sexual tension. They were alone at the edge of a pond, large shrubs sheltering them to either side. His body stirred, aware of her closeness, and he remembered the sleek column of her neck with the strand of red hair lying against it. She swayed almost imperceptibly toward him and the urge to kiss her rose in his blood.

He cleared his throat and stepped back, seeking firm ground. Their working relationship made a kiss a huge mistake. And this was Kelsey. He had no wish to be romantically involved with her.

She blinked and looked away. "I've been thinking

about Step Two for how you can find peace in your garden," she said, her voice starting at a squeak but reaching normal level by the end.

"I already failed Step One—turn off the cell phone," he said, his own voice cracking. He'd almost kissed her. *He'd almost kissed her.* Jesus Christ.

"You'll get there. Step Two might help you."

They moved away from the pond, and the dangers of seclusion. "Okay, Zen Mistress. What's Step Two?"

"Grasshopper," she said in a kung-fu movie voice, "to know peace in your garden, you must work in your garden."

"I don't like the sound of that."

She grinned. "Think of it this way: You won't need your gym membership anymore."

"You look harmless, but you aren't, are you?"

Her grin widened. "You have no idea."

CHAPTER NINE

Kelsey knelt on the floor and pulled the metal box out from the back of her closet. It had been four weeks since she and Jack had gone to Kubota Garden and come so close to a kiss, and for four weeks she had been waiting for that almost-kiss to become real. Every few days she dragged the box out and stared at its closed lid, wanting to open it and fearing to at the same time.

Jack had starting working with her and Bridget in the garden, sometimes early in the morning, sometimes in the late afternoon, and other times not at all as he left town for work. When he was there, though, he worked at whatever job she set for him, never complaining but often asking questions. He chatted easily with them both, and when Bridget wasn't near he let the conversation with Kelsey verge nearer on the personal. He often asked her how things were going with Mark, and she hated to answer. Every date with Mark, every marker of it being a relationship made it less likely that Jack would cross the line from friend to lover.

She could have Jack if she wore the shoes. Without them, it was a schoolgirl fantasy.

Mark was reality.

The phone rang.

"Hi, Kelsey, it's Mark."

Speak of the devil. "Hi. I think I recognize your voice by now, silly," she said. They'd been seeing each other about twice a week for a month: Dinners out had progressed to dinners and rented movies at Mark's, and a few make-out sessions on his couch that hadn't yet led to him touching her anywhere below the waist. She let him set the pace for the relationship, but was a little puzzled that it was going as slowly as it was. Didn't he want to have sex with her? She had felt his erection hard under the zipper of his jeans, but he hadn't yet unleashed the demon.

Either he was a bit old-fashioned, or there was something wrong with his penis. She hoped it was the former. She was becoming fond of Mark, and from some things he'd hinted at about the future— talk of flying back to Wisconsin to meet his family, asking her if she wanted kids, and when—she guessed his own feelings for her were strong.

"Are you free next Friday night?" he asked, sounding a bit nervous.

"Yeah. What's up?"

"Nothing, I just want to take you out to dinner."

"Oh. Okay. Or I could make you dinner here. I'd like that."

"No, I want to treat you to a nice dinner, somewhere special. I . . . I want to talk about our future."

"Oh!" Good lord, was he telling her he wanted to propose? "All right. I'll find something nice to wear."

"Don't buy anything new; just come as you usually are."

"Okay." That was kind of sweet: He wanted her as she was. "Do you want to do anything this weekend?"

"I, uh, I've got some things I have to take care of," Mark said.

"Oh. Okay." Was he going ring shopping?

"But I'll see you next Friday. I'll pick you up at eight."

"Okay."

"Have a great week," he said.

"You, too."

She hung up feeling strangely flat, and a bit anxious.

Shouldn't she be giddy?

Instead, she felt a vague but growing pressure. She didn't love him. She might someday grow to love him; she could imagine them being compatible, and building a life together despite a few petty annoyances and disappointments. She did mostly enjoy the time they spent together, and even more, she enjoyed the physical affection. If he declared his devotion to her, she was either going to have to be honest and hurt him with her lukewarm response, or she would have to lie and commit herself to him.

She sat on the floor and pulled the box between her outstretched legs. There were only two weeks of work left at Jack's house and then she'd move on to her next project. No more working with him by her side, chatting, laughing, every moment pregnant with possibility in her mind, but obviously not in his.

Next Friday Mark might propose, and she might give him a tentative yes. If she did, then she would never again don the shoes. She knew it was morally wrong even to do so now, but she couldn't make herself care. Her lust for Jack was her secret, was her private passion, separate from anything to do with Mark. She would indulge it and expunge it at will.

Tonight was Friday. Jack had mentioned that all day Thursday through Saturday, until ten P.M., he'd be at a gamers convention downtown. His company had given him a suite in a hotel nearby.

Perhaps Rosa had a game *she* wanted to play on Saturday.

Kelsey put her hand on the lid, imagining she could feel the power of the shoes within.

"Who's your goddess?" Shoestra whispered naughtily in Kelsey's mind.

"I am," Kelsey said, and opened the box.

CHAPTER TEN

"I swear Kelsey, I'm beginning to wonder if you're not bipolar. You've got a weird light in your eye," Holly said, glancing away from the road for a moment.

"I'm not manic. It's these shoes: They make me feel sexy. They make me feel like Rrrr-osa," Kelsey said, rolling the *R*. "Rrrr-osa Rrrr-ugosa."

Holly snorted. "I don't know why Rosa wants to spend Saturday night at a gaming convention."

"Because of all the *es-sexy* men who like to play games," Kelsey said in her best Latina accent.

Holly choked. "You're going to make me pee my pants." She pulled over to the curb near the entrance to the convention center, looking worriedly out the windshield at the twilit sky. Although it was almost nine thirty, the long spring day still held a trace of light. "So your friend Carol and her husband are meeting you inside?"

Kelsey nodded, unhappy with the lie but unwilling to tell the truth. Holly seemed to like Mark and to think Kelsey had a possible future with him. Seducing another man didn't fit into that vision.

"Don't wait up for me; we might end up staying in a hotel." She'd timed her arrival to the end of the convention day, hoping there'd be nothing to stop Jack from spiriting her away.

"Okay. Call if you need me."

"Thanks, Hol." Kelsey felt a warm burbling of love for her protective sister. She leaned over and kissed her cheek. "You're too good to me. I love you, you know."

"Monday morning, it's off to the shrink with you. But I love you, too."

Kelsey grinned and got out. "Thanks for the ride."

As Holly drove off, Kelsey straightened her tight Chinese dress. It was peach silk brocade with a delicate design of white chrysanthemums with green stems. It traced her body from its mandarin collar to the hem at her ankles. A slit to midthigh on either side made it possible to walk. Erica had again worked her magic on Kelsey's hair and makeup, transforming her from bland landscaper to femme fatale.

Or, in the case of this convention, transforming her to the living incarnation of every male gamer's video fantasy. The shoes told her it was true, and the gaping jaws of men as she strutted into the convention hall were confirmation.

"Ready, shoes?" she said under her breath as she stopped to survey the hundreds of booths arrayed in aisles. "Find Jack."

She pivoted right and started walking. The shoes took her deep into the convention hall, moving her like she knew where she was going and wasn't going to let anyone stop her. Men and women seemed to sense her approach, turning and gawking, then falling back to make way.

"Who is that?" people whispered.

"She's that actress from what's-it, isn't she?"

"No, she's the model they used for Sex Vixen III."

Kelsey made eye contact and smiled as she glided by. *Tonight I say yes to everything that brings joy. Tonight I say yes to Jack.*

It was with that thought fresh upon her that the last of the crowd parted, leaving him standing alone in the center of the aisle, his back to her.

She stopped a dozen feet away. The crowd around them quieted, not sure what was happening or even why they themselves seemed to be playing a role.

Jack slowly turned, as if sensing a tiger behind him. "Rosa," he breathed, as if not believing his eyes.

She walked slowly toward him, feeling her desire in every pulse of her blood.

He dropped the paper cup of water he was holding. It splashed and rolled aside, ignored.

She came face-to-face with him, her body only inches away, and leaned forward until her mouth was beside his ear. "I've been waiting so very long for you," she whispered. "I can't bear it." She heard him swallow, and felt his quickened breath on her hair. "Make love to me, Jack."

"You ran away last time," he rasped.

She leaned in the last few inches until her body touched his. "I didn't know what I wanted. I was frightened."

"But you know now?"

"I've thought of you every day since." Her hips

pressing against his, she draped her arms around his neck and leaned her upper body back so she could see his face. She met his eyes and slowly raised her lips to his. When her lips brushed his, his control finally broke. His arms went around her and he crushed her to him, his mouth bruisingly hard on her own. He bent her backward until she was barely on her toes, her arms clinging to him for support. Around them the crowd roared approval, women clapping and men whistling.

Jack broke the kiss and, with his arm around her waist, half ran with her toward the exit. When that was too slow, he scooped her up in his arms and carried her. "You don't have to stay and work?" she asked.

"I should spend another half hour with these guys," he said, nodding at a couple of gaping techies in a booth they were passing, "instead of with you?"

"Hell, no!" the techies answered for him.

Kelsey blew them a kiss over Jack's shoulder.

He put her back on her feet when they got outside, and with her hand firmly in his he pulled her a block and a half to a hotel. "I have a room," he said as they went through the revolving doors. They were the first words he'd spoken since the trade show, but the hovering disbelief in his eyes and his death grip on her hand both loudly said that he did not trust she would not disappear if he should let go of her for so much as an instant.

Kelsey let herself float on the current of his grasping passion, feeling a deep thrill in the possession of his hold on her. She was giving herself over to his will and wanted him to do anything and everything he wished to her.

They reached the suite and Jack put the DO NOT DISTURB sign on the door and bolted it. Kelsey stood in the doorway to the bedroom, watching him, waiting with a tremble in her belly for him to come over her like a storm and sweep her onto the bed behind her. She wanted the thundering rain of his desire to pour upon her until she was aware of nothing in the world but Jack.

Instead, he stopped a few feet from her. Joy struggled with distrust in his eyes. "How did you know where I was?"

"I talked to someone who knows you."

"Who?"

She shook her head. "It was a voice in passing." *It was my other self, the self you cannot see even though she's right before your eyes.*

He took a step closer. "You vanish and appear as if out of nothing. Surprises aren't easy on a man."

She wet her lips, the trembling moving into her limbs, afraid now that it was anger moving through him as much as lust. "Not even the good surprises?"

"I don't like it when I don't understand what's happening," he said, taking another step closer. "I want to get to the bottom of it."

"You'll destroy the mystery."

"You can't hold on to a mystery."

"You can hold on to me, Jack. I'm right here. You can trust in my body beneath your hands, can't you?" She undid the silk frogs that ran from her neck to her arm and let the fabric fall from her shoulder. "There's nothing more real than that."

He closed the distance between them and lifted his hands to her face, holding them to either side without touching her, as if framing a vision. "Why do I feel that I know you so well, when we're all but strangers?" he asked hoarsely. "How do you do this to me?"

"It's because you are all that I want in this world."

His fingertips touched the sides of her face and she felt his own trembling.

"Say yes to me, Jack," she breathed, the words less than a whisper. She tilted her face toward his, her lips parted. "Say yes."

"Yes." His mouth came down on hers, his arms around her waist. She wrapped her arms around his neck as he lifted her off the ground, her hips pressed against his, and walked her back to the bed. He lifted her onto it, lying her on her back atop the sheets that had already been turned down. He grabbed the chocolate on the pillow and tossed it aside.

"I might want that later," she said.

He smiled, and pulled her dress down as far as it would go in front, revealing one half-peach breast. "Chocolate is going to be the last thing on your mind."

She shivered, and he bent his head and rasped his tongue against her nipple. "*Jack,*" she breathed, looking down at the dark hair of his head. It was finally happening; he was finally here with her, wanting her, and nothing was going to stop them from joining their bodies together. She arched her back at the thought, the pressure of two months of waiting making her impatient.

She found his hand and put it on the side zipper of her dress; his mouth never left her skin as he pulled it down. His lips brushed round her aureola, his tongue found the well above her collarbone, his teeth grazed the side of her neck, nipping at where it joined her shoulder and sending shivers through her body and straight to her loins. With both hands he peeled the dress off her, down her arms and past her hips, Kelsey arching to release the fabric beneath her. She wore no undergarments, and when the dress was barely past her mound he held it there, a thick confining band of fabric that would not allow her legs to part.

He trapped her legs under one of his, binding them further, and lay against her side. She raised her hands above her head, invitation in her eyes. He lay one strong palm across both of hers and she grasped his hand, creating her own willful bondage.

His face above and to the side of hers, he watched her reaction as with his free hand he stroked her cheek with the backs of his fingers, then trailed them down her neck. His exploring touch traced around one breast and into the vulnerable pocket of her underarm, then down her side over the valley of her waist and hill of her hip. He skimmed across her lower belly, tripping lightly through the edge of that nether hair, the touch sending off alarms of arousal through her sex.

He tortured her with his slow voyaging, his finger-tips stroking the top of her thigh, the back of his hand teasing her and setting off hunger contractions in her passage, only to abandon her loins to again play with a nipple or slide over the edge of her lips, where she couldn't resist sucking on his fingertip as her whole body wished to do with his cock.

With his finger wet from her own mouth, he slid his palm firmly down the center of her body and lay it over her mound. He put his lips to hers and opened her mouth with his tongue, and when she received him he lightened his hand and gently slid the length of his fingers over the edges of her folds.

She moaned into his mouth, her hands tightening on his. When she arched against his touch he pulled back, forcing her to lie passive if she wanted his stroking. Her thighs tensed with the effort not to move as his fingers worked their magic in the tight confines of her pressed-together legs. The desire to have him deep inside became visual, her mind imagining his cock sliding deep within her, filling her, stroking in and out. When at last his fingertip touched the entrance to her core, her body released itself in waves of pleasure. He pressed his mouth more firmly to hers, his tongue thrusting deeper as she shook against him, her thighs clamped tight to his hand.

When the last spasms had died away he released her. She lay relaxed and lazy as he slid the dress off her legs, but when he touched the strap of one shoe she jerked her foot away. "Leave them on," she said.

He grinned. "I won't complain."

He stepped into the bathroom and she guessed he was looking for condoms in his toiletry bag. She rolled over on the bed and shoved the sheets and blanket down to the foot, baring the bottom sheet as she had done at his house. She sat up and waited.

He emerged a moment later with shiny packets in his hand and as naked as the day she'd first met him, his erection even larger than she remembered. Her sex, so recently sated, tingled anew.

"How do you want me?" she asked huskily.

"Six ways from Sunday. But I'll start here." He pulled a straight-back chair away from the wall and sat down on it.

Kelsey got off the bed and walked slowly toward him, placing her shod feet precisely one in front of the other, aware of the swollen anticipation between her legs. Her hair brushed sensuously against her shoulders and she lifted her hands to cup her breasts and play with her nipples between her fingers.

Jack groaned, his rubber-encased erection bobbing in appreciation. Kelsey felt the power of her sexuality expanding within her, blooming like the rose for which she had named herself when taking on this guise.

She reached Jack and stood with one foot to either side of his, then bent forward and braced herself with her hands on the tall back of the chair. She kissed him, and as she did she straddled him, her legs forced wide by the width of the chair seat. He grasped her hips in his strong hands and guided her down. She helped him find the angle and then closed her eyes and threw back her head as he slowly filled her, her body lowering onto his, coming to rest with the nub of her desire pressing against the firm flesh above the base of his rod.

Jack's hands on her hips set the pace, her thighs lifting and rocking her in response to his demands, the high heels of her shoes giving her the leverage she needed. As desire built again in her, she took over the pace, grinding against him in search of her own peak. Her pace was too much for his control and his arms came around her, holding her tight against him as he shuddered to his own climax.

When at last he relaxed she kissed the side of his head, and then could not resist a gentle rocking upon his cock still deep inside her.

"Don't worry, sweetheart," he said against her ear, and laughed softly. "There's plenty more to come."

He spent the next four hours proving he told the truth.

Kelsey woke in the dawn hour, her body half-sprawled against Jack's. He was snoring lightly.

They'd fallen into slumber with the lights on, and the room revealed itself to Kelsey's bleary eyes in a chaos of displaced furniture and pillows used for reasons no future guest would want to know about. Her feet were sticking out the bottom of the blanket they'd pulled over themselves sometime during their sleep. She raised one foot into view and thick red rose blossoms fell from it.

The roses on the vamp had not only grown and bloomed: they were spent.

Just as her night with Jack was finished, so were her shoes.

She eased off the bed, then bent down and unfastened the footwear, shedding petals all the while. She stepped out of them, expecting to feel a sudden nakedness and shame, but instead a mix of joy and sadness flowed through her. She would never regret a moment of this night, and her only grief was that she must now leave it behind. Rosa was part of her, but only part. She needed a man who could love all of her. Jack couldn't help not being that man.

She found her dress and pulled it on. Jack continued to sleep, his face relaxed in peace. She resisted the urge to kiss him, fearing he would wake.

Kelsey picked up her shoes; then, after a moment's thought, she placed them on the bedside table, a memento to prove to him that this had been real.

She left on feet as silent as the falling of a petal.

CHAPTER ELEVEN

"We need eighteen *Woodwardia fimbriata*," Kelsey said, putting her truck in park and hopping out onto the dirt road that wound through the wholesale nursery.

"Eighteen *what?*" Jack asked. He had Monday off after having spent the weekend working the gamer's convention and had surprisingly accepted Kelsey's half-hearted invitation to come with her to the nursery.

"Giant chain ferns," Kelsey said flatly.

"Eighteen giant chain ferns—yes, ma'am." He shut the passenger door and went to work selecting ferns in black gallon buckets and sliding them into the bed of the truck. "What are you getting over there?"

"Fifteen *Polystichum munitum*, twelve *Adiantum pedatum*, and ten *Blechnum spicant.*"

"Go ahead, keep it secret if you want to," he said, annoyance in his voice. He obviously knew she was being intentionally opaque with the names.

"They're all ferns."

"What's the matter with you today?" he asked, coming over to where she was picking through the specimens. "You've been getting increasingly sour by the minute."

"You haven't been Mr. Cheerful, either."

"I told you why."

Kelsey tightened her lips. Yes, he'd told her all about the most amazing night of his life—with gentlemanly discretion about the details, of course—and each word fired Kelsey's fury. If Rosa was so frickin' unforgettable, a face never to be found again, a body beyond compare, then why was she so invisible in Kelsey Safire? She thought she had accepted that Jack could not be the man for her; but if she had, she wouldn't be so angered by his continued blindness.

"Maybe I'm angry at your reluctance to see the truth," Kelsey spit out.

"What truth?"

"About your precious Rosa! She abandoned you *again*, Jack. No explanation. You're hurt, you're angry, but you're still in love with her."

"Why should that make you so mad? What does it have to do with you?"

"Nothing! Except that by now I think I've become your friend, and I don't like to see my friends get screwed over."

He looked at her for a long moment. "Love's a funny thing," he said at last, in a calmer voice.

Kelsey colored. "Meaning what?"

"It comes in different shades. Friendship, admiration, respect. Lust, longing. Protectiveness."

Her cheeks burned, and she dropped her eyes, certain he had divined her crush on him.

"There are many ways to love," he went on, "but

it's a mistake to think that they all lead to the same real-world destination."

"What destination is that?" she mumbled.

"A life together. Marriage. People can love each other without that ever being in their future."

Kelsey squatted down and fussed with a fern. He was telling her in the most delicate of indirect terms to lay off; that he and she would never be we.

"I don't know what's going to happen where Rosa is concerned," he said, "but that doesn't mean I can't take joy from what we shared. You'll let me have that, won't you?"

She nodded, too embarrassed to look him in the face.

They gathered more plants and trees throughout the acres of the nursery. Eventually there was only one thing left on her list, and Kelsey chewed her lip as she stared at the words in her own handwriting, jotted down as a necessity for Jack's garden long before she had ever visited Hiheelia.com and cat-walked her way into so much trouble.

"Please don't get mad at me for this," Kelsey said as she stopped the truck and got out.

"For what?" Jack joined her in front of a dense mass of unusual rosebushes with thick, rough green leaves. They were blooming in colors ranging from white to deepest red, their heavenly fragrance wafting on the breeze, attracting bees and butterflies. "What's to get mad at? They're beautiful."

"They're *Rosa rugosa*." She watched his face for a reaction, detecting only a twitch of muscle near his eye. "We need some for your garden."

"*Rosa rugosa*," he repeated without apparent emotion. "I saw that name was a type of rose when I Googled her after that first night. I ignored it." He touched a silken yellow petal. "Rosa Rugosa probably isn't *her* real name, is it?"

"I suppose it's possible," she said, feeling bad about the hurt she sensed under the surface of his expression. " 'Rugosa' sounds Italian."

"What's it mean here?" he asked, gesturing to the flowers.

" 'Rugose.' Which means wrinkled, or with ridges. They're named for their leaves. They're beautiful, hardy, self-sufficient plants, which is why I wanted them for your garden," she babbled, hating the silence when his face was like stone. "They've always been one of my favorite plants. Maybe they were one of hers, too."

"Which ones do you want?" he asked flatly.

She winced at his tone. "We could find something else; we don't *have* to use rugosas."

"Tell me which ones you want. These yellow ones? The pink?"

"Jack . . ."

"I'm not going to let her ruin my garden! God dammit, it's just the name of a freakin' bush! I'll put the things in my garden if I damn well please!"

"Then get one of the God damn pink ones, and one of the God damn red ones," she shouted back, "and three of the God damn white ones! Because they smell really God damn good, okay?"

He gaped at her, and after a long hanging moment of tense silence a chuckle formed in his chest, building until laughter came spilling out in a wave of mirth that washed her in shock. "Kelsey," he said on a laugh, and came over and hugged her, smooshing her goggled face against his shoulder. "How did I ever get along before I knew you?"

"I don't God damn know," she muttered, and felt his laughter in her whole body.

CHAPTER TWELVE

They were back at his house unloading the collection of plants when Kelsey dropped her bombshell on him. "I think Mark is going to ask me to marry him this Friday."

Jack dropped a pot of *Gaultheria shallon* on his foot. He knew that's what it was because he'd been reading the tag when she spoke. "He *what?*"

"You heard me."

"But you've only been going out for a month!"

She shrugged and dragged a five-gallon pot off the bed of the truck and carried it over to her staging area, working with a speed and ease that gave no hint of the true weights involved. They were doing the work alone, Kelsey having sent Bridget home when they went to the nursery. "He's been talking about flying to Wisconsin to meet his parents, and he was all nervous on the phone, saying he wanted to take me somewhere special and talk about our future."

"You're going to say no, of course."

"What do you mean, 'of course'?"

"You don't love him."

"How do you know?" she asked accusingly.

"Because I have ears. You don't talk about him like a woman in love."

She gave him a dark look, visible despite the orange goggles she always wore on work days. "I doubt I'll say yes, but it doesn't mean I have to say no, either. There might be something there, if I give it time."

He snorted.

"What?"

"You don't give this type of thing time. You know already whether or not you could ever marry him. Don't torture the guy."

"So, feelings never change over time? What about all those arranged marriages where people grow to love each other, when they originally thought it impossible?" she countered.

"*You* have choice. People in arranged marriages don't. Big difference."

"Feelings can change for the positive as you get to know a person, I'm sure of it. If they can change for the negative—which happens all the time as you get to know someone you're dating—then I don't see why they can't change for the better. You have to keep your eyes open to who someone really is, instead of only seeing the bits that conform to your first impression."

"Even if that's so, you've known Mark long enough to know he's not the one for you. You're young, there's no reason you should settle."

"There's no knight in shining armor out there for me, Jack. It's only hobbits that come to my door."

He pictured Mark and burst out laughing.

"Hobbits are good people," Kelsey said. "Don't mock them."

"They *are* good people. But you're not one of them."

"So I'm bad?" she asked, slanting a sly look at him.

"You're not a *hobbit*. Just don't settle, okay? You deserve someone who thrills you, not someone who's 'good enough.'"

She made a noncommittal noise.

"Promise me."

"But I like their little furry feet."

He caught her grin and knew she was having him on. "Why you—" He threw a clod of dirt at her.

She laughed and nailed him in the chest, dirt spraying across his shirt. In moments they were running up and down the slope, chasing each other like puppies, both of them laughing so hard they could barely run.

Jack swooped his arms around her from behind and lifted her off the ground, spinning her in circles, girlish squeals piercing her laughter. He set her down and they both staggered with dizziness, then mock-fell to the ground. Jack rolled over on top of her, pinning her panting beneath him. She grinned up at him, and without thought he lowered his mouth to hers.

It felt like the most natural thing in the world. Her grin relaxed into the kiss, her lips answering his as if they'd done this together a hundred times before. She wrapped her arms around his neck, and when he traced his lips down to the corner of her neck she sighed into his ear with the trusting abandon of a longtime lover.

He lifted his head and looked at her. The white zinc on her nose and orange bug-eye goggles were as ridiculous as ever, but her eyes met his with clarity and calm acceptance, as if she could see this thing between them with a perfect understanding that he as yet lacked. Her lips beneath his had felt every bit as good as Rosa's, but with Kelsey there was something else, as well; something that added a richer layer compared to the sheer pleasure of Rosa.

Kelsey would not disappear with the dawn. She was as real as real got, a woman literally of the earth. And when he was with her, he realized now, he felt the peace and joy that had eluded him for so long. It wasn't the garden that Kelsey built that would bring him happiness: It was Kelsey herself.

"Kelsey," he said in faint surprise, "I think I'm falling for you."

"You think, or you know? Make up your mind, Jack."

He chuckled. "You're not a romantic, are you?"

"I'm not fond of ambiguity when it's my heart on the line. You think, or you know?"

"*Is* your heart on the line?" he asked, his own heart beating faster with the sudden question of what her feelings were.

"You think, or you know?" she repeated softly.

He lowered his lips next to her ear. "*I know,*" he whispered.

"Prove it to me," she whispered back, and arched her body against his.

He groaned deep in his throat, his body going hard with desire. He would prove it to her right here on the ground, if he had a condom handy. Instead, he picked her up off the ground and pulled her toward the house.

"I'll prove it when you get rid of *this*," he said, snatching the legionnaire's hat off her head and tossing it to the ground.

She grabbed at her bare head. "Jack!"

They went through a side door and paused to kick off dirty shoes. Jack pinned her against the wall and kissed her again; then when she was dazed and helpless he lifted the hem of his shirt and wiped the zinc off her nose. "And when you get rid of *that*."

She covered her nose with her fingers. He grabbed her hand and dragged her through the kitchen and living room. "And *this*," he said, snagging the elastic around the end of her French braid and tugging it off.

"Jack, wait!" she protested, reaching up to protect her hair.

He trapped her inside his embrace and used his free hand to gently loosen her hair until it spread in red waves over her shoulders. She had so much in common physically with Rosa, and yet was so different.

Kelsey ducked her face against his chest; then when he loosened his hold she darted from him, down the hall to his room.

"You know I'm coming for those damn goggles next!" he said, chasing after her.

"I know, I know," she said, panic in her voice.

He reached the room as she closed the last of the curtains. There was still enough light to see his way by, but the room had gone to shades of gray and the shadows were deep. "I'd rather see you," he said.

"If I can barely see you without my goggles, then this is only fair."

"Are you really that shy of my seeing you?" he asked, coming close to her. He could see the shape of her face, and the glint of lighter gray reflecting off the goggles.

"Just this first time," she said softly. "Please."

He carefully removed her goggles and set them aside. "All right."

The darkness amplified their breathing, and with small exhalations and moments of held breath they undressed each other, piece by piece. They were both damp with sweat beneath their clothing, especially between Kelsey's breasts, confined as they had been by the sports bra. He ran his fingertip down her sternum, feeling the droplets and dragging them in a trail down to her belly.

He put condoms on the bedside table and together they tumbled onto the mattress. Their hands explored each other in the dark, her eager hands touching him without shyness, his own hands roaming her lithe body and marveling at the catlike sleekness of her muscles. As his eyes adjusted to the dark he could see her shape more clearly, and it was eerie how similar she was to Rosa. He tried to shake off the thought, not wanting thoughts of another woman to intrude on this moment with Kelsey.

They touched each other until their breathing grew heavy, and he donned protection. She surprised him then by pushing him onto his back and climbing on top, sliding herself onto him without further preamble. She was a demon, her hair hanging wild about her as they rocked together, her back arching and breasts rising as she leaned back to change the angle. In the semidark her body merged again and again with his memories of Rosa, until even her face began to look like Rosa's.

Kelsey reached down to touch herself, shameless in her need for gratification, and when her climax came, his came, too. When their motions eased she slowly leaned forward, her hands on his chest, and kissed him while he was still inside her. In that moment he thought that even her eyes had lightened from black to blue, and he was so appalled with himself for thinking of Rosa that he closed his eyes against the image.

She fell asleep tucked against his side, but he could not rest easy, his mind wide-awake and sick with dread that he had led Kelsey down a false path. Even as his heart said that the woman sleeping beside him was the one that he wanted, his vision of her atop him as Rosa made him doubt the truth.

Did he think he loved her *because* she resembled Rosa?

But wait. He laughed with Kelsey; they talked; they worked together and were silent together; and he looked forward to her arrival every morning. Those many hours had not been a lie. Her adorable wit and weirdness and incomprehensible fondness for Little Bastard were not a lie.

He wished he'd never met Rosa Rugosa, if it meant she was going to taint what he could have with Kelsey.

He slipped from under Kelsey's hold, unable to lie still any longer with the thoughts and feelings that were torturing him. He stood beside the bed and looked down at her, so serene in her trust.

She moved, startling him, and then rolled over so that her face was toward the windows. The dim light fell more strongly upon her, and he stared at her face in growing disbelief. There couldn't be two women roaming Seattle with the same features and same body, who would both go to bed with him in the space of three days.

Kelsey had known he was going to be at the convention. Kelsey, who had never let him see her without her hat and orange goggles, or glasses so big that he wouldn't recognize his own mother in them.

"You have to keep your eyes open to who someone really is, instead of only seeing the bits that conform to your first impression," Kelsey had said not an hour ago.

He stepped to the curtain and slowly pulled it open. A wedge of light stretched across the bed, widening as it moved up her body, then falling at last upon her face.

Kelsey squinted in her sleep, then slowly opened her eyes.

They were the intense blue-green of a tropical sea.

His heart thudded in his chest, a flush of adrenaline flooding through him, although he didn't know if it was for anger, fear, or relief. His vision throbbed to his own heartbeat, and he sank to the foot of the bed, staring at her.

"Jack?" she said sleepily.

"Right here."

She pushed herself upright, her hair in glowing copper tangles against the perfect whiteness of her skin.

"Can you see me?" he asked.

"A smudge," she said, and yawned.

"I can see you."

She tensed, one hand flying to her face as if seeking the disguise that obviously wasn't there. She dropped her hand. "Then you know."

"Why, Kelsey? That's all I want to know. Why?"

She drew her knees up to her chest, as if to protect herself. "I didn't think you could ever see me as anything more than your landscaper. I didn't think you could ever love Kelsey Safire. But Rosa—any man would want Rosa."

"Then why play the Rosa role so little, if that was what you wanted?"

A wry smile touched Kelsey's lips. "She seemed bigger than life, but in truth she was only a small sliver of it—too small a sliver to inhabit for more than a few hours."

He continued to stare at her, astonished how blind he had been to the obvious. "You must have thought I was so shallow to be attracted to Rosa but apparently not to you."

She tilted her head in reluctant acknowledgment. "And you must now hate me for lying. So what did it get me?" she said sadly.

He laughed softly. "I'm not angry. I fell for you both times, didn't I? I have the feeling I'd be fighting the inevitable if I ended things over this." He moved forward until he could reach her, and with the tip of his finger raised her chin until her face was fully in the light. "I don't suppose you could live your life somewhere in between orange goggles and dancing all night at clubs? I'd hate to see *all* of Rosa disappear from you. She did have her merits."

"I know what *merits* you're talking about," Kelsey said, an eyebrow raised suggestively. "I was there while you were appreciating them." Then she smiled, and the aqua light in her eyes spoke of mischief and love, and the hope that maybe they did have a chance together; that maybe all was well that ended well.

"I kept the shoes, you know. Want to put them on?"

She laughed, and he knew he would be hearing that laugh beside him for the rest of his days.

EPILOGUE

"What do you think, Little Bastard? Do you think they'll be impressed?" Kelsey asked the goat. She'd bathed him and cleaned his hooves, and tied him firmly to an eyebolt embedded in the patio. As a worker on the Lovgren garden project, he deserved to be present for the festivities.

"Nay," Little Bastard declared.

"That's what you always say. Try saying yea once in a while, you might like it."

Guests were starting to arrive for the house-warming Jack was throwing to show off not only the house and garden, but as he put it, "the hot babe I found in the ivy outside my window."

Bridget, Derald, and Mark came out onto the patio, and Kelsey hurried over to greet them, giving Mark a hug to make sure he knew he was welcome as a friend. She'd called him to cancel both their dinner date and their relationship. His surprise had quickly given way to relief: It turned out that his talk about the future had meant he wanted to break up, and to send her off with a nice meal as a consolation prize. "I don't think we have that 'spark,'" he explained again and again on the phone, even as she told him that no, it was okay, she felt exactly the same.

"It's beautiful, Bridget honey," Derald said, wrapping his arm around his wife's waist. "You did a marvelous job."

Bridget giggled. "Kelsey did quite a bit herself. I can't take all the credit, you know, although there *are* some of my own touches on display."

Actually there weren't, as Kelsey had removed the plants that Bridget had installed in a burst of uninformed horticultural creativity. It was no skin off her nose to let Bridget be the genius in her husband's eyes, though. On such illusions were grand loves built.

She found Holly and Erica in the kitchen, Holly adding tequila to the pitcher of margaritas and Erica looking annoyed as Jack's friend Richard chatted her up. "Erica, Mark is suffering out on the patio. Would you mind bringing him a drink?" Kelsey asked. She knew that Holly had eyes for Richard, and wanted her to have a clear shot at him.

"I'd be *delighted* to," Erica said, pouring a glass for the hobbit. "I always thought he was kind of adorable," she whispered to Kelsey as she passed by. "Like a teddy bear."

"Kelsey, I meant to tell you!" Holly said. "That shoe site is back up. You're right, it *is* weird. I think I ordered something, but heck if I know what it was! Guess I'll just have to wait and see."

Kelsey glanced at Richard, who was wandering

after Erica, oblivious to the brunette goddess in the room. "Holly, I promise you won't regret your purchase."

"Good. So, when do you turn on the waterfall? I'm dying to see it run."

"As soon as Jack stops abusing the snails."

"Hey, serving them was not *my* bright idea," he said, struggling to get a sheet pan of mushroom caps stuffed with snails into the oven. "We should tell people they're clams. I don't think the truth is going to be a big selling point."

"If they refuse to eat garden snails, it just means there will be more for us. Admit it: You love them."

"With a bit of Tabasco they aren't half bad."

"With an apron on, neither are you," Kelsey said, putting her arms around his waist and giving his butt a surreptitious squeeze.

"You and your costumes."

"Don't pretend that you're complaining."

He kissed her, and they went out to throw the switch to the waterfall pump together.

"There's something very sexy about those shoes," he whispered in her ear as they crossed the patio. "Every time you wear them, I get the strangest urge to take you behind the bushes and ravage you."

"I don't see the problem with that."

Jack growled his approval, and together they threw the switch to the falls.

First they heard the faint rumbling of the motor, and then several seconds later the first gurglings of water somewhere up the slope, the source hidden by carefully placed greenery and stones. The gurgling turned to splashing, careening down the bends and drops of the waterway, and then finally a sheet of water spilled over the top of a stone and dropped five feet to the pond below, in which a half dozen koi milled, waiting for food.

The guests applauded, and Little Bastard said nay.

Thinking of Jack's words, Kelsey glanced down at the Hiheelia shoes she wore, and she sent a private word of thanks to Shoestra. She was not the same woman who had started work on this garden, hunched behind a goat and longing helplessly for a man. The shoes had brought out a sensuous, confident side of herself she would never have known she had. And Rosa was not gone now, whether or not Kelsey wore the shoes: She had taken her proper place amongst the facets of Kelsey's character.

The red blossoms had all fallen off the shoes, but in so doing had revealed the structure of the vamp beneath: a gold filigree of roses, in permanent bloom.

GEMMA HALLIDAY

So I Dated
an Axe Murderer

For the Romance Divas, the most fabulous friends a girl could ask for.

And for our fearless leaders, Kristen, Jax, and Lisa, three amazing ladies who know that true bliss really can be found in a pair of sexy stilettos.

CHAPTER ONE

They were beautiful.

I stared down at the box in my hands, recently delivered via one UPS guy whose name I could never remember. My fingers had trembled as I'd opened it up. I never did things like this. Bought such extravagant, silly things for myself. But these—these I hadn't been able to resist. The second I'd seen them on the Hiheelia website, I knew I had to have them.

The site had featured a woman in a short, black cocktail dress, about fifteen vava-voom points higher than anything I'd dare to wear, standing in the middle of a crowded room. All eyes were on her—every woman wanting to be her, every man wanting to own her. But I could tell by the look in her eyes that no one owned her. Not a manager breathing down her neck from nine to five, not an ex-boyfriend who couldn't tell her from a doormat, not a mother relentlessly pointing out a multitude of shortcomings. No, she was a woman unto herself, and she answered to no one.

On her arm was a man who made my mouth water. He personified the tall, dark, and handsome look—square jaw, rich, chocolate-colored eyes, broad shoulders beneath a blazer that was airbrushed onto a physique that obviously spent a lot of time at the gym. He was like an orgasm on screen.

Yep, the woman in the Hiheelia ad had everything. Everything I never would. I just wasn't destined for that kind of life. Me? I had a real-person life. A cat. A cubicle. A hatchback that was nearing the hundred-thousand-mile mark and had certain parts held together with duct tape. But for the most part, I was okay with that. My life wasn't the worst, right? I mean, who really has a supermodel's life anyway?

But as I stared at the website, somehow it was like I was five years old again watching Disney's version of *Cinderella* on TV and wishing I was the princess. Somehow, despite my thirty years of experience telling me differently, I once again believed in fairy tales—that I, plain-Jane Kya Bader, web designer, Silicon Valley single, and Match.com subscriber, could be that woman.

Even after I got home from work, changed into my favorite pair of drawstring flannels with the little Corona bottles on them and a faded UCSC sweatshirt, ate my Lean Cuisine in front of a rerun of *Seinfeld*, and checked my e-mail while Tabby the cat tried to molest my laptop screen, I couldn't stop thinking about the website. And somehow, the page popped up on my screen again. That woman. That man.

That life.

The site sold shoes. Hundreds of websites did. But these shoes were different. On Supermodel's feet were a pair of insanely high, red stilettos. Ankle straps embedded with tiny, sparkling rhinestones, toes pointy in a way real feet never were, heels ending in a dangerous silver tip. Totally impractical. Totally beautiful.

The caption beneath them read: *Shoes that will change your life*.

I knew it was utter crap. A pair of shoes is a pair of shoes. The only way those things would change my life was if I broke my neck trying to walk in them.

Still . . .

The more I looked at them, the more I sat at my computer screen alone in my one-bedroom apartment browsing Match's online profiles of guys I'd never even have the nerve to e-mail let alone meet in person, listening to canned laughter from the TV and still smelling the remains of my microwave dinner for one, the more I *wanted* to believe in the fairy tale. The more I envied her. The more I wanted to be like her. I wanted a life like that.

I wanted *her* life.

I don't know what came over me, but I found myself clicking the "add to cart" button, my fingers walking through the motions of buying the stilettos, size seven, express shipping, sent via UPS to my cube at OmniWeb the next day.

And they were every bit as beautiful as they'd promised to be.

I carefully unwrapped the layers of tissue covering the red shoes. Patent leather, so they shone even under the dull florescent lights above my desk. I ran one finger over the surface. A sort of tingle shot through me and for a moment I almost believed they did posses some magical powers. They were certainly the polar opposite of anything I usually wore. I looked down at my jeans, brown loafers, and black sweater. Did I even own anything red? I ran another finger down the length of the heel. God, how did anyone walk in these? How did she? I was pretty sure I'd stare at them for a day and then send them back. I mean, they were ridiculous. Where would I even wear them? And with what? It wasn't like I had a tall, dark, and handsome model just dying to take me out to some expensive dinner on the town.

"Hey, Kya."

My head snapped up, my hands immediately covering the shoe box as if to obliterate my dirty little secret. I bought fairy tales off the Internet. How pathetic was that?

"Yeah?"

My co-worker Danielle cocked her head of brown, corkscrew curls at me. "You okay?"

I bit my lip. A terrible habit that Ex-Boyfriend had nagged me about to no end. *If I wanted to kiss raw hamburger, I'd go to McDonald's.*

"Yeah, fine." I quickly shoved the box onto the floor, kicking it under my desk next to my humming PC tower. "What's up?"

Danielle locked one finger in her thick hair and started twirling. "We're having an all-hands meeting. Peterman wants to 'interface,' " she said, letting go of her hair long enough to do a pair of air quotes with her fingers, "about the new 'team building strategies' laid out by the 'interpersonal accessibility consultant.'" She finished by rolling her eyes—big brown ones lined in heavy black makeup that never smudged, never ran, never looked like it was applied in a hurry while juggling a latte and rush-hour traffic.

"Yeah. K. I'll be right there," I responded.

"Good. 'Cause we need all the solidarity we can get against management on this one. Whoa, who's he?" Danielle pointed to my computer screen.

I'd forgotten I'd left Hiheelia up. Ms. Supermodel and her Orgasm-on-Sight boyfriend were still suspended there, his adoring eyes still firmly rooted on her. I felt myself go warm, as if she could read my ridiculous thoughts about the man.

"No one." I quickly closed the window.

"Damn, he was hawt! Can you make me a screen saver of that guy?"

"Sure, maybe," I mumbled, ducking my head to cover my embarrassment.

"Cool. Hey, listen, I wanted to ask if you were busy tonight?"

"Why?" I narrowed my eyes at her. Danielle was fine as co-workers went, but she had an annoying habit of scheduling hot dates on nights when major projects were due. Leaving yours truly to pick up the slack. Which, of course, I always did. It's not like I had anything else to do, my steady date being twelve inches tall and covered in orange fur.

"Maxie and I are trying out this new club in the city tonight. You know Maxine in accounting, right? Tall, redhead, total crack-up."

I nodded. I'd run into her once or twice in the break room.

"Anyway, I need to leave a little early, 'cause I've got nothing to wear and need to hit the mall. So, I was hoping you could cover for me. Pretty please?" Danielle clasped her hands in front of her in a begging motion.

"Yeah, sure," I agreed. As if either one of us thought I wouldn't.

"Thanks, Kya!" She leaned in and gave my shoulders a little squeeze. "You're the best. I heard this club is off the hook."

I'm not sure why, but my eyes strayed down to the shoe box tucked at my feet. A nightclub. That was the place you wore a pair of heels like those. A hot new nightclub in the city. If I had someplace like that to go . . . I mean, not that I was thinking about *keeping* them.

But would it be terrible to wear them just once?

"Um, Danielle?"

"Yeah?"

"What if . . . I mean, I could still cover and all this afternoon . . . but, you know, it's Friday night and . . . well . . ." My heart suddenly hammered in my chest, my cheeks growing hot, my palms sweating. Was I really going to do this? This was so far outside my comfort zone. I felt my lips moving but almost couldn't believe the words pouring out. "Maybe I could go with you?"

Danielle froze. Then cocked her curls to the side again, picking up that errant strand. "You?"

I should have been offended by her shocked tone, but, honestly, I couldn't blame her. It wasn't that Danielle hadn't ever invited me out. She had. In fact, when I first started working here last year, she'd always included me in her Friday night plans. I'd just always declined. I don't know why. Somehow an evening with Tabby always seemed . . . safer. I guess I just never saw myself as the partying-until-dawn type.

I stole a glance at the box by my feet.

But *she* was.

"Yes. Me."

"Um, yeah, sure," Danielle said. "Yeah, if you want to come, that would be great." She perked up and almost looked like she meant it. "We're meeting at my place at seven. You need directions?"

I nodded, too shocked by my own behavior to say anything.

Danielle plucked a bright pink Post-it from the pad on my desk and proceeded to write down her address.

I'd wear them just once, I promised myself. Then I'd return them.

Just once.

I stared at my reflection in the mirror. Wondering if, in fact, it was *my* reflection. Same ash blonde hair, a little too long to be stylish, a little too short to be sexy. Same stick-straight frame, legs too long, arms too thin, chest way too flat. But that was where the Kya I knew ended.

I'd put the heels on as soon as I'd gotten home. And somehow they'd spurred me to rummage

135

through my closet until I hit the back, pulling out all the things I never wore. Because tonight I didn't want to be me. I wanted to be *her*.

I found a black skirt that ended just below my knee. Plain, stretchy material, but it hugged my hips in a way that almost made curves. I found a white blouse with ruffles down the front that my mother had bought me for Christmas. I'd never worn it. Too frilly, too clingy, too . . . noticeable. I slipped it on and buttoned it up the front. Then undid the top two buttons. Then the third. My black bra showed through beneath, but for some reason, I didn't mind.

Once I'd dressed, I dug out the only makeup I owned: a tube of black mascara left over from my cousin's wedding, black eyeliner I'd used to draw a mustache on myself last Halloween when I'd gone to the office party as a pirate, and a tube of red lipstick I'd gotten free with a bottle of shampoo.

Unfortunately, I had no idea what to do with any of it. I did a quick Google on makeup and came up with enough not to poke myself in the eye while applying the stuff. The effect wasn't the totally polished look Danielle achieved each day, but it wasn't bad. In fact, the red lipstick was pretty nice. It made my lips look more plump, full. Almost . . . sexy.

"What do you think, Tabby?"

My cat stared at me and meowed. No doubt asking where his Fancy Feast was. A whole lot of help he was.

I studied my reflection. The look was almost there. But it didn't quite do the heels justice.

I leaned down and fingered the hem of my skirt. *She* wouldn't wear something this long. Before I could stop myself, I felt my fingers taking hold of the hem, grabbing tight on each side of the seam, and ripping until a slit ran up the length of my thigh, ending a good six inches above my knee.

I should have been mortified. I should have been embarrassed beyond belief to go out in public in something this revealing.

Instead, for some reason, my reflection just smirked back at me.

Club Ecstasy in San Francisco was packed by the time we got there. Not that I knew a packed club from anything else. I'd honestly never been out to a real nightclub before. I'd seen them on TV. But never actually set foot in a real one. It was a lot warmer than I'd thought. Wall-to-wall bodies, all packed against each other like refugees shown on CNN. All sweating, gyrating, moving en masse like some giant orgy. I admit, I wasn't totally getting the appeal.

"Isn't this place fab?" Maxine yelled over the techno music pulsing through hidden speakers.

I nodded. *Liar.*

"Here we go, three cosmos," Danielle shouted, returning from the bar with three wide-brimmed glasses of pink liquid. She handed one to Maxie, then me.

"Oh, no, I don't . . ." I paused. Maybe *I* didn't drink. But *she* would. "Uh, thanks," I said instead. I took the glass and sipped gingerly. Then coughed. It was sweet yet like drinking liquid fire all at the same time. I forced myself to take another sip. This one went down a little smoother. A little.

"You okay, Kya?" Danielle asked.

"Yeah." I covered my mouth with my hand, coughing again. "Dandy. Just fine."

"Cool. Then let's go dance!" Danielle yelled over her shoulder, not waiting for an answer before threading her way through the mob.

Maxie followed, bobbing her head in time to the eardrum-busting beat.

I was left with no choice but to do the same, holding my glass above my head to keep from spilling on the strangers who kept rubbing up against me.

The club was separated into different levels—the main floor, which had the bar, and a loft section accessed by a pair of spiraling, chrome staircases. We were on the main floor where strobing lights and pink-and-green lasers cut through the air, overloading my senses. A DJ cranked out music from the center of the room on an elevated platform suspended just above the dancing crowd. Flanking him were four more elevated platforms, where scantily clad women danced go-go style, moving their hips in a way I'd only seen on late-night Cinemax specials. I couldn't help staring as I followed Maxie and Danielle.

"You guys do this every Friday?" I asked, in awe.

Only I got no response. I turned around. I'd been so engrossed in watching the go-go girls I'd totally lost my friends.

Oh. Shit.

"Danielle?" I called out. But my voice was lost in the sea of noise. I whipped my head around, suddenly feeling like a lost little kid at the mall.

Okay, stay calm. I was a grown woman. I was fine. I could handle this. I looked at the pink drink in my hand. Then downed the liquid courage in one horrifying sip.

"Hey, darling, you wanna dance?"

I lowered my glass to find a salt-and-pepper guy, forty-ish, wearing a black shirt and chinos, and gyrating in front of me.

I bit my lip. And shook my head violently from side to side. *Oh, bad idea.* The cosmo shot straight to my head, making the room sway.

"Come on, sugar, with legs like those, I'd bet you're a natural." The guy turned and did some sort of weird hand signal to the crowd behind him.

"No, actually, I'm just looking for my friends. They—"

But before I could finish, the crowd had responded to Chino Man's prompting and I felt my feet lifting off the ground.

Holy hell!

"No, really, I'm just . . . please, I'm only . . . I don't think I can . . ."

Yeah, like anyone was listening. My protests were completely swallowed up by the DJ, spinning a new song with a lot of bass and wailing lyrics, as a dozen hands shoved me up onto a raised platform. Once they let go it took me a minute to get my balance. Especially with the cosmo still whirring through my system. I stood up on shaky legs.

"But I don't even know how to dance!" I shouted, scanning the crowd for any glimpse of Danielle's curly head.

What I saw instead was a sea of expectant faces. Raising their fists. Cheering me on.

Me?

Panic rose like bile in my throat. Shit. What did I do?

I looked down. My red stilettos shone against the flashing strobes and lasers, the patent leather reflecting the pulses of light like shiny red mirrors. I focused on them. Beautiful shoes. Daring.

Sexy.

I looked out at the crowd again. Maybe I didn't know how to dance. But I bet *she* did.

I closed my eyes, letting the rhythm of the bass beat fill me. I lifted one arm over my head. Then the other. My head start to bob in time with the music, my hips swaying. The crowd's roar turned up a notch. I was keenly aware of the cool leather hugging my feet as I took one step to the right, then one to the left, the shoes guiding me, telling me how *she*'d dance.

And then I was moving. Dancing. Swinging my legs beneath the ripped skirt, the revealing slit riding up my thigh, shimmying my flat chest at the crowd like I was some stacked Playmate, moving my hips like I belonged on MTV.

In hindsight, it was probably the strong cosmo on an empty stomach. But right then I blamed the shoes.

"Wooo, baaaaaby," I yelled out, ripping off my ruffled blouse and dancing on the platform in my black lacy bra. And the crowd loved it. In fact, I think Chino Man even whistled at me. I whistled right back.

I have no idea how long I was up there. It felt like only seconds, yet an eternity, before Danielle and Maxine appeared in front of me, their arms outstretched to help me down. Reluctantly I went, clearing the platform for a woman in strategically placed spandex and thigh-high fuck-me boots to take my place.

"That was awesome," I panted, as Danielle steered me away from the action.

"Ohmigod, what were you doing up there?" she asked, laughing. Clearly this was not the woman she was used to seeing in the next cubicle.

"Dancing," I managed to get out. I grabbed the drink in her hand and sipped eagerly. "You guys have got to try that."

Danielle threw her head back and giggled. "Wow, Kya cuts loose."

I shook my head. "No, I'm not Kya tonight. I'm her."

"Who?" Maxie asked, scrunching her ski-jump nose.

"The woman on the website. I'm the shoe lady." I pointed down at my feet.

Danielle and Maxie looked down, then at each other, clearly not getting it. It didn't matter. All that mattered was that for tonight—just one night—I could leave boring old Kya's life behind.

"Excuse me."

I turned around, flipping my hair over one shoulder the way I envisioned *she* would, to find Chino Man standing behind me, his face spread into a grin that was all teeth.

I would have stammered. *She* didn't. "Hey there, cutie," I flirted without missing a beat. Okay, so he wasn't her Mr. Orgasm by a long shot—too short, too eager, and somehow too overly polished. But he wasn't a bad start.

"Hey, gorgeous. You put on some show."

I should have been mortified. Instead, I laughed. A deep throaty thing that I didn't know I could do.

"Listen, doll," he went on. "My name is R. J. Alexander." He slipped a hand into his pocket and pulled out a business card, handing it to me. "I'm a talent agent with Parker Models."

I squinted down at the card. Plain white with a little red logo in the corner that looked like a catwalk.

"Your performance out there was stunning. Hot. Sexy as hell."

"Oh, that was nothing. You should see me when I'm warmed up." Wow. Did I say that?

"Ha! I knew you'd be a natural." He beamed at me.

"Well, I always say when you got it, flaunt it." I sipped at my drink and gave him a wink. Good God, where was I coming up with this bullshit?

But R. J. ate it up. He laughed, slapping one knee with his hand. "That's the perfect motto for a model, honey."

"Oh, I'm not a mod—" I stopped myself. I looked down at my feet. Why the hell not? "It is, isn't it?" I finished instead.

"What's your name, doll?"

"Kya—" Again I faltered. "Star. Kya Star."

"Gorgeous. Listen, Kya, honey, I've got a shoot coming up this weekend that I think you'd be perfect for. Tell me you don't have representation already?"

I shook my head.

Again with the full-bodied grin. "Perfect! Tell you what, swing by my office tomorrow and I'll give you the particulars." He didn't give me a chance to respond, instead leaning in and air-kissing me on both cheeks. "A natural, doll!" And then he disappeared, swallowed by the mob.

I looked down at the card in my hands. I bit my lip, tasting waxy red lipstick. Tomorrow? Little did he know that by morning I'd be back to plain old Kya Bader, designing Sholtskie Plumbing's website and talking to my cat for company.

A tug of regret pulled at the back of my mind.

But I quickly shook it off. So what? Tomorrow was an eternity away. Tonight I got to be Kya Star.

I slipped the card into my bra and downed the cosmo in my hand before turning to Danielle and Maxie again.

"Come on, girls. Let's dance!"

CHAPTER TWO

So this was what a hangover felt like.

I rolled over in bed and stared at the alarm clock, rudely blaring David Bowie at seven-fifteen on the dot. "China Girl" had never before been so painful. I lifted my arm and flung it in the general direction of the clock, managing to hit the snooze button. Then I flopped over on my back and contemplated the ceiling. Ow. Everything hurt. And my mouth felt like sandpaper. How many cosmos had I drunk last night? Four? Five? I'd lost count. But obviously the answer was too many.

I thought about getting in the shower for a full ten minutes before I realized it was just too much work. Instead, I reached for my cordless and dialed OmniWeb's number. I was taking a vacation day. Considering I never went anywhere, I had plenty saved up and I figured this was a prime time to take one. Hell, the way I felt, I might even take two.

After mumbling something semicoherent to my manager, I pulled the covers over my head and went back to sleep.

I woke up again sometime around noon, feeling a little better, but still vowing never to touch another pink drink again. I took a long, hot shower and dressed in my favorite pair of sweats, an old concert T-shirt from college, and fuzzy pink Hello Kitty slippers before flipping on my computer. I made a pot of very strong coffee while it booted up, then poured myself a cup as I sifted through my e-mail. Hmm . . . two from Match.

"See how popular I am?" I asked Tabby.

He looked up, meowed, then went back to licking his privates. Master conversationalist.

I sipped my black coffee and opened the first e-mail. A guy named BigLarry69 asking if I was a "nawty girl."

I shuddered. Delete.

The next was a guy in Canada asking if I would consider marrying his cousin to get him a U.S. visa.

I was so pathetic I paused for a moment, wondering what his cousin looked like, before hitting the delete button.

I took a long drag from my cup, leaning back in my chair. My hunk-of-the-month calendar hung just above my TV, a half-dressed fireman this month's eye candy. My living room was crammed with mismatched furniture I'd had since college, a sofa with a pronounced dent in the middle because it was the only place I ever sat and I was the only one who ever sat on it. On the scarred coffee table sat copies of *Cat Fancy*, *PC World Magazine*, and a printout detailing my World of WarCraft character, a female troll shaman.

Jesus, I was a geek.

Then my eyes rested on the red heels.

They were on the floor next to Tabby's favorite squeak toy, the first in a breadcrumb-like trail of discarded clothes that led to my bedroom. Somewhere around three AM Danielle and Maxie had dropped me off, and I vaguely remembered shedding layers like a snake as I stumbled to my room, flopping on the bed naked to dream about flashing lasers and go-go cages.

Even though I was a geek, I was neat geek. I set my coffee down and picked up my skirt. The slit had worked its way higher as the night wore on and I was pretty sure my panties had been showing by the end. I examined the seams. Ruined. I threw it in the vicinity of my trash bin. The blouse had a couple of pink stains. I battled a round of nausea at the thought of those evil cosmos and quickly tossed it into the hamper. Underneath my black bra sat a rectangle of white paper. I bent down and picked it up, turning it over in my hand.

Parker Models. R. J. Alexander. Chino Man.

Funny, I'd been half sure I'd dreamt that part last night. I wondered how drunk I was when I'd talked to him. Had he really offered me a modeling job?

No, Kya, I reminded myself. He'd offered *her* a modeling job.

I looked down at the heels. Man, what those shoes had done to me last night. In one way, it had been freeing. In another, scary. Who knew that I had an inner hussy?

I looked back at the card. R.J. had called me a natural. Had last night been a fluke? I wondered if I could pull it off again. I know, I know, it was only supposed to be for one night. I mean, it had been dark, I'd been drinking. Chances were if I showed up at his office this afternoon in the harsh light of day, he'd laugh in my face. He'd throw me out.

Wouldn't he?

I looked down at the shoes again. I slipped them on. Amazing how even after a full night of dancing they didn't hurt my feet in the least. That in itself was magic. Maybe even reason enough to keep them.

I walked over to the full-length mirror hanging next to my cardboard cutout of Mulder from the *X-Files*. They were hot shoes.

I sat down behind my computer, pulled up a Google screen, and typed in *Parker Models*. Immediately I got a hit for their website, a sleek black and gray design with lots of flash videos of catwalks. Their "About Us" section listed lots of high-profile accounts. Well, they seemed legitimate enough.

And it wasn't like I had anything else to do today.

Parker Models was located in a three-story Victorian on Van Ness, sandwiched between a Starbucks and a head shop. Its stucco façade was pale taupe, though I could tell from the layers of paint it had been a virtual rainbow of colors in its lifetime. I walked up the half dozen steps leading to the door, my hands sweating as they skimmed the wrought-iron railing. God, what was I doing here? I paused halfway up, taking a deep breath and contemplating turning around and getting a latte next door instead.

I'd spent a full hour rummaging through my closet for something to wear with the shoes. The skirt from last night was toast, so I finally settled on a pair of faded jeans with holes in the back pockets. They were the grubbies I'd worn when painting my apartment last fall, but shabby chic was all the rage, right? Besides, they were tight and lean and ended two inches above my ankles, perfect for showing off the red heels. I'd paired them with a black tube top that my sister had gotten me as a gag gift one year for Christmas. (Yes, I get it. I have no boobs. Ha, ha, sis.) My hair was piled in a black clip up off my neck. I'd looked surprisingly decent when I left the house.

But now on the threshold of Parker Models, I was having second thoughts. Okay, fine—third and fourth thoughts, too.

I took a couple more deep breaths.

"Excuse me." I stepped to the side as a woman in a black dress hurried past me up the stairs, disappearing through the door. I only caught a glimpse from behind, but I could tell by the long legs, slim waist, and graceful Hepburn-like walk that I was staring at the backside of a runway diva.

These are the kind of people who model, Kya. Not boring little techies like you.

I bit my lip. Then quickly released it, hearing Ex-Boyfriend's taunts about hamburger meat ring in my ears as I stared at the door.

I looked down at the heels.

Hell, I'd come all this way, might as well go inside, right?

I squared my shoulders and lifted my chin as I navigated the last few steps and pushed open the front doors.

The inside of Parker Models was a stark contrast to the outside. Sleek lines, bold colors, modern furnishings. A woman wearing a headset sat at a reception desk in the shape of a giant red kidney bean, simultaneously chatting away while her fingers danced across a keyboard. I approached her desk, trying to hold on to some of the confidence I'd felt last night. Maybe I should have downed a couple of cosmos before coming over.

"Uh huh. Tuesday, three fifteen, and make sure you bring three changes for the casting director to look at. He's going to want to shoot you right away. Ciao!" The receptionist clicked off and looked up at me expectantly. "May I help you?"

I licked my lips. "Uh, yeah. I mean, yes. I'm here to see R. J. Alexander."

"And do you have an appointment?"

"Um, no."

"Who, may I ask, is here?"

"Kya. Star." I licked again. "Kya Star."

"Just a moment, Ms. Star," she said, her fingers flying along the keyboard again as she informed someone on the other end of the line that a Ms. Star was here to see R.J. She paused for an answer then turned back to me. "Mr. Alexander will see you now."

Now? I took another cleansing breath. God, what was I doing here?

"Down the hall, first door on the left," the woman

indicated before clinking back to the phones with a cheerful, "Parker Models, how may I help you?"

Thusly dismissed, I made my feet walk the short distance down a hallway and left, toward a frosted glass door with ALEXANDER stenciled on it. I lifted my hand to knock. Then paused. Would *she* knock? No. *She*'d walk in like she owned the place. So I did.

"Kya, honey, a pleasure to see you." R.J. was again dressed in khaki chinos paired with a black shirt, matching black jacket, and that same Cheshire cat smile stretching across his face. He came out from behind a massive cherry desk to greet me, laying an air-kiss above each of my cheeks.

"R.J., what a fabulous office you have. Is that jacket Armani?" I asked. Yeah, right. As if I knew Armani from Target.

But R.J. seemed to eat it up. "It is. You've got a good eye, doll."

Wow, lucky guess.

"Please sit," R.J. instructed. "I'm so glad you came down today."

"Well, of course! You think I'd stand up a handsome fellow like you?" I gave him a wink. I have no idea why.

"Ha! Aren't you a flirt. But, look, this is business, doll. I think you're fantastic. That body, that face." R.J. nodded, his hair sprayed so perfectly into place it nodded with him as his head bobbed up and down. "Look, my job around here is to sniff out new talent and you, my dear, you are talent times ten."

I stared at him. Me? But instead I shot back a saucy, "Looks like you have a good eye, too."

"Ha! Listen, I've got a shoot this weekend that I think you'd be prefect for. We've been having a bit of trouble casting it and let me tell you, you are *it*, baby. What do you say? You want to be a Parker girl?"

I cleared my throat. "What exactly does being a Parker girl entail? Because, I have to be honest with you, Mr. Alexander, I don't really have any modeling experience."

"Please, call me R.J." If it was possible, his grin widened. "And no experience necessary. Honey, I saw you last night. You're a natural. The camera will love you. Believe you me."

"Okay."

"Okay? Great." R.J. pushed a button on his intercom. "Julie, I want you to get paperwork together to sign Miss Star. Fast track it. We need her for the Sunday shoot."

Wait, had I said "okay"?

"Uh, Mr. Alexander—"

"R.J."

"Right, R.J. Look, I'm really not sure about all—"

But I didn't get to finish as the door to his office swung open behind me.

"R.J., we need to talk to you about—Oh. Sorry. I didn't realize you were with someone."

I swiveled in my seat to get a look at the intruder.

He was tall, lean, somewhere in his late forties if I had to guess, but, from the fit of his thin sweater, obviously someone who still kept in shape. Blond hair, tan skin, weathered just the right amount. He reminded me of Robert Redford—timelessly hot yet ready to break into a grin at any second.

But it was his companion who made my heart lurch into my throat.

It was *him*.

The man with the model in the shoe ad. Mr. Orgasm on the Spot. The same dark hair, dark eyes, the same square jaw, by God, even dusted with that fine sprinkling of stubble that hinted he was too manly to shave every day, yet too sophisticated to let a beard get out of hand. I think I stopped breathing.

"Ah, Alec. Come on in. Kya, I'd like you to meet my partner, Alec Davis."

"Pleasure to meet you," the Redford clone said, offering a hand my way.

I took it, still trying not to stare at his friend.

"Alec handles all the contracts and accounting at the agency," R.J. explained. "I'm the face man, and he's the brains."

Alec grinned. "Just think of me as the silent partner," he joked.

"Nice to meet you," I finally managed to get out.

"And this," R.J. said, gesturing to Mr. Orgasm, "is Blake Stone. He's one of our many talented male models here at Parker."

Blake stuck his hand out toward me. For a moment I just looked at it. Wow. He was even better in 3-D.

"Nice to meet you, Kya."

Kya. He said my name. Why did that suddenly make me want to doodle *Blake + Kya* in big hearts?

"Uh, hi," I said lamely, shaking his outstretched hand. It was warm. Big. Mine almost disappeared in it. And his grip was strong. Yet familiar somehow. Inviting. I felt myself go warm in completely inappropriate places.

"I'm actually glad you two had a chance to meet," R. J. continued. "Blake will be doing the shoot with you on Sunday. Don't worry, he's a pro. He'll walk you through everything, honey."

I licked my lips, my mouth suddenly dry. "Okay."

"Okay, great. Listen, Kya, why don't you go fill out those papers with Julie, and once Alec looks over everything, I'll have someone give you a call with all the particulars about Sunday."

Alec nodded.

"Uh, okay."

"Great, see you later, doll."

"Nice to meet you," Blake said, flashing me a smile that could melt the panties off a nun.

I smiled back. I should have worn my hair down. I had a feeling he would have liked that. I blame the hangover and the night of brazen hussiness that I had a sudden vision of his hands fisted in my hair as he trailed his lips down my neck.

"I'll see you Sunday."

"What?" I blinked, feeling my cheeks go warm as Blake waved to me. "Right. Sunday. Um, bye."

I slipped out, closing the door behind me.

I took a few deep breaths, trying to get my heart rate under control as I walked back down the hallway and out to reception.

"Ms. Star?"

I paused halfway to the front door as the receptionist called my name. "Yes?"

"If you could just fill out these forms, we'll get you on the books."

I turned around. She had a neat stack of papers sitting at the edge of her desk, arranged on a clipboard. I glanced at the first page. An agency contract between Parker Models and Kya Star. I scanned it. While I couldn't totally make out all the legal mumbo jumbo, it seemed like a pretty standard fare, a lot like the ones OmniWeb had our clients sign when we did web work for them. I scanned the second page. And felt my breath catch in my throat. It was the agreement for the modeling job on Sunday. And apparently models made a whole hell of a lot more than web designers. Seriously, someone was going to pay me this much just to throw on some clothes and smile?

I stared at the last page and a line just waiting for my signature.

Okay, get serious, Kya. One wild night at a club was one thing. Even coming here today had been, well, a little on the crazy side. But actually going on a modeling shoot? How long did I think I could keep up this charade?

The reality of it was that I'd show up, they'd put the clothes on me and nothing would fit right, because, duh, being a flat-chested stick of a woman, nothing ever fit right. Ex-Boyfriend had once said sex with me was like making love to a tree. Chances were they'd fire me on the spot.

But if they didn't . . .

Visions of all sorts of gadgets I could buy for my Dell with that kind of money started dancing before my eyes. I took a deep breath. And before I knew it, I was signing *Kya Star* on the bottom of the page and initialing here, here, and here.

I felt my heart hammering in my chest as I pushed the clipboard back at Julie.

She smiled. "Thanks, Ms. Star. I'll call you once we have the particulars about where and when you're to show up on Sunday."

I nodded, not trusting myself to speak.

"Kya?"

I turned. Blake was just coming down the hall. I cleared my throat. "Uh, hi."

"Hey, glad I caught you."

Oh, you can catch me anytime. "Oh?" I cocked one eyebrow at him.

"R.J. told me you're kind of new to modeling."

I nodded. "Between you and me," I said, leaning in, "I'm a photo shoot virgin."

Ohmigod, did I just say "virgin" to the hot guy?

He grinned. "Don't worry, I'll be gentle."

Hell. I think my womb just clenched.

"Listen, I was wondering if maybe you'd like to grab dinner some night? I could give you a few pointers before the shoot?"

I blinked. Dinner? As in with *him*? As in *he* and *I* together?

"Are you asking me out on a date?" I asked, looking up coyly at him through my lashes. Probably a move I'd seen in an Angelina Jolie movie.

One corner of his mouth lifted up, producing the most adorable dimple on the planet in his right cheek. "Maybe. Only if you say yes, though."

I sucked in my lower lip seductively. "Yes."

The other corner lifted up. What do you know? He had a pair of dimples. Absolutely adorable. "Great. I'll get your number from R.J. and call you. Tomorrow night sound okay?"

"Perfect. Looking forward to it, Blake," I said. Then, before he could change his mind, I turned on my heel and walked out the front door, giving my hips just a little more sway than normal.

As soon as I was outside, I ran down the front steps two at a time, doing a cross between hyperventilating and giggling like a kid with a serious pop-star crush. Had I just flirted with a hot model? Did I have a date with one? I had never flirted before. I'd tried once. With Ex-Boyfriend on our first date. He'd told me later it was so pathetic that he'd felt sorry for me and taken me home. Kinda like a little lost puppy.

So, how had I done that? It was like I knew exactly the right thing to say. For once in my life.

I looked down at my heels. Maybe they really would change my life.

I walked down the block, toward my car parked on the next street over, and pulled out my cell, keying in Danielle's extension at work.

"Danielle Greene," she answered on the first ring.

"Hey, Danielle, it's me. Kya."

"Kya! Hey, girl. Maxie and I were worried about you. Peterman said you took a vacation day. You okay? Those cosmos hit you hard last night, huh?"

She didn't know the half of it. "Yeah, I'm fine. Listen, I was wondering if you're busy tonight?"

Danielle laughed. "Don't tell me you want to go clubbing again?"

"No, actually, I was wondering if maybe you could help me do a little shopping. I need something to wear tomorrow night. I—" I paused, feeling my face break into a goofy grin. "I have a hot date."

CHAPTER THREE

He was late.

I pulled my cell out for the fourth time in as many minutes, checking the screen. 7:05 PM. And no calls. Blake had said he had a photo shoot that afternoon and to meet him at La Cucina restaurant at seven for dinner. I was sitting in my car (too nervous to go into the restaurant alone) waiting for any sign of him in the parking lot. None so far. I was beginning to think I'd been punked. I mean, had I really thought he wanted to go out with me? Maybe it was "haze the new girl," or maybe he and R.J. had been in on this little joke from the beginning. Let's see how far we can push the plain girl into actually thinking she's really something. I'll offer her a modeling contract and you ask her out on a date. Hardy har har.

I shifted in my seat, tugging at the hem of my dress as it rode up my thigh. I had a feeling I'd be doing a lot of tugging tonight. The dress was at least six inches shorter than anything I'd ever worn. Slinky, tight, and cut into a low V in the front. And red. Not maroon or mauve but bright fire-engine red. I'd protested about a dozen different ways when

Danielle had plucked it off the rack at Macy's yesterday, but once she shoved me and the dress into a fitting room, I'd had no choice but to put it on. Oddly enough, it actually flattered my shape. It *gave* me a shape. Almost a miracle. And it had been on sale. Discounted 50 percent as the new season's styles were about to come in. But the deciding factor had been the color. It perfectly matched my red heels. Yeah, I was wearing them again. Call me superstitious, but I was starting to think of them as my good luck charms. I know, I know, I'd have to get a new pair at some point or people were going to begin to wonder if I only owned one pair of shoes. But for now they fit perfectly, matched perfectly, and looked smoking hot for my date.

That is, if he ever showed up.

I glanced down at my cell again. 7:10. Hell, was I being stood up?

I was about to call it quits when at 7:14 a blue convertible BMW roared into the parking lot, circling once before finding a space under a blinking overhead streetlight. The door opened, and Blake emerged, dressed in a dark blazer over a pair of butt-hugging jeans. My stomach bottomed out, and I took a deep breath, getting out of the car just as he spotted me. He waved, then jogged over as I locked my hatchback.

"Hey, terrible traffic on 101. Sorry I'm late," he said, leaning down and brushing the slightest touch of a kiss on my right cheek.

I was never washing that cheek again.

"Were you? I just got here myself," I lied.

"Perfect timing then." He grinned, a one dimpler this time. "You look beautiful." His eyes scanned me head to toe then back up, resting on my hair. "I like your hair like this. Long and loose. Gorgeous."

I licked my lips. "Thanks." See? I'd known he was a long-hair kind of guy.

"Hungry?"

"Starving," I replied honestly.

"Shall we then?" He placed a hand at the small of my back, gently steering me toward the restaurant. His touch was tingling, all consuming. It was all I could do to place one foot in front of the other as my entire body focused on the heat coming through his palm. Again I got that odd sense of familiarity. I could easily imagine those hands gliding up my back, kneading the nape of my neck, spinning me around for an intimate kiss as they tangled themselves in my hair.

"Did you have any trouble finding the place?"

"What?" I said the word on a sigh, pulling myself out of the vivid daydream.

"The restaurant? You said you lived in Sunnyvale. Any trouble getting here?"

"Oh, no. No, your directions were perfect."

"Yahoo maps." He winked at me. "But I'm happy to take credit for them if they earn me a brownie point or two."

"Very cute."

"I try." This time the grin was a two dimpler.

I couldn't help smiling back as the waitress guided us to a table for two near the back. White linen tablecloths, beveled wineglasses, a single votive candle flickering in the center. All we needed now was shared strand of spaghetti and it was the picture of a romantic Italian restaurant.

Blake pulled out my chair, then sat opposite me.

"What are you in the mood for?" he asked, picking up the wine list.

"Oh. Uh . . ." I bit my lip. As I may have mentioned, I wasn't much of a drinker. Wine came in three kinds in my world: red, white, and from a box. I wracked my brain to come up with anything that didn't sound like I was twelve. What had Danielle ordered when we'd gone out to lunch for her birthday? What kind had they served at the office Christmas party? Come on, anything. "How about a . . . Riesling?"

Blake looked up from the menu. "A Riesling?"

Shit, had I picked the wrong one? "Yes. Something light, a little fruity?" God, please let Riesling be light and fruity! I was so pulling this out of my ass.

Again he paused. Then slowly put the menu down. "A Riesling it is then." But he continued to give me an odd look.

I felt my cheeks burning and hoped Blake couldn't tell under the dim lights. "Unless you'd rather have something else?"

He shook his head. "No, no. It's just . . ." He looked down at his hands, clasped on the table in front of him. "My last girlfriend. She always ordered Riesling. It's not that common."

Great. Leave it to me to pick the ex's favorite. "Oh. Well, we can order something else if you'd like."

"No. It's fine." He blinked back some emotion, then turned his sixty-watt smile on again. "Sorry, didn't mean to bring that up. Bad first-date form, huh?"

I smiled back. It was hard not to. He was charming without even trying. "No problem. You get one free pass. In fact, I might even let slip what an ass my ex-boyfriend was just to make you feel better."

He laughed, throwing his head back with a warm, low chuckle that sent my stomach on a roller-coaster ride. I had a vision of that sound waking me up after a long night of staring into Blake's eyes. His breath on my ear, lips murmuring against my neck, his body nuzzled against mine as we slept.

"Thanks," Blake said, pulling me out of my fantasy. "I needed that."

"Anytime."

"So, tell me something about yourself? R.J. says you're new to modeling. What did you do before?"

"I worked in high tech. A little of this, a little of that. How about you? Are you originally from the Bay Area?" I asked, switching the subject. The last thing I wanted to talk about tonight was any part of Plain Kya's life.

"No. Actually, my family moved here from Denver when I was a kid."

"I bet you miss the snow."

His eyes shot up to meet mine. "Yeah. I do. Actually, it's the one thing that I really miss about Denver."

"Well, at least you can get up to Tahoe a few times a year to ski."

He cocked his head to the side. "I was just going to say that. I rent a place up in Tahoe every winter.

Are you reading my mind or something?" he asked, a teasing note in his voice.

My turn to grin. I wasn't sure what it was about him—maybe the fact that I'd spent an embarrassing amount of time staring at his picture—but I felt oddly comfortable with him. Not the nerve-wracking sweaty-palms mess I usually was with strangers.

"Maybe I am reading your mind," I responded coyly.

"Okay, then, what am I thinking right now?" he asked. He trained his eyes on me, his mouth twitching at the corners as if it were ready to lift at any moment. Then he let his gaze fall from my face, trailing lower, resting on my cleavage. Then slowly rising again to meet mine. His eyes went dark and glazed over.

A vision hit me of that look across a big white bed. I felt a raw hunger that had nothing to do with the plates of pasta whizzing by our table. His big, warm hands slowly undressing me, sliding the strap of my dress down my shoulders, his heated gaze never leaving mine . . .

I felt my cheeks blaze, this time sure it was apparent. I ducked my head to cover the X-rated daydreams filling my head.

"I don't think I can voice those thoughts in public."

His lips quivered into a full fledged grin. "Damn. You're good."

The Riesling was excellent. As much as I hated to think of Blake with any woman other than me, I had to admit, his ex had good taste. I had a second glass. Then a third. Then the shoes started to work their magic again and I flirted, fawned, and made amazingly not-geeky conversation all the way through the meal and the decadent tiramisu dessert we shared.

Afterward, Blake walked me to my hatchback, not even raising an eyebrow at the dented back fender courtesy of an errant shopping cart at Safeway last year, or the fact that my stereo sported duct-tape edging.

"I had a great time tonight," he said, taking one of my hands in his.

"Me, too. Thanks for dinner."

"Thanks for showing up."

I threw my head back and laughed. "Are you kidding? I was here twenty minutes early, I was so eager." Crap. I knew my run of intelligent conversation had to end sometime.

He cocked an eyebrow at me. "So you weren't late then?"

"Busted. No. I just said that so you wouldn't feel bad."

He leaned in, one hand reaching up to brush a strand of hair from my face as the breeze picked up. "Wow."

I licked my lips, my throat growing dry at his touch. "Wow?"

"Beautiful and sweet. Not a combination a guy finds very often."

I opened my mouth to respond, but I didn't get the chance. His lips were suddenly hovering over mine. Nipping. Tasting. Sampling. They were soft and warm.

Tentative at first, but quickly growing firmer and more insistent. Not that I resisted. I melted on contact. My mind going on vacation, my body taking over as I lifted my arms around his neck. His hand circled my waist, heat resting at the small of my back, then slowly traveling upward as his hand snaked up my spine to knead the nape of my neck, then thread into my hair as his kiss deepened.

Just like I had imagined.

My breath caught in my throat and I pulled back, feeling an odd sense of déjà vu prickle my skin.

Blake was panting, his pupils dilated, his lips wet and slightly pink from my lipstick. "Sorry. I guess I got a little carried away."

"No, no, it's okay," I stumbled, trying to shake the odd sensation. I'd daydreamed about kissing him, then actually kissed him. No biggie, right? So what if he moved just the way I'd imagined he would? That was a good thing.

"Kya, I'd love to see you again. I mean, you know, more than see you. Take you out. Again. Somewhere."

I smiled, glad I wasn't the only one made stupid with lust. "I'd like that."

His face lit up with a two dimpler, and I felt an answering light flip on inside me. God, he really was gorgeous.

"How about Sunday after the photo shoot? We could drive over to the coast, maybe have a little picnic there?"

I nodded. "Sounds great."

"Great." He leaned in and gave me a peck on the

cheek, his lips resting on my skin just a moment too long. "I'll see you Sunday then."

I nodded again. "Sunday," I repeated. Then I watched him get in his BMW and drive away.

The first thing I did when I got home was kick off my heels and change into a pair of sweats and fuzzy slippers. I booted up my computer, shaking a handful of Meow Mix into a bowl for Tabby as I scanned through my e-mail. A few work-related items, a couple of ads promising to end my erectile-dysfunction problems for good. Two new messages from Match members. But I didn't even read them. I didn't care. Yeah, I was that ga-ga over Blake. I know, it was just one date, but I felt like a middle schooler with her first crush. I swore every time I licked my lips I could still taste him there.

Instead of reading my Match messages, I pulled up a Google screen and typed in: *Blake Stone*. Immediately my screen was filled with images of Blake. In a tuxedo on a runway, in a Speedo doing an ad for sunscreen (I think I drooled a little on my keyboard at the vision of his six-pack), lying in a field touting the merits of a certain cologne. I physically pinched myself at the thought that I had been in a serious lip-lock with this same man.

I went back to Google and couldn't help adding a word to the search: *Blake Stone girlfriend*. Yeah, I know, we all have exes. But the way he'd been so upset at the mere hint of her, I had to see who she was. I steeled myself against the idea she was some gorgeous European supermodel. Or worse yet, a gorgeous rocket scientist. I waited as the results came up. Not nearly as many, but among the ads, I found a celebrity gossip site that looked promising. I clicked on the link and an article came up about Blake Stone seen at a nightclub with girlfriend Angel Cressley.

I typed her name into the search engine and prayed she was some homely kindergarten teacher.

No such luck.

Dozens of images immediately filled my screen. Images of a tall, long-legged blonde in a skimpy black dress, an itty-bitty bikini, an evening gown.

And a pair of red patent-leather ankle-strap rhinestone-studded stiletto heels.

It was *her*.

Blake's ex-girlfriend was the woman on the Hi-heelia website.

CHAPTER FOUR

It was cold. Freezing. The breeze from the bay cutting through the air. I was shivering, standing in the dark, waiting. Waiting for what, I wasn't quite sure. But I knew it was coming. And not in a good way. A feeling of dread grew by the second as I stood there, my teeth chattering against the wind. And then I felt him. I felt him long before I saw him. He was there, behind me. Closing in. But somehow I couldn't make my legs move. My feet were glued to the spot. And he was getting closer. I tried to scream, but no sound came out. Tears started to roll down my cheeks as I stood there, freezing. And then I felt him. I mean really felt him. His hands on my shoulders. Clamping down on me, pushing me. I tried to move away, to lash out with my arms. But they moved in slow motion like I was underwater. And that's when I realized, I *was* underwater. Cold, wet, shivering, I looked up and saw the glassy surface of the water above me, saw bubbles rising from my mouth as I tried to scream again and again, his hands holding me under, the pressure building in my throat, in my head, behind my eyes. I thrashed, but it didn't do any good. I could feel myself slipping away as his grip grew tighter and tighter. My vision started blurring, my eyelids growing heavy. And that's when I looked down and saw the red patent-leather heels on my feet.

And this time I did scream.

I sat straight up in bed, panting, my head whipping wildly to check my surroundings. Alarm clock. Pink-striped comforter. Tabby lounging on the windowsill. No large body of water, no faceless man in the shadows.

I gulped in large breaths of air and fell back on my pillows. A dream. That's all it was. Vivid, but just a dream.

I rolled over and looked at the red blinking numbers on my clock. 7:12. I looked up at the ceiling.

Would it be wrong to take another vacation day?

Actually, once I called in and asked for another vacation day, Peterman informed me that the Sholtskie Plumbing account I'd been working on was having server troubles so I might as well take the whole week. I didn't argue. The thought of going back to Kya's life wasn't appealing. I wanted to put it off as long as I could.

I'd much rather spend my day shopping for a hot new outfit to wear for my picnic with Blake on Sunday. Because, despite my realization that *she* was Blake's ex, I was still looking forward to it. Granted, it was a little unnerving that he'd dated my idol before me, but so what? Obviously things hadn't worked out, right? Maybe he preferred slightly mousy web designers to jet-setting supermodels?

Yeah right, a small part of my brain told me. The world is full of men who hate supermodels. But I told that part of my brain to shut up. I was going to enjoy this while it lasted.

Sunday morning I was dressed in a pair of hip-hugging white capris, a hot little red spaghetti-strap top, and my red heels. At some point I was going to have to wear other shoes or Blake would start thinking I was whacked. But I was still too superstitious for that point to be now.

I followed the receptionist's directions to the shoot up 880 North through the east bay to a warehouse in Oakland. It wasn't a great neighborhood—definitely not one where I'd walk alone at night—but it wasn't in the worst part of town, either. A handful of cars were already parked in the lot, and I added mine to the row, then made my way inside.

I was immediately assaulted by bright lights mounted on tall metal stands. All five towers focused on a stage in the middle of the warehouse. A back wall—painted a light blue, like a cloudy sky—was laid out behind a giant four-poster bed swathed in layers of gauzy white sheets. Off to the side a folding table held photographic equipment and a laptop, and beyond that sat wardrobe racks and makeup tables. A handful of peopled milled around a wardrobe rack while others toyed with the lights, moving them half an inch to the right or left.

"Kya!"

I tuned to see R.J. approaching, his chinos pressed

with crisp lines down the front, his smile as wide as ever. "Kya, doll, I'm so glad to see you. Emmy, this is Kya Star." He gestured to a women with red hair held back in a ponytail, a camera in her hand. "Kya, Emmy McDonald is the photographer today."

"Nice to meet you," Emmy said, extending one hand.

I shook it. "You, too."

"And of course you know Blake." R.J. gestured to where Blake was walking onto the bedroom set. I felt drool pool in the corners of my mouth as I saw he was dressed only in a pair of pale blue boxer shorts. Through my insta-lust I managed a feeble wave. Blake returned it, giving me a lopsided grin in the process.

"Okay, let's get you into wardrobe, yes?" R.J. bustled me over to the rack of clothes where a man with frizzy hair and a metallic shirt thrust a negligee at me. I looked from the scrap of fabric (and I do mean *scrap*) to R.J.

"I'm modeling this?"

He nodded. "It's an ad for Jessica Simpson's new perfume. Didn't Julie tell you?"

I nodded. "Yes, but I didn't know . . ." I trailed off, my eyes going to the faux bedroom where Blake was lounging on the bed as someone held a light meter to his face.

"Don't worry, it's all very tastefully done. Emmy won't let you down. Now, hop into this, we've still got to get you made up and," he added, fingering a lock of my hair, "we've got to do something about this hair."

"R.J.?" Emmy called, lining up shots through her camera. "How long?"

"She'll be ready in five minutes, love." He turned to me. "Let's get a move on, Kya."

I looked from the negligee to R.J. to Blake's nearly nude form. Not exactly how I'd envisioned our first time in bed together . . . but what the hell? I'd gone this far.

I slipped on the negligee and was whisked to the hair expert, who painted gold highlights onto my ash blond locks and worked some kind of goopy stuff into it that made it shine under the bright lights. Then the makeup person threw about fifteen different shades of eyeshadow on me that, when he was done, seemed to blend together seamlessly to give me those kind of sexy bedroom eyes that only girls in Maybelline commercials have. I hardly recognized myself when he was done. Even my too-long legs and too-skinny arms almost looked right in the soft, white lingerie.

"Ready, Kya?" Emmy prodded again.

My heart pounded like a jackhammer in my chest as I stepped out onto the stage.

"Hey there, gorgeous." Blake lay on the bed, his head propped up on one arm as he grinned at me. "I have to admit, I didn't think it would be this easy to get you into bed."

I couldn't help the giggle that escaped me. "Likewise." I stared at his straight-out-of-a-movie abs. Vaguely I wondered how many crunches a day he did to keep those things looking like that. They ended in a perfect tight V, his boxers covering just enough from view to keep me from jumping him on the spot. He looked positively amazing. I had the carnal urge to reach out and lick him. For the hundredth time I wondered just what I was doing here.

"Kya, would you mind getting on the bed with Blake? We're going to try a few different positions."

I almost laughed out loud. Would I mind? Hell, I'd died and gone to heaven. If it weren't for the camera, lights, and handful of crew members watching our every move, I'd be living out every woman's fantasy.

I gingerly lay down on the bed beside Blake, trying not to smudge my sexy makeup on the white sheets.

"That's good. Now put your arm up over your head, right like that," Emmy directed. "Now if you could tilt your head just a little to the left. There, now look at Blake."

I did, feeling my heart beat double time. His face was inches away from mine. His eyes dark and intent—though whether he was playing for the cameras or feeling a fraction of the pure animal lust rushing through me, I'd be hard pressed to say.

"Blake, shift a little to your right. Great, now put your arm around her."

He did. I felt his legs brush against mine, his arm encircling my waist. *Oh, mama.* My breath started to come out in quick little pants as I tried to get my surging body under control.

Blake must have noticed, as he gave me a little wink. "You know, I'm *really* looking forward to our picnic now," he whispered, barely moving his mouth as Emmy began to click away.

I tried not to smile. "Me, too," I whispered back.

"You've got beautiful eyes, Kya."

The compliment threw me for a moment, and I froze.

"Kya, move a little to your left. There, perfect. Blake, could you move in a little closer?"

He did. I felt something hard press against my thigh. Was that what I thought it was?

I licked my lips.

"Perfect, Kya, do that again."

Do what? My brain was in a total fog, all I could do was focus on Blake's dark, chocolate eyes. And the thick bulge pressing into my right thigh.

He gave me another wink. "Can't help it," he whispered. "You're too damned hot, Kya."

I think I laughed.

But masochist that I was, my mind immediately went to the pictures I'd seen last night of him and Angel. Had he said the same things to her? I knew they had worked together. I suddenly wondered if they'd done any lingerie shots. Had she been in this same position? Hearing the same sweet nothings murmured to her out of the corner of his mouth as the camera clicked away?

"Kya, you're stiffening up on me. Relax, try shifting over to your side," Emmy instructed as she continued shooting.

I rolled over, my back to Blake.

"That's it, Blake. Come up behind her, maybe nuzzle at her neck a little."

His warm breath was on my ear. I shivered, my

eyes fluttering closed for half a second. God, that felt good.

"That's it. Perfect, Kya."

Little did she know, I was no actress.

"You taste good," Blake murmured, his lips grazing my neck.

I sighed out loud, arching my back, trying not to become a total sex kitten on camera. I wondered if he was this good when the camera wasn't rolling. I wondered if I'd get a chance to find out.

Had Angel found out?

Damn. I was obsessed with her.

I gave myself a mental shake and tried to focus on the latest direction Emmy was giving me, on the crew, on R.J. standing to the side, beaming like a proud parent.

Somehow I made it through the shoot without driving myself nuts thinking about Angel or having an embarrassing orgasm on the set. When we were done, Blake gave me a quick peck on the cheek and said he'd meet me outside. Then he walked off set to find his pants.

"You done good, kid," R.J. said, slapping me on the back as I threw on a robe. "I knew you were a natural."

"Thanks. You think the pictures came out okay?"

"Do I think?" R.J. laughed. "Honey, I know. I was watching the monitors. You rocked that set, doll. Hell, you had me wanting to buy a case of that perfume."

I knew he was pumping me up a little, but I

couldn't help the smile that hit my cheeks. I'd actually pulled it off. Me!

"Drop by the office in the morning and Alec will have your check ready for you."

"Thanks. Hey, R.J.?"

"Yes, sweets?" he asked, steering me over to wardrobe.

"Can I ask you something? Something about Blake?"

He nodded. "Sure, toots."

"His . . . his girlfriend. Angel. Do you know what happened between them?" I bit my lip, not sure I really wanted to know the answer. But somehow unable to stop myself from asking anyway.

R.J.'s brow furrowed, his lips pursing together. "What do you mean?"

"Well, just that when he mentioned her, well, he kind of got this look on his face. Like he'd swallowed a bad oyster or something. I don't mean to pry I just . . . I guess I'm just a little worried he's not really over her, you know? Did she break things off with him or what?"

R.J.'s jaw tightened. He glanced over both shoulders. Then he leaned in. "Look, I wouldn't mention Angel around Blake again if I were you. She didn't break up with him. She died."

I sucked in a breath. "Died?"

He nodded, his voice hushed. "Six months ago. Blake took it really hard. He . . . well, he was depressed. Didn't get out of bed for days. He's only come back to work again the last couple of months. It was . . . it was a real tragedy for us all."

"I'm so sorry," I said, genuinely meaning it. I suddenly felt like an ass. How could I be jealous of a dead woman?

I glanced over at Blake, smiling and chatting with Emmy. I couldn't imagine what he must have gone though.

"Yeah, it was hard on us all for awhile there."

"Did you know her, too?"

R.J. nodded, an unreadable look behind his eyes. "Yeah. I was the girl's agent. She was the one who introduced me to Blake in the first place. A terrible tragedy. She was so young, so vibrant. She had such a great career ahead of her. What a waste."

I put a hand on R.J.'s arm, unsure what to say. "I'm so sorry," I repeated.

He nodded. "Thanks."

"What . . . I mean, if you don't mind me asking . . . what happened to her? Was she ill?'

"Ill?" R.J. asked. He shook his head. "No, she wasn't ill. She drowned."

CHAPTER FIVE

My skin went cold, the hairs on the back of my neck standing on end as I remembered my dream from the night before. It was probably coincidence. I'd probably heard about her death on the news at the time and my subconscious had pulled it up again last night. It was nothing.

"She drowned?" I asked, my voice shaky.

R.J. nodded. "In Blake's swimming pool. She was spending the night, must have wandered out for a midnight swim, because the next morning Blake found her there. Dead."

"Oh my God." I covered my mouth with my hands, tears pricking the back of my eyes. I couldn't image what a horrible moment that must have been for him, finding a loved one that way.

R.J. continued, "He did CPR until the paramedics arrived, but they said she'd likely been dead for hours at that point. He was a wreck. Felt completely guilty that he hadn't heard her, hadn't woken up in time to save her."

I shook my head. "But there's no way he could have known! What could he have done?"

R.J. shrugged. "I know, darlin'. But guilt isn't a logical emotion."

"Ready?"

I spun around to find Blake smiling at me, a picnic basket in one hand.

"Uh, yeah. Just . . . just let me change."

His smile faltered. "You okay?" he asked.

I blinked, sniffing back unshed tears at his loss. "Yeah, fine. It's just . . . it's been quite a day." I forced a smile I didn't really feel.

But I guess it was convincing enough, as his two dimples showed up in response. "Well, it's not over yet. Come on, let's get out of here."

I scuttled behind a makeshift curtain and quickly pulled my own clothes back on. I did a cursory wipe down on my face, getting off the heavier of the pancake makeup, then shoved my feet into the heels and met Blake at the door.

We agreed I'd follow him across the bay to a beach he knew just west of the Golden Gate. But as we crawled through traffic, all I could think about was what R.J. had told me. I was right when I'd assumed Blake wasn't over his ex-girlfriend. But it wasn't the relationship, it was the loss. I mean, how did one ever get over that? I wondered if I was the first girl he'd seen since Angel. Likely. R.J. said he'd only been back to work a few months. I bit my lip as we wound down the coast.

The water was a crystal clear blue, the sun sparkling above it like one of those famous California days captured on a postcard. Blake pulled into a spot along the curb and I followed suit, deeply inhaling the crisp, salty air into my lungs as I stepped out of the car. I hadn't been entirely dishonest when I'd said it had been a hell of a day. Keeping up the Kya Star charade was beginning to wear on me. I was looking forward to a nice afternoon on the beach. Blake grabbed my hand and led me to a spot near the ocean, then spread out a thick blanket on the sand.

"You did great today," he said, pulling items out of his picnic basket. A bottle of wine (not a Rielsing, I noticed), cheese, fruit, a baguette.

"Thanks. It was . . . um . . . a new experience."

He cocked an eyebrow at me. "Oh?"

I felt myself blush. "I mean the cameras. Not being in bed with a man. I've done that lots of times before."

There went the eyebrow again.

I paused. "I mean, not a *lot* of times before. Some. A few. A perfectly respectable amount."

Blake grinned, obviously enjoying this. "Uh huh."

"I'm just digging the hole deeper, aren't I?"

He laughed. "Yep. Quit while you're ahead, kid."

"Am I ahead?" I asked, biting my lip.

His grin went from amused to wicked in seconds flat. But instead of answering, he leaned in and planted a soft, long kiss on my lower lip. "It's adorable when you do that," he murmured.

"Do what?"

His mouth traveled down, nipping at my pulse. "Bite your lip like that."

A laugh bubbled up in my throat. "My ex hated it."

"Then he was an idiot."

I had to agree with him there. "Blake?"

"Uh huh?" he mumbled, his mouth opening to let his tongue tickle the hollow of my throat.

I let out a long sigh. "R.J. told me about Angel."

He froze.

Shit. Why had I brought that up?

Blake pulled back, his eyes unreadable, his expression suddenly guarded. "He did."

I nodded. "He told me what happened. I—I'm so sorry."

"Yeah." He looked out at the ocean, not meeting my eyes. "Me, too."

"Listen, I understand if you don't want to talk about her, but . . . well . . . I just wanted to let you know that if you do, it's okay. I mean . . . I'm here."

He didn't say anything, just stared at the sun casting perfect crystal shimmers on the cresting waves. He sat that way so long I began to worry. Finally he just said a simple "Thanks."

I reached out a hand and gingerly took his, squeezing when he responded to my touch. Finally he turned his gaze back to me, any trace of his sad thoughts gone, his genial smile replaced. "You hungry?" He nodded toward the picnic basket.

"Famished. Posing is more of a workout than I thought."

He laughed deep in his throat. "No kidding." Then he winked at me. "You should try it with a raging hard-on some time."

It was late before Blake and I finally left the beach, the sun long melted into a dusky purple glow on the horizon as he gave me a good-night kiss that ended in me letting him round second base. The entire drive back to the freeway I had a goofy grin pasted on my face as I followed his taillights. I was two exits from my turnoff when my cell rang out from my purse.

"Hello?" I answered.

"Hey, it's me."

Blake. If it were possible, my grin grew wider. Damn I had it bad for this guy.

"Hey, you."

"Listen, I hope this doesn't sound too presumptuous, but I really don't want this day to end yet."

I looked at my reflection in the rearview mirror and I think I smirked. "Oh? What did you have in mind?"

"Interested in coming back to my place for a nightcap?"

Oh yeah, that was definitely a smirk. "Are you trying to get me in my skivvies, Mr. Stone?" I teased, flirting shamelessly. I passed my turnoff, continuing to follow his BMW.

He chuckled on the other end. "Nope. I've already seen those."

"Good, as long as we're clear."

"Follow me home?"

"Yes," I said. Then quickly hung up before he could change his mind.

I followed as he surged into the next lane over, a ball of anticipation building in my stomach. I tried to remember the last time a guy had invited me over for a nightcap. I couldn't. Probably because it had never happened before. Not that I'd never been with a man. As I'd so eloquently put it on the beach, I was not a virgin. I just didn't get out all that much. And when I did, it wasn't like this, for romantic picnics and nightcaps. The last guy I'd been with, I realized as I searched that cobweb-ridden section of my brain, was the rebound guy after Ex. He'd been living with his mom at the time so we'd had to do it in the back of his car. Something I hadn't done since I was sixteen. And it hadn't gotten any more comfortable with age, let me tell you.

But I had a feeling tonight would be different.

By the time Blake turned onto a tree-lined street just south of the city, the anticipation was so high I was fairly floating off my seat. And, man, did I have to pee. Nerves did that to me. I pulled in behind him in front of a one-story bungalow on a modest-sized lot. It was a nice neighborhood, set up on a hill, obviously well cared for. Cosmopolitan without being too flashy. It suited him. The house was all glass on one side, capitalizing on the view of the valley. And probably the swimming pool.

I shoved that thought to the back of my brain as Blake got out of his car and walked over to open my door.

"Home sweet home," he said, gesturing to the place.

"It's nice."

"Thanks. I like it here."

He led me inside, where simple, tasteful furnishings filled the modest space. Wood and leather dominated with small glass accents here and there.

Overall a peaceful, homey feeling. Beyond the living area sat a kitchen fitted out with stainless appliances and pale, smooth cabinets. A pair of glass doors led out to a backyard—a small stretch of patio surrounding a brilliant blue swimming pool that overlooked the valley. I quickly turned my gaze away, shuddering as if I could almost feel that cold water washing over me.

"Mind if I use your bathroom?" I asked.

"First door on the left."

"Thanks," I called over my shoulder.

He had an amazingly clean bathroom for a bachelor. Once I finished, I walked out to find Blake in the kitchen.

"Would you like something to drink?" he asked, pulling a bottle of wine from a wrought-iron rack on the counter.

I nodded. If I didn't watch it, I was going to become a lush.

"Merlot all right?"

"Fine."

"Good. This is from a new winery up the coast I've been meaning to try. I think you'll like it. It's a little more mellow than most. Could you hand me a couple of glasses?" Blake asked, his back to me as he rummaged in a drawer for a corkscrew.

I pulled open the cupboard on my right and grabbed a pair of long-stemmed, blue glasses.

"They're in the first cupboard down the . . ." He trailed off, turning around to give me an odd look.

I looked at the glasses. "What?"

"How did you know where they were?"

I blinked, looking from the glasses to the cupboard I'd just pulled them from. I shrugged. "Lucky guess?"

Blake gave a little shake of his head. "Very." He poured merlot for us both, then corked the bottle and set it on the counter.

"You live here alone?" I asked.

"Yep, just me and Rufus."

"Rufus?"

He shot me a grin over his glass. "My dog. He's next door with the neighbors. He hates being alone too long, so they watch him if I'm going to be out all day. They've got three kids, and Rufus just loves them."

"So, you're a dog person?"

"Yeah. Why?" He paused. "Oh no. Don't tell me you're a cat person?"

I nodded. "Tabby. An orange-striped monster that doubles as my therapist."

Blake made a tsking sound as he sipped his drink. "That's it, this is never going to work then," he said, a teasing glint in his eyes.

I couldn't help the corners of my mouth jerking up. "No?"

He set his glass down, then slowly advanced on me until his lips were inches from mine. "Nope," he whispered. He kissed me. Softly. Tenderly. I responded instantly, my body going loose, my lips parting to meet his until our movements escalated into hot and needy. His hands snaked up my back, my arms went around his neck and he danced me backward toward the bedroom, shedding clothing as we went.

I never did get to try the merlot.

It was dark when I woke up. At first I couldn't remember where I was. Then I heard Blake's soft, even breath beside me. His arms were still twined around my waist, our limbs tangled. I smiled in the dark. Wow. I didn't know what I'd done to deserve this night, but, man, I hoped I kept doing it.

I slowly slipped from his grasp, careful not to wake him, and stood back, admiring his bare body. A more perfect specimen I could not imagine. I felt myself go all tingly again as I reached for his discarded shirt and slipped it over my head, padding out to the kitchen on bare feet.

I went to the sink and poured myself a glass of water, looking out the back door at the perfect picture of the valley of twinkling lights laid out before me. Like thousands of stars fallen down to earth. The sight was so alluring, I slipped open the back door and stepped out onto the patio.

The stone was cool beneath my feet, the air hitting me like a sudden refrigerated blast, causing little goose bumps to rise onto my arms. I looked out at the valley.

Then down at the swimming pool in front of me.

It lay uncovered, the surface a glassy dark blue, appearing almost like a shimmering mirror reflecting the sparse moonlight. I walked over to the edge, looking down at my reflection.

That's when I felt him.

Hands on me from behind, shoving me forward as I watched my horrified reflection stare back at me. Before I could scream, water covered me, the sounds lost in the waves of the perfect blue swimming pool. I tried to push upward, to reach the surface, but something was holding me down. Someone. I thrashed my legs back and forth, my arms lashing out, my vision blurred by the water, everything growing darker and darker as I felt my lungs slowly losing air, screaming for the surface of the pool I could see just inches above me. I tried to reach it but couldn't move. The hands. They still held me from behind, firm, strong, menacing. Pushing me under as my vision went black. I tried to scream one last time.

"Jesus, Kya, what's wrong?"

I jumped as Blake materialized in the doorway, clad only in his boxers.

I looked down. I was dry. I was alive. I was sitting at the edge of the pool, my knees tucked up under me, cold sweat pouring down my back. I was shivering, my teeth chattering.

"What are you doing out here? God, you scared me half to death. Why were you screaming?"

In one quick stride Blake was crouched at my side, his warm arms wrapping around me, chasing away the chill.

"I . . . I don't know." Which wasn't entirely a lie. I shook my head, trying to remember what had happened. I'd gone to the kitchen for water, went outside. I was standing at the edge of the pool when someone pushed me in. Only . . . I looked down. My clothes were still perfectly dry. Obviously I hadn't been in the water. A dream?

"I . . . I came out to look at the pool," I said, lamely.

Blake's face was a deathly shade of white under the moonlight. "Why?" he asked, his voice shaky.

"I . . . I don't know." I shivered again despite his arms around me as I remembered the feel of those hands pushing me under the water. It couldn't have been a dream. I'd been wide-awake. A hallucination? But it had felt so real. Even as I grasped Blake's arms in a death grip, I could almost taste the chlorine on my tongue, feel the burn in my lungs, the desperation bubbling up in my throat again.

"Hey, you're shivering," Blake said, helping me to my feet. "Let's get you back inside."

I nodded and let him lead me through the glass doors and back to bed.

Both of us curled up into silent little balls as soon as we got there, each lost in our own thoughts.

CHAPTER SIX

Blake had an early shoot, something out in Half Moon Bay for a fitness magazine. He slipped out at dawn with a chaste kiss to my forehead and a promise to call me later. Which was fine. After the midnight interlude at the swimming pool, I could tell some of the magic of last night had worn off for both of us.

As soon as he left, I got dressed and went to the kitchen in search of coffee, pausing just a moment at the back door to look out at the pool.

The odd thing was that I'd never thought of drowning before. I'd learned to swim at my cousin's pool when I was five, practically lived at the water park in the summers, and grew up just minutes from the ocean. I'd never feared the water before, never given a second thought outside of basic safety to the idea of being sucked under the surface. But suddenly I was consumed by it. First the dream, then last night . . . that. Whatever that was. Can you even call it a dream when you're wide-awake? Part of me wondered if the stress of being Kya Star wasn't getting the better of me. Maybe the wine on the beach had been too much. Maybe my never-before-abused liver had been tipped over the balance last night.

Had Angel been afraid of the water? R.J. had said she'd gone out for a midnight swim. I took a step closer to the pool. People who were afraid of the water didn't usually go swimming by themselves at night. She must have known how to swim.

So what had happened to her?

I glanced across the room at Blake's laptop, set on a slim pine computer desk in the corner. I crossed the room without even thinking and turned it on, feeling just the tiniest bit intrusive using it without asking. But he had said to make myself at home. And I wasn't sure I could survive the entire ride back to Sunnyvale without knowing.

Telling that guilty niggle at the back of my mind to shut up, I opened a Google window and typed in Angel's name. Again, the images of the perfect model filled the screen. I couldn't help staring a little, that same feeling of awe that I'd first had when I'd seen her on the Hilheelia website rushing over me. Only this time it was colored with a profound sense of loss.

I tried to shake it off, amending my search to include the word *death*. Fewer hits this time. Apparently she hadn't yet reached the celebrity status of the Kate Mosses of the world. A few articles in the local papers and a short mention in the *NY Times*. I started with the *SF Gate*. The archives held a series of three articles, none longer than a few paragraphs, about the tragic death of the young model.

Angel Cressley was born in Indiana, then moved out to California after high school to earn a degree in accounting from UCLA. That's where the acting bug bit her and she'd landed a minor part on a soap opera. She abandoned her studies for stardom and moved north where she'd signed on with Parker Models almost immediately. She'd started working the local fashion shows and quickly landed her first big account: Hiheelia shoes.

I felt a lump form in my throat, remembering just how powerful that image of her in the red heels had been. If everyone else responded to her photos that way, it was obvious she'd been destined for big things.

I skimmed the next paragraph about her other accounts and skipped ahead to the part about the night she'd died. According to her boyfriend at the time, Blake Stone, he and Angel had gone out to a local club, then come back to his place where they'd both fallen asleep. Sometime in the middle of the night, Angel had gotten up for a dip in the pool. Blake claimed he'd had too much to drink that night and didn't hear a thing. The next morning, he'd awakened to find Angel floating facedown in the swimming pool.

I bit my lip, doing everything I could not to look out the window. Instead, I clicked on the next article.

This one detailed the police's findings the following week. Angel had died of suffocation and water in her lungs—drowning. At first the police hadn't been sure whether they were looking at a suicide, homicide, or accidental death. My heart clenched as I read that Blake had initially been questioned by the police but let go due to lack of evidence. Eventually the coroner had ruled accidental death by drowning and the case had been dropped.

An accident.

I closed my eyes and immediately felt those strong hands on my shoulders again. My breath froze in my throat. The report had said there was no sign of trauma, she hadn't hit her head going into the water, and Blake had told police that she was a strong swimmer.

No matter what the coroner had said, it didn't feel like an accident.

I got up and walked to the sliding door, watching the morning sunlight shimmer off the pool's surface. Blake had been home alone with Angel. He claimed he hadn't heard a thing. I glanced at the bedroom door. It was only a few feet away. An ugly thought entered my head: How well did I really know Blake?

I bit my lip. I'd like to think I got to know a guy pretty well before falling into bed with him, but the reality was that I'd only just met him a few days ago. He seemed normal enough, but, as I well knew, a person could fake anything for a few days. Could Blake have been pulling off a charade of his own? Playing the normal, attentive man while underneath lurked a cold-blooded killer?

I shivered despite the sunlight pouring in the wall of glass and grabbed my keys from my purse. Even though I was 90 percent sure I was letting an over-active imagination run away with me, I was sud-denly eager to escape the bright sunny bungalow.

It was Monday and, while I should have gone to work, I called Peterman and told him I needed an extra week away. He wasn't quite as happy with it this time, saying he'd have to give the Sholtzkie Plumbing account to Danielle, who was already working on the Olsen's Bakery site. But consider-ing I had about three years' worth of vacation days saved up, there wasn't much more he could do about it than whine. Besides, I figured with all the times I'd covered for her, Danielle owed me this one. Instead I took a long, hot shower, fed Tabby a can of seafood delight, and dressed in a light cot-ton sundress I'd picked out at the mall the week before. White, sleeveless, with little eyelet details along the neckline. Very soft, very feminine. Very unlike anything I'd ever owned before. But as I looked at myself in the full length mirror, it kind of suited me. Even better when I added the red heels.

I grabbed my purse from the end table and, with-out even glancing at my e-mail, got in my hatch-back and drove up the peninsula to Parker Models.

Unfortunately, R.J. was at a go-see with one of his young hopefuls, but the receptionist directed me down the hall to Alec's office. In contrast to R.J.'s mas-sive desk, Alec's office was decorated in slim, sleek furnishings—pale woods and lots of chrome. The walls were dotted with framed head shots, mostly models whom I assumed the agency represented, though I spotted a couple that were clearly younger versions of Alec.

"Kya, lovely to see you again," he said, leaning over his desk to pump my hand. "How are you?

"Good. Great," I lied.

"So, how did you like your first shoot? Exciting, yeah?"

I nodded. "Yes." I gestured to the framed head shots. "You used to model, too?"

Alec's face broke into that easy grin. "Eons ago. But I still remember that thrill of making love to the camera for the first time. R.J. tells me you did a fantastic job."

He reached into a file and produced an envelope, sliding it across the desk to me. "Your check." He gave me a wink.

I took it and slid it into my purse. "Thanks."

"So, you ready for another one?"

"Another? Oh well, I . . ." I hadn't thought ahead to doing any more. Quite honestly, I hadn't expected to last through one. The idea of doing it again had never even occurred to me.

But Alec didn't wait for an answer. He riffled through a stack of papers on his desk, finally holding one up as he squinted at the writing.

"R.J.'s got you scheduled for tomorrow afternoon. Three PM. It looks like it will be fairly short. But Blake's booked on it already. Sound good?"

Somehow the fact that Blake would be there again settled the anxiety in my stomach. I found myself nodding.

"Great. I'll give R.J. a call this afternoon and let him know you're on board."

"Just, uh . . . it isn't lingerie again, is it?" I asked, feeling my cheeks heat.

Alec laughed, throwing back his head. "Nope. Shoes. Think you can handle that?"

I thought of my newfound love of red heels. "Definitely."

"Great, why don't you check in with Julie on your way out to get the particulars."

Alec moved to stand as if our little visit was over. But for some reason I couldn't move.

"Um, actually, I was wondering if I could ask you about something else."

"Oh?" He sat back down, clasping his hands together in his lap. "Shoot."

"It's about Angel."

His smile faltered, emotion flitting across his eyes before he composed himself again. "Oh," he said slowly. "Okay, what about her?"

I took a deep breath. This was harder than I'd thought. Somehow I really needed to know but really didn't want to hear the answers. "What exactly happened to her?"

Alec's tanned brow furrowed. "She had an accident. She drowned."

"I know. I mean, R.J. already told me that. What I meant was . . . well, I read the articles about her death online. At first they suspected that she . . . that she was killed. They even questioned Blake."

Alec abandoned all pretense of a smile. "They

questioned all of us. Everyone who knew her. Was she depressed? Suicidal? Where were we that night?"

"The papers said there was a lack of evidence. That they *had* to rule it an accident."

Alec nodded. "Yes."

"But they also said she was an excellent swimmer and there was no sign of head trauma or any other reason for her to have drowned."

"What are you getting at?"

"Do you think it was an accident?"

Alec sat back in his chair, steepling his fingers together under his chin, his Redford-blond brows drawn together. "She had been a little upset. We'd given one of her accounts to a younger girl. Angel just didn't fit their image. But I hardly think she'd take her own life over that."

I shifted in my seat, distinctly uncomfortable. "Actually, I wasn't thinking suicide. I was thinking . . ." I somehow couldn't bring myself to say "murder." It seemed too melodramatic, too *CSI*. Too . . . final. "I was thinking someone else was there. Someone who may have pushed her in."

Alec's eyebrows headed north. "But you said yourself, there was no sign of trauma."

"He held her under."

"He?"

I bit my lip. Here it was. The real question. God, I didn't want to hear the answer. "Do you believe Blake's story?"

Alec cocked his head to the side. "You think Blake killed Angel?"

I chewed furiously on my lower lip. Bad habits be

damned. "I don't think she fell in the pool. I think someone held her down. Under the water." I shivered despite the heat being pumped in through the air ducts as I remembered the feel of those strong hands on my shoulders.

Alec shook his head. "I don't know what to tell you. Yes, I believe Blake's story. I mean, why would he lie? He was obviously in love with Angel. He'd never have done anything to hurt her." He leaned forward, taking one of my hands in his. "Kya, I know being the new girl around here must be hard for you, but you've got to know that the police looked into all this. They had every technology at their disposal. They found nothing. It was an accident. A terrible, tragic accident, but that's all it was."

Alec stood, walked to his office door and threw it open. I followed. But the look on my face must have said I still wasn't convinced.

"Kya, for your own sake. Let it go, huh?" Alec said.

I did an unconvincing nod again, this time trying to force a smile I didn't feel.

I stopped at the reception desk only long enough to sign the contracts for tomorrow's job and grab the info sheet—which I shoved into my bag without even looking—before pointing my hatchback toward home.

The drive down 280 was quick at that time of day. Just me and the rolling hills. I sped up, pushing eighty. My shoes even looked hot pressing down on the accelerator. But if I wore these to the shoot tomorrow, people were likely to think I didn't own a second pair of shoes.

Had Angel owned a pair of the red heels? Sure, she'd worn them in the ad, but had she had a set of size sevens in her closet at home? Had they made her feel the way they did me? Bold, powerful, sexy. Almost as if I were stepping outside myself into someone else's life. Into Angel's life.

It hit me hard, jarring me so that I swerved into the next lane. Thankfully, the only thing I collided with was those little yellow safety dots. But it made me slow down and focus on the road. My heart beat fast, harder and stronger, as I realized just what I'd thought.

I had Angel's life. I had her job, her agent, her boyfriend. God, I'd even spent last night in the same place she'd died. I was running around town quite literally filling her shoes.

I started to feel my pulse speed up as I mentally ran through the events of the last week. I'd been obsessed with Angel's ad. With her. I wanted to *be* her. And as soon as I'd put those red heels on, I'd known exactly how to move, how to dance, how to charm every man in the nightclub as she would have. Including charming R.J. into hiring me on as her replacement. I'd known just what to say to Blake. I'd even ordered her favorite wine at dinner. I'd known exactly how Blake wanted me to wear my hair, exactly how he'd kiss, what it would feel like to be in his arms. I'd known my way around his kitchen.

And I'd known how Angel died.

I wrenched the steering wheel to the right, pulling over to the shoulder and sticking my head between my knees as my breath came out in ragged pants.

Only that didn't help much as it brought me face-to-face with those damned red heels. I quickly ripped them off my feet as if they were on fire and threw them into the backseat. I opened the car door, setting my bare feet down on the asphalt, and took in welcome gulps of fresh air. In. Out. In. Out. I closed my eyes, telling myself it was all coincidence. Some weird, bizarre chain of coincidences. That nothing about Angel's death had anything to do with me.

And I almost believed it as my breathing started to regain a normal tempo, my pulse slowing.

Almost.

Until I spied my purse sitting on the seat beside me and remembered the job I'd signed on for tomorrow. Modeling shoes. No, it couldn't be . . .

But as I reached across the console and ripped the info sheet from my purse, my heart caught in my throat as I saw that it was.

Tomorrow I was shooting an ad with Blake for the Hiheelia website.

CHAPTER SEVEN

It was a breezy night. The wind whipping at my bare skin. I looked down. I was clad only in an oversized T-shirt with a big red Stanford *S* on it, my legs exposed beneath. And the wind was picking up, rushing over me so that little goose bumps appeared on my arms. Why was I outside, dressed like this?

The noise. That's right, I'd heard a noise. I was afraid it was the dog. Blake's dog. Sometimes he got out at night.

I called his name softly. "Here, boy. Here, Rufus."

Only the wind answered, gusting through the trees, making little ripples on the surface of the pool. I tiptoed closer to the edge of the water, squinting through the darkness at the thick bushes that flanked the patio. Were they moving?

"Rufus?"

Or was it just the wind? I couldn't tell. It was so dark, the moon a tiny sliver in the sky, giving off no more light than a flickering candle. I should have brought a flashlight with me. Where did Blake keep his flashlight?

I was about to turn around and go back into the house to get one.

But I was too late. A pair of hands on my shoulders. Strong and rough, shoving me forward. So unexpected, I lost my balance immediately, pitching forward, arms out to break my fall as I hit the water.

The cold sent a shock through me and I involuntarily took a breath. Only water came rushing into my mouth instead of air. I tried to cough it out, to propel myself upward. But it was no use. Those hands were still holding me. Pushing me down. Instead, I tried to turn around. I needed to see him. Who was doing this to me? Why? What had I done to them? I thrashed to the left and right, unable to see anything in the dark, the water clouding my eyes, my lungs stinging, burning, begging for just one little sip of air.

But he wouldn't let me have it.

I felt my eyes closing, my limbs growing heavy, the fight slipping out of me. I focused everything I had left into one more movement and flipped my head around to see him watching me. Watching the life slip out of me as his hands held me under the water. I couldn't believe it.

It was him.

"You!" I screamed.

I blinked my eyes against the darkness. I was dry. In my apartment. Alive. Breathing. Air was pushing in and out of my lungs, not chlorinated water. Pushing quickly, too, on the verge of hyperventilating. I bit my lip, steadying myself to get my bearings.

I'd fallen asleep on the sofa, the TV on, a *Cheers* rerun blaring as Tabby curled up at my feet. I wasn't sure how long I'd been there, but it had been light when I'd fallen asleep. Fully dressed. I'd dropped the red heels on the floor when I walked in. I quickly kicked them away from me now as if I could kick the dream away, too.

His face. I'd seen his face.

Only I couldn't. I mean, *she* had, but it had been dark. I could only see the outline. It had been a man, tall, close-cropped hair, Caucasian. But that was all I'd been able to see. Or maybe that was all I wanted to see.

It had to have been Blake. If he'd really been asleep and she'd fought that hard, he would have woken up. He would have heard and come out to the pool, saved her. There was no way he could have slept through that struggle.

I strained my memory trying to get more details out of the face, but nothing came.

But she'd seen him. Angel had known who her killer was as she'd watched him drain the life out of her.

The thought sent a shiver up my spine, and I quickly got up and turned on the light. In fact, I turned on every light in my apartment. How could he do something like that? Actually watch the life go out of someone. It was beyond me. But one thing I knew for certain.

"I won't let him get away with it, Angel," I said to my empty apartment. "I promise."

I dressed with determination the next day, putting on the sexiest thing I owned: a white, clingy dress that ended just south of my derriere and plunged just north of my belly button. I contemplated the white slingbacks Danielle had prompted me to buy, but instead I picked up the discarded red heels. They had started this whole thing. It seemed only fitting I wear them to end it.

I pulled up in front of the Victorian on Market that Julie had directed me to and was quickly ushered into a room decorated like a scene from ancient Greece. White columns, grape vines, and lots of gold streaking through the background. Crew members ran back and forth putting the finishing touches on the set and arranging the array of lights as a man in all black stood behind a camera lining up shots.

Blake was already there, next to a wardrobe rack, being fitted in a white toga. I had a moment of doubt as he flashed his lopsided grin at me, raising a hand in greeting. But I swallowed it down. Angel did not kill herself. And Blake had been the only other person there.

I pasted a fake smile on my face, holding on to that thought as I waved back.

"There you are, my love," R.J. said, bustling up beside me. Alec followed a step behind, his hands in his pockets as he surveyed the set.

"And don't you look fabulous today?" R.J. exclaimed, giving my dress a once-over. He shot me a grin showing off all 500 of his teeth. "Got a hot date later?"

I glanced over at Blake. "I hope so."

"Well, let's get you in wardrobe," Alec prompted. "As promised, you will be fully clothed this time."

"You're the Goddess Shoestra of Mintandia," R.J. said. "And Blake gets to be your love slave." He winked.

I felt bile rise in my throat. My love slave. Like he'd pretended to love Angel? Like he'd made love to me? God, I wasn't sure I could pull this off. I looked down at my heels. But I had to try. For her.

"Great," I forced out.

R.J. continued to fill me in on the mythology behind my character as a thin, mousy wardrobe girl whisked me into a white, draping dress that ended just below my knees. It was shot through with gold accents that the hairdresser mirrored in my locks, gold ribbons pulling my curls up into a crown around my head. And on my feet were a beautiful pair of gold heels—a strikingly modern touch to the ancient scene. The photographer led me out onto the set and posed me against a white pillar. Blake appeared a moment later.

I bit my lip, squelching the rush of emotions at being so near him. Disgust at what he'd done mingled with the memory of the night I'd spent in his arms. How could I have been so wrong about him?

The photographer told Blake to kneel at my feet. He did, giving me a secret smile that said he was enjoying the intimate pose. I did my best dominatrix look back.

"Perfecto!" the photographer yelled, and started clicking away.

"You look hot in a toga," Blake whispered.

"Shh. I'm working, slave boy."

His mischievous grin grew. "Yes, goddess."

I turned my head the other direction, hardly able to look at him without wanting to throttle the man.

Somehow I made it through the shoot without vomiting. Even with Blake giving me moon eyes the entire time. By the end, I felt like I'd run a marathon, though the shoot had lasted only a couple of hours. When it was over I quickly rushed back to wardrobe, changing into my own clothes. I took a few deep breaths, telling myself I could do this.

"Hey, kid, you okay?" R.J. asked, coming up behind me as I was strapping my shoes on.

"Yeah, fine," I lied. "Why?"

"You sound like you're hyperventilating. What's wrong? Something going on between you and Blake?"

I shook my head. Then paused. If there was anyone who might have insight into Blake and Angel's relationship, it was R.J.

I leaned in close. "R.J., I think Blake killed Angel."

His wide smile dropped. "Alec told me you'd been asking questions, but I didn't believe you seriously thought Blake could have anything to do with this. I told you, he tried to save her."

I shook my head. "I know, but . . . but I'm certain."

He leaned in. "You have proof?"

"Yes." I bit my lip again. "Well, not exactly. I mean . . . look, you're going to have to trust me on this. I know who killed Angel."

R.J. stared at me for a moment, his expression unreadable. He opened his mouth to say something.

But didn't get the chance as Alec joined our little group.

"That was fantastic, Kya. I'd be surprised if I'm not looking at the next Heidi Klum."

"I don't know about that," I said, my eyes still on R.J. His brow was furrowed, his lips set in a thin line, digesting what I'd just told him.

"Wow, killer dress, Kya."

I froze, feeling Blake come up behind me, his hand skimming the small of my back.

He let out a low whistle. "That thing should come with a warning label."

"Thanks," I said, putting on my best poker face.

"Got plans tonight?" Blake asked me.

"No," I said, slowly tearing my gaze from R.J.'s furrowed brow. "Why? Did you have something in mind?"

Blake's eyes twinkled with a look that could only be called wicked, that dimple creasing his left cheek. "One look at that dress and I've suddenly got just one thing on my mind."

I pasted a smile on my face and gave him a playful swat on the arm. "Down boy."

"Tell you what, come back to my place and I'll cook you dinner. Ask the boys here, I'm an excellent cook."

I turned to R.J. He'd seemed to regain his composure somewhat, though his mega-watt smile was still absent. "Oh, it's true. The man is a wonder in the kitchen. Have him make you his mushroom lasagna. It's to die for."

I'll bet.

But instead, I gave a grin that was all teeth. "Blake, I'd love to."

Maybe going home alone with a killer didn't top the list of smart things I'd done in my lifetime. But visions from a dead woman were hardly conclusive proof of his guilt. If I wanted to get any sort of justice for Angel, I had to get something real. I had to get Blake to confess. My only hope was that I could get him comfortable enough to confide something damaging to me. And if I was going to do that, I had to get him alone.

After two plates of, I'll admit, delicious lasagna, Blake and I retired to the living room. I sat on the sofa with my legs tucked up under me as Blake handed me a glass of cabernet. Which I had no intention of drinking. I needed all my wits about me to pull this off.

"That was delicious. I can see a girl's going to have a hard time keeping her figure around you."

Blake grinned, sitting down beside me. Close beside me. I involuntarily inhaled his warm scent and couldn't breathe for a moment.

"I don't think that will be a problem for you," he replied, running a finger lightly down my arm. It was a small gesture, soft and intimate.

I sucked in my lower lip to keep from pulling away.

"So, have you done a lot of work for Hiheelia?" I asked, trying to steer the conversation toward Angel.

He nodded. "Yeah. They like to keep familiar faces in their ads."

"Like Angel?"

Blake's eyes clouded over. "Yes. She worked for them."

"I know." I held up one foot. "I bought these because of her picture."

His eyes hit the floor as he idly swirled the cabernet in his glass. "Yeah. I remember that shoot."

"It must have been hard dating her."

His head lifted. "Hard?"

"Dating a model I mean. Men always looking at her. The jealousy. I bet you two fought a lot?"

His eyebrows drew together in confusion. "No. Never."

Liar. Who never had a fight with his girlfriend? After date number three, Ex-slimeball and I had fought like cats and dogs.

But instead, I said, "Hmm. That's nice."

I took a swig of wine. This was going to be harder than I thought. How did those guys on *Law & Order* do it?

"Working together and dating was never a strain? I mean, that's a lot of together time."

He grinned. "You and I work together, you know."

I bit my lip. Touché.

"Did she stay here a lot? At your place?"

Blake cocked his head to the side. "Why do you ask?"

"No reason. Just curious about her, I guess."

He paused, staring at me for a moment. "Yeah, I guess she did. Especially in the summer. She . . ." He trailed off, his eyes cutting to the swimming pool outside. "She loved the water."

"Odd that she couldn't stay afloat that night then."

Blake's face froze. Absolute granite. His eyes went deadly flat, their dark chocolate depths turning black.

Great, so much for my couth.

"What are you doing?" he finally asked, his voice low.

I'd pushed it too far. I felt my heart racing, adrenalin pumping through my veins. "Nothing," I said, doing some serious backpedaling. "Nothing. Sorry, I didn't mean to bring her up." I held up my glass. "I get a little funny when I drink sometimes."

He stared at me with unreadable black eyes for what seemed like an eternity. Then his features slowly relaxed. "No," he said, "it's all right. I'm just . . . it's been hard. I'm not really ready to talk about her, you know?"

I nodded, relief flooding through me. "Right. No problem."

"Listen, it's been a long day. I'm gonna get some sleep." Blake rose, setting his glass down on the coffee table. Then he gestured toward mine. "I think you better stay here tonight, huh?"

Only there was no hint of seductiveness in his voice.

I nodded. Grateful. I didn't want to leave until I got what I'd come here for, but the thought of sleeping with him again churned my stomach. No way could I do it, not after knowing what he really was.

Instead, I borrowed an old T-shirt from his closet and slipped into the other side of his bed, trying to make myself as small as possible.

No such luck.

Blake rolled over, laying an arm across my stomach. Despite my disgust at what he'd done to Angel, my body instantly responded to his touch, going warm and soft beneath his hands.

I closed my eyes, telling myself my body was a traitor of the worst kind.

I waited until I heard the deep, even sounds of Blake's breath before slipping out of the bed. I tiptoed out of the room in the dark, afraid to turn on a light. It wasn't until I made it to the living room that I let the tension drain out of my muscles.

I blinked, letting my eyes get used to the dark as I scanned the room. Somewhere here there had to be evidence of why Blake had done it. Some e-mail, some note, something that told a different story from the one Blake had spun about their perfect relationship.

I started with his laptop, holding my breath as the welcome screen lit up the room. With one eye on the bedroom door, I quickly opened his e-mail program. Luckily, he didn't take advantage of all his browser's security features and his password was still in the system, showing up as a neat little row of asterisks. I hit "log in" and quickly scanned the contents of his inbox. The oldest message was dated three weeks ago. Damn. I tried to do a word search through his archived messages, but without knowing what I was searching for, came up with nothing. If he'd had e-mails from Angel, they were long gone now.

I moved on to his hard drive, checking for recently deleted files. I came up with only a couple of old bank statements. His personal files were just as mundane. A few financial records, a note to his aunt thanking her for the sweater she'd knitted for his birthday, some photos of him and his buddies in Stanford T-shirts somewhere warm and tropical, a couple of letters to R.J. Nothing that even hinted at Angel.

I checked his browser cache to see what websites he'd been visiting recently. Most related to modeling, though I was surprised to see World of WarCraft listed. I couldn't help it. I clicked on the link and sure enough, his password was stored there as well. I smirked as I saw his character. He was a night elf hunter, just barely at rank seventy. I could so kick his butt.

Resisting the urge to mess with his character, I closed the site, instead scanning his hard drive again for anything that gave any indication that he and Angel might have been on the outs. I came up with nada. And I knew my way around a computer. If it had been there, I would have found it. Admitting defeat, I turned the laptop off, plunging the room into darkness again.

I waited a couple of beats for my eyes to readjust, then set to work on his desk.

I pulled open the first two drawers, coming up with the usual fare—pens, rubber bands, loose change, stamps. Though his file drawer held some promise. I flipped quickly through the tabs marked *Bank Accounts* and *Insurance* until I got to one marked *Contracts*. Maybe it hadn't been a personal issue that had led Blake to kill. What about professional jealousy? I pulled out the folder and scanned the contents. It held contracts from the previous year, all in the same legal mumbo jumbo mine had been. All I could really tell from them was that Blake made way more than a beginner like myself. Like a couple zeros more. No wonder he could afford vintage merlot.

But nothing to suggest he held a grudge against Angel.

I put the folder back, pausing to listen at the bedroom door. No signs of movement, just the sounds of his even breathing.

I tiptoed back to the living room, desperation starting to bubble up in my throat. What if there really wasn't any evidence? What if the police were right and Blake had truly committed the perfect crime? It wasn't fair. Angel deserved better.

I slid open the glass doors and stepped out onto the patio. The night was still, a rarity off the bay. The air was cool, but without a breeze, it almost felt like summer again. The valley twinkled below, lights winking back at me, reflecting off the calm, glassy surface of the swimming pool.

I hugged my arms around myself. "I'm sorry," I whispered to the night. "I tried."

I closed my eyes and tried to imagine Angel. To feel her. *Come on, girl, tell me where to look. What to look for.*

I was concentrating so hard, I could swear I almost

felt her as I stood there at the edge of the water. A presence. Someone else on the patio with me.

Of course, I didn't realize it wasn't Angel until I felt a pair of strong hands grab my shoulders and push me into the pool.

CHAPTER EIGHT

The cold water hit me like a punch in the gut, knocking the wind out of me as I went under. Instinctively, I kicked upward, surging toward the glassy surface above me. But I never got there. Two hands clamped down on my shoulders, stopping my progress just below the surface.

I panicked, felt my arms flailing, legs kicking, my body thrashing side to side using up precious oxygen. None of which did any good. My attacker only tightened his grip, his long fingers digging into my shoulders, pinching as my lungs began to burn.

I tried to twist around to face him, but he held fast. I reached up, ineffectually pawing at his hands. My throat stung, my head started to fill with a thick fog as my lungs begged for the air I could see right above me. So close, yet an eternity away. I felt tears sting the back of my eyes even through the strong chlorine.

Was this it? Was I going to die here? God, I wished I'd never seen those shoes. Angel's life hadn't been all that great. And I could tell you firsthand that her death had sucked big time. What had been so wrong with my old life anyway? I had a good job, good friends, a damn good cat.

Poor Tabby! How long would he be cooped up in my apartment alone before someone found him? Then what? The pound? I'd be leaving him an orphan.

And that's when I got mad. No one did that to my cat.

With my lungs on fire, my limbs heavy and numb with cold, I summoned up what strength I had left, turned my head to the right and bit the hand on my right shoulder as hard as I could.

I heard a muffled yell, and his grip loosened. I quickly wiggled free, kicking up toward the surface. I almost cried out the relief was so great when I felt the cool night air on my face. I dragged in one deep breath after another.

But it was short-lived. His hands were back, grabbing for my throat this time. I thrashed to the left, feeling his fingers graze my neck, water splashing in front of my eyes, blurring my already clouded vision. I tried to swim for the side, but I was disoriented. I didn't know where it was. Where I was. All I knew were those hands grasping for me again. They seemed to be touching me everywhere, dozens of them. Finally they caught hold, fisting in my hair, yanking me backward under the water again. I fought back a cry as pain erupted on my scalp. Instead I reached up with both hands, grabbed hold of one of his wrists, and kicked forward as hard as I could. I must have thrown him off balance because the next thing I heard was a loud splash as his grip loosened again.

I pushed off from the bottom of the pool and hit the surface. I sucked in air as I swam forward, trying to put distance between us. I got two good strokes in before I felt his hand wrap around my ankle, pulling me back under again. I kicked hard with the other foot, colliding with something soft, and heard an answering grunt. But he didn't let go. Instead he grabbed me by the throat, pushing himself up to the surface as I watched it grow farther and farther away.

I clawed at his hands, feeling myself break the skin, but he didn't budge. I thrashed, kicked, squirmed, but it only made his fingers tighten. Bubbles poured out of my nose and mouth as my last bit of air floated to the surface. I watched them break the glassy calm through blurry eyes, feeling my arms and legs grow heavy, my eyelids start to close. My entire body begged for sleep.

Was this how Angel had felt? So tired. So heavy. Had she fought? Or had she been caught off guard, never had a chance? Had she been grateful when her eyes had finally closed? Not to feel the pain in her lungs, in her limbs, in her head?

I wondered if she was with me now, watching as I slipped out of this world and into the next.

And then it happened. A loud boom, like a cannon going off, and the grip on my throat disappeared. It took a second before my foggy brain registered my freedom, but as soon as it did I kicked toward the surface with an energy I didn't know I still had, breaking through the top with a grateful gasp. I took a second breath, then another, my lungs burning with each one, my throat on fire, as I kicked toward the side of the pool, twisting to see if Blake was following me.

I twisted around. And let out a scream. Instead of Blake chasing after me, I saw a body laying face-down in the center of the pool, a large red stain slowly spreading out from beneath it, coloring the water a murky pink. I thrashed wildly, splashing, kicking, trying to get away from the macabre pink water.

A pair of strong hands reached down and lifted me from the water. On instinct, I pulled away, twisting out of their grasp before focusing my eyes on the person they belonged to.

Blake.

I blinked. He was standing at the edge of the pool, skin white as a ghost, eyes dilated to an unhealthy size. A gun in one hand.

My eyes shot to the body. If Blake was standing here, then who was . . . ?

I forced myself to look more closely, fighting off nausea as I took in the man floating in the pool. Blond hair, tanned skin, lean build. I sucked in a breath.

Alec.

"Kya?" Blake asked, taking a tentative step toward me. "Are you okay?"

I shook my head, my fuzzy brain trying to make sense of it all.

"Y-y-y-you shot Alec," I said. My teeth were chattering, my words slurred.

Blake ran a hand through his hair, making it

stand on end. "Christ, Kya, he had you by the throat. I thought . . . God, I thought he was going to kill you. Tell me you're okay?"

I licked my shivering lips. Then finally nodded.

Blake dropped the gun on the patio with a clatter, closing the gap between us and crushing me to him in a fierce hug. Which was a good thing. Because as the adrenalin wore off, I felt my legs give out completely, my body sagging into his embrace.

It was dawn before the police left. As soon as he'd gotten me inside and out of my wet clothes, Blake had called 911. I wasn't totally sure that what he'd told them made sense, both of us bordering on hysteria by that point, but a uniformed officer arrived ten minutes later, followed by a whole posse of others as soon as he called in the body.

Blake was swabbed for gunshot residue and DNA and put into the back of a squad car. I was shoved into an ambulance where EMTs went over every inch of me, examining the dark purple bruises I could already feel forming on my throat. Once they determined I was relatively okay, a plainclothes police officer in a fedora that looked like he'd seen one too many episodes of *Dragnet* told me he'd like me to come down to the station to answer some questions. Since it wasn't really a request, I agreed.

It was light out by the time I'd relayed the events of the evening in triplicate to Dragnet, who'd then had me sign a statement and asked that I be available for follow up questions should the need me. Again, not really a request, so I nodded and promised I wouldn't leave town as a uniformed officer led me through the lobby.

That's where I finally saw Blake. He was promising much the same to another detective, this one a spitting image of Kojak. My heart clenched as I saw his pale cheeks hadn't gained much color since he'd fished me out of the swimming pool. I walked toward him and gingerly put a hand on his arm as the detective walked away.

"Hey."

He spun around, the lines around his eyes softening as he saw me. "Hey. You okay?"

I nodded. Great would have been an exaggeration, but I was breathing, so I figured okay was a good description.

"You?"

He took a deep breath and let it out slowly. "I will be. Jesus, Kya, I shot a man."

I nodded. "I know." I paused, then asked the question I'd been dying to have answered all night. "What happened, Blake?"

He scrubbed a hand over his face and sat down on a wooden bench by the wall. "I . . . I'm not really sure. Something woke me up. I don't know what, but I realized you were gone. My head was all fuzzy, I couldn't really focus for some reason. And at first I kind of freaked out, remembering you by the pool the other night. I walked to the sliding door and saw someone in the water, thrashing around. I . . ." He faltered, then looked at the ground. "At first I thought it was Angel and I lost it. I tried to grab you, pull you out of the pool. But you kept twisting away from me. And then I realized there was someone else in the water with you. I saw him grab you by the hair and pull you under. I tried to stop him, but I couldn't." He looked down at his hands. "It was like I was moving through a fog, my body felt so heavy. Then I remembered the gun I'd bought after Angel died. I ran into the house to get it, then came back out to see him with his hands around your throat. I didn't even think. I just aimed and fired."

Guilt hit me full force. How could I have been so wrong about him? He'd saved my life. I should have known there was no way he could ever have hurt Angel. "Thank you. I thought I was a gonner."

"Yeah, me, too." He attempted a little half smile. It was pretty feeble, truth be told, but I was glad he was even attempting.

"Let's go home," I said, the fatigue I'd been fending off suddenly getting the better of me.

He nodded, taking my hand in his. It was warm, soft. Comforting.

"How about my apartment?" I offered.

Blake nodded. "Yeah, I'm pretty sure I'm never going back to my place again."

I didn't blame him. "Well, in that case, I hope Rufus likes cats."

He grinned at me, this one closer to genuine, even showing a little dimple, as he gently brushed a kiss along my lips. "He'll learn to love them."

CHAPTER NINE

I sat forward in my cubicle, leaning my elbows on my desk as I moved my mouse to the "next" link and clicked through to the rest of the Yahoo News story about the death of Alec Davis.

It had been one month exactly since the attack. I can't say I'd really gotten over it, but the bruises around my neck had almost faded. A good thing, too, as I'd just about run out of turtlenecks to wear to work.

Yeah, I was back at OmniWeb. After my agent tried to kill me, I figured my modeling days were over. While it had been nice to play the center of attention for awhile, Kya Star was no more. Because, honestly, there really hadn't been anything all that wrong with Kya Bader to begin with. Sure, she'd had ample practice at being a doormat in her lifetime, but that didn't mean I had to throw her out entirely. She had a lot of good qualities, too. And the moment I'd seen death hovering on my horizon, I'd made a promise to myself to discover them all.

The news page loaded, Alec's Redford good looks filling the screen. I tried to ignore it, instead focusing on the print beside it.

According to the reporter, the police's first order of business had been to go over every inch of records at Parker Models. The conclusion: Alec had been skimming funds. As soon as the detectives confronted the receptionist, Julie, she'd broken down and admitted to everything. Alec had had her draw up two copies of contracts for every model— one with the real amount they were being paid, one with a fake number that left Alec with a commission bordering on 75 percent. Apparently once his own modeling jobs dried up, he hadn't been content with a mere 15 percent of the profits. He'd had the models sign the fake ones, then transposed their signatures onto the real documents before sending them in to his accounts. Poor R.J. had been clueless about the whole operation running right under his rose.

But Angel hadn't.

As an accounting major, Angel had noticed discrepancies and caught on to his scheme. According to Julie, she'd had a heated argument with Alec just days before her death, but Julie claimed she had no knowledge of what happened next. The police speculated that Angel confronted him and he'd killed her to keep her quiet.

That's when I'd popped on the scene, asking questions about Angel and making Alec nervous that the whole thing would be dragged up again. But what had tipped him over the edge was that R.J. had told him I had proof of her killer. (Little did he know it was in the form of creepy visions—hardly admissible in court.)

Alec had freaked and followed me to Blake's, where he'd waited for the right opportunity. Clever me, I'd walked right into it.

Blake had eventually been cleared of any wrong-doing in Alec's death, though, according to his tox screen, he'd ingested large amounts of sleeping pills. After going over Blake's place, police found the half-empty bottle of wine he'd drunk that night, laced with enough drugs to put an elephant out. Blake admitted Alec had given it to him before leaving the set that day.

The police surmised that Alec must have used a similar MO in Angel's murder, first making sure Blake was knocked out, then killing Angel. Though, the reporter finished by saying that whether Alec lured Angel outside or it had been pure opportunity to find her at the pool, we'd probably never know.

I bit my lip as I stared at the screen. Well, maybe some would never know . . .

Ever since Alec's death the dreams, visions, whatever they'd been, had stopped. I'd like to think it was because Angel was at peace now, but I wasn't about to try to analyze it. I'd come to terms with the fact that what happened to me didn't make a whole lot of sense. In fact, it was bordering on *Montel* episode weird. But Alec was gone, Angel's murder was solved, and my life was back to its normal routine of cubicles, web layouts, and cat fur on my black sweaters.

So I wasn't complaining.

"Kya?"

I snapped my head up, quickly closing the

news window as Danielle ducked her head around my cube.

"Oh hey, Danielle. You scared me, I thought you were Peterman."

"Yeah, you're on his shit list for taking three weeks vacation in a row."

I shrugged. "I was due."

"Hey, Maxie and I are cutting out early to go to Club Ecstasy. You wanna join us again?" She poked me in the arm. "I know how much fun you had last time."

"Oh, uh, sorry, not tonight."

"Ah, come on, Kya, you've got to learn to live a little, girl."

I grinned. "Actually, I've already got plans."

Danielle cocked her head to the side, fingering a corkscrew curl. "Oh yeah? With who, your cat?"

I should have been offended, but instead, I couldn't wipe the smile off my face. "Nope." I nodded behind her. "With him."

Danielle spun around just in time to see Blake step off the elevator.

Okay, so maybe there was one thing about Kya Star's life that I wasn't totally ready to give up. Could you blame me?

After Kojak and Dragnet had cleared Blake of all charges, he'd gone back to his place only briefly to pack up a few things and collect Rufus from the neighbors before moving in with me. I'll admit, it was an adjustment for both Tabby and me to not only have a man, but also a huge Saint Bernard, suddenly in our space. But so far we were adjusting nicely. Okay, maybe Tabby was a little more reluctant than I was, but the first morning I'd woken up in Blake's arms, I knew there was no other place I'd rather be.

"Ready, gorgeous?" he asked as he approached my cube, giving a cursory glace to Danielle, who looked like her eyes were about to pop out of her head.

"Ready." I flipped off my monitor and grabbed my purse from the floor beside my tower.

"See you tomorrow, Danielle," I called, waving over my shoulder at her.

She did a feeble little wave back, shaking her head in disbelief as a smile crept across her face. I knew I was going to have to give her mega details tomorrow in the break room.

"What do you feel like doing tonight? Movie? Dinner?" Blake asked, taking my hand in his.

"Hmmm . . ." I bit my lip. "Or we could spend the night in?"

He grinned down at me, showing off both dimples. "Oh yeah? And just what did you have in mind?"

"My shaman kicking your elf hunter's butt. He is so weak."

Blake threw his head back and laughed as he hit the elevator button. "Hey, that elf hunter saved your pretty little shaman behind last week, if I recall. Remember that troll? With the rampant crossbow?"

"Damn. You got me. I guess I owe you then, huh?"

He nodded. "Big time."

"Okay, tell you what? We'll order in Chinese, lock the animals in the bathroom, turn down the lights, and I'll let you play with my spells."

"Your spells, huh? Hmm . . ." he said, getting a wicked gleam in his eyes. He leaned in and grazed his lips along the nape of my neck. "It's a deal."

I giggled and went warm all over.

Blake squeezed my hand as the elevator doors slid open and I stepped one shiny red patent-leather heel over the threshold of the elevator.

Oh, yeah.

I guess there was one other tiny part of Kya Star's life I was keeping, too. What can I say? They were *hot* shoes.

MELANIE JACKSON

And They Danced

*For my sister, Monica,
who also loves to dance.*

CHAPTER ONE

. . . I need a vacation but that would be hard with the cat. He gets carsick.

Faith looked at what she had just typed on her portable computer and reached for the delete key. Her hand hovered in the air, reluctant to erase yet another draft of the letter for her middle sister, but a girl had her pride and she was not going to send home another pathetic e-mail. This one wasn't as pathos-filled as the last one, but it was hovering near the low-water mark, and she knew her sister would share the news with her parents and siblings. Too many more unhappy messages and her family was going to think it had been a mistake for her to take this job. Actually, they already thought it was a mistake, that she had only fled to California because of a broken heart. It had to be that, they insisted. They had a flatlander's mistrust of the coastal regions that had both mountains with yearly winter mud slides and unpredictable earthquakes that happened in any season. Also, a lot of very strange people lived in California. Faith's parents thought it arrogant of Man to build straight out to the coast when the coast was slowly eroding away—and so it was. But Faith wouldn't give up living by the sea for anything in the world.

Around her, the seaside community she had recently adopted bustled on its busy way. That was Santa Cruz for you, she thought. It gave the impression that everyone was heading off for a party, even at eight o'clock in the morning on a cloudy Monday when by rights people should be looking downtrodden. But no one looked unhappy. The summer fog was already thinning and everyone seemed certain the weatherman's promise of sun and heat would be honored. As she watched, the first glimmerings of morning light pushed through the salt sky, warming their faces as they talked on their phones and listened to their iPods. Even the homeless walked about in shorts, some with cell phones, and all with smiles. This was a magical place where anything could happen. Every last person seemed smug in the knowledge that it was another perfect day in paradise and they were going to enjoy every minute of it. That was very different from Faith's childhood upbringing where everyone understood that weather was something you endured, something that would try and kill you. No one expected to actually take pleasure in it.

The Internet café where she wrote was a popular one and therefore constantly filled with the cheerful roar of coffee grinders, shouted orders for double lattes with extra cream, and the giant espresso machines that left the atmosphere thick with noise and the glorious smell of roasting coffee that blended well with cappuccino scones, which were the specialty of the house, and the ocean, which was a specialty of nature.

The two-story building was set back some thirty feet from the busy street where traffic crawled by at the pace of the bicyclists, roller skaters, and those in motorized wheelchairs who asserted their right to use the same road as the motor scooters, golf carts, three-wheelers, and SUVs, whose large tires hissed loudly on the fog-damp tarmac as they rolled toward the highway. The paved and planter-boxed open space outside the broad doors was used by various performance artists and orators or the usual religious, political, and alien-among-us persuasions. The populace that wasn't indoors drinking chai and coffee—and that included the many canine companions—were having passionate discussions about every imaginable subject, including the café's decision to sow the giant brick planters with real opium poppies.

Faith peered over her portable's glowing screen and looked out the large glass doors that were standing open in order to lure the caffeine junkies inside its faux brick portal. At one time the gateway had been built of actual bricks, but the original structure had toppled during the Loma Prieta earthquake and safety regulations had triumphed over aesthetics during the rebuilding process.

She took a quick sip of her decaf-nonfat-café mocha and skimmed her note. Mocha was her favorite morning drink, which she used to bridge the gap from her morning oatmeal to her first carbonated, caffeinated beverage at noon. If it happened to be Wednesday, a busy time when lunch would be had from a vending machine, she also added *pain au chocolat* to the order.

Faith sighed and hit the space key. As she reached for the keyboard she noticed that she still had a daub of orange paint on her left thumbnail.

> *. . . But at least my social calendar is filling up. In fact, next weekend I have to decide whether to attend a dance competition or the D&D championships at the office. Ha! Like there's any real danger of me going to the dance. Yes, my to-die-for cute neighbor will be there, but after all, it's more important for a girl to defend her Dungeon Master title from the other nerds she works with. Seriously, though I'd love to see Mister Tall Dark and Dancing, unless the gods send me a sign, I doubt we'll ever go out again. You know me. I'm not into artists and performers. Give me a stable nine-to-five nerd any day.*

That was a little better, if slightly untrue. Actually, very untrue, but at least it held out hope to her family that she was willing to see some real, living men, and not holding out for some modern-day Prince Charming. And she would date again eventually. Her breakup with Brad had been painful but not soul scarring; her mother had taken the end of their relationship harder than Faith had. Brad's pragmatism and utter lack of imagination suited her practical nature. Faith just needed some time to adapt to the new place and the new job before diving into the dating scene again. Not unnaturally, moving away from her family had left her feeling a bit low at first, but as the weeks passed, she had found the burden of being the youngest and least conventional of the Fleetwood children slipping off her shoulders. Her spirits were gradually lightening. And she was in Santa Cruz, living near the beach! She even had a pet cat that she had inherited with the apartment. Life was going to be very good. Eventually. Especially if Avel could somehow be a part of it.

Faith shoved her glasses back up her nose. The thick black frames were fashionable but she had a suspicion that they had been a mistake. There was a fine line between brainy and geeky, and she might have just crossed over it, no matter which designer name was displayed. She might have to go back to contacts or her wire frames, though she was certain that glasses made her look grave and intelligent.

In fact, it was these glasses that had gotten her in trouble the last time the to-die-for Avel had asked her out. Avel was an accountant, but he seemed to spend little time actually accounting, at least during the day. She had met him by chance at a Dougie MacLean concert where they had noticed each other because they were the only nonsilver-haired people in the crowd—excepting some whiny redheaded kindergartener dragged there by his grandparents. Of course, there had been no overlooking Avel anyway; he was, hands down, the best-looking man in the crowd. Avel had the excessive good looks that some Frenchmen are gifted with—a genetic present, he told her later, from a maternal grandfather who had been an actor. The rest of him was Russian Jew. Avel's real passion was dancing, and because he was foreign it made the pastime acceptable to his American male friends who had the traditional distrust of men who liked such activity. Not that anyone would mistake Avel's grace for being effeminate or weak. There was just too much self-assurance and lean muscle there. Extreme beauty did that for a man. Probably for a woman, too, but Faith wouldn't know about that. She was most often called cute.

After the concert they had gone for ice cream and Avel had convinced her to visit the dance club where he taught a Thursday evening line-dancing class to visually handicapped children. She had been dazzled by extra fudge sauce and Avel's amazing eyes, and said yes without thinking.

The class had gone well until break time. Asked by one of the students if she could dance, she admitted to having had a few Latin-dance lessons in college. Avel had immediately invited her to take a turn about the floor and she'd said yes again. Someone popped Santana's "Smooth" in the CD player and they had taken to the floor. Faith thought that she had been doing pretty well—only stepping on his toes once or twice with her Birkenstocks, which were de riguer pedestrian footwear for the city but lousy for two-stepping—but once he had taken her hand and spun her into a fast turn her new glasses had come flying off and gone skittering across the glassy wood floor. Being a gentleman, Avel had dashed after them. The children hadn't been able to see clearly what was happening, but there were other people there who did, and they had giggled.

Faith shuddered at the memory. She was always a bit klutzy around handsome men, but she had truly exceeded herself that day. The moment he had taken her back into his arms for a second try, she had been overcome by self-consciousness and completely forgotten how to cha-cha. The legs did rumba, the feet were doing tango, and the arms . . . well, they had been doing The Swim or something. She would always be grateful that Avel's students couldn't see her humiliating performance. It was bad enough that he had been there.

Things might have ended thusly, but Avel had hired her to design a website for his business. That meant spending time together while they talked about his requirements. She'd poured her heart into that webpage and Avel had been impressed with the results. He convinced the dance studio to hire her as well and offered to act as liaison. Besides spending even more time with Avel, this had the added benefit of getting her noticed at work. New hires didn't usually get requested by name their first few weeks on the job.

But they hadn't tried dancing again, and their lunches and dinners had always had involved at least some business. There'd been no kissing, not even of the cheek-planted, good-night-and-thanks-for-the-dinner variety. Frankly, it was amazing that Avel had actually asked her to enter the dance competition with him.

Of course, his regular dance partner had gone snorkeling in Hawaii last week and liked it so well that she'd decided not to come home, so he was at loose ends this weekend. And the competition was for charity, a literacy project. The newspaper said that the organizers were trying to make it into the *Guinness Book of World Records* for the longest conga line. Since Avel was one of the studio's best students and a huge supporter of their after-school dance program for disadvantaged kids, he was bound to ask everyone in the neighborhood to come to the event and dance the conga, even the neighborhood spastics.

Faith sighed and checked her watch. It was time to go. Work whispered and, lo, she had to answer. She began to wrap up her note.

> *So, you see, though I may be putting in too many hours and perhaps going to have to repaint again (because that mango orange really is a bit overpowering) I am having fun and getting quite good at meeting new people outside of work. Tell Mom to stop worrying. I really am fine.*
> *Love you all,*
> *Faith*

She clicked the send icon. Relieved to have that weekly chore done, Faith finished her mocha and closed up her computer. Of course she had high-speed Internet access at home as well as at work, but she preferred being out with her colorful neighbors when she did e-mail, especially when her apartment was thick with paint fumes. Which it often was, because she seemed unable to decide on just the right colors for her new place.

Taking her mug back to the counter, she said good-bye to the owners, Mario and Ellen, and then started off for Web Spinners. She didn't use her car much anymore because her office was only three blocks away, and her workplace and home were the only places she spent any time these days. Maybe she should sell the Honda and get a bike like most of the locals used. She could save herself the expense of the twice yearly insurance payments, and would be able to afford a home all the sooner.

Of course, the first step was keeping her job, and the best way to do that was to not be late. She sighed, wishing she were more of a morning person.

CHAPTER TWO

That night, after a long day of work, Faith juggled her computer bag, oversized purse and Lee Fook's Nook take-out bag as she coaxed the stiff deadbolt lock on her front door to open. The nightly salt fogs corroded everything metal and the lock needed replacing. All the apartments in what used to be a motor court inn faced the ocean, and they all had sticky locks. That was the price of living by the sea. The landlord would get around to fixing it eventually; maintenance wasn't really his thing when the surfing was good. Faith was learning to have a laid-back attitude.

It took some effort and threats of bodily harm, but the door finally saw reason and let her inside. It was only as she tripped going over the threshold that she realized there was a large box waiting on her doorstep.

Putting her paper bag and computer case down on the table by the door, she went back to the front step and fetched in the large lion-colored box that now had a dent in its side. The handwritten label was blurry, as if the box had been out in the rain. Packages were supposed to be left in the manager's office, but it was rarely open and people complained about having to fetch them, so the postman had taken to leaving things on the doorstep. There were no other markings on the box to say whether it had been delivered by the postman or UPS. Perhaps someone here in town had just left it for her.

Feeling suddenly cheerful and wondering who could be sending her a gift weeks before her birthday, Faith went into the kitchen to fetch a pair of scissors. Cutting carefully through the gold strapping tape, she pried open the cardboard flaps and then lifted out the sheets of antique gold tissue paper. Nestled inside was a satin bag in a delectable shade of seafoam green with gold embroidery.

She recognized the slip-sack. It was the kind that exclusive boutiques supplied for exotic purses or even more exotic shoes.

Heart pounding in anticipation, she lifted up the sack and opened it carefully.

"Oh my!" she said. And then: "Ooooooooh."

Faith removed the shoes one at a time. She recognized the pumps. She had looked at them last night at an online shoe store. They had a name. They were called Cabbage d'Orsay and they were created by the king of shoemakers, Manolo Blahnik. Except, these shoes were a little different. They didn't say Manolo Blahnik. And the heel was higher and even narrower than the one in the picture. Could this be some prototype, a sample of a design that was altered before it went into production? Surely it wasn't some knockoff. The shoes were made of a pale green silk and adorned with cabbage leaf bows of the most delicate mauve pleated silk. The heel was high, a nearly transparent spire, a place where wood nymphs would stand in a garden bower and be adored by passing mortals.

"There's got to be some mistake," she said to Ambrose, who was twining about her ankles. The cat also liked Lee Fook's Nook takeout, and he was reminding her that it was dinnertime. Carefully she set the shoes aside and looked at the box again. She had been right the first time. There was no return address and no invoice, just a card in the very bottom that read:

www.Hiheelia.com
Home of the Goddess Shoestra
The place where wishes come true.

She looked at the label again. It was blurry, but this definitely had her name and address. The shoes were also her size. But who on earth could be sending her pumps that cost more than her monthly living expenses?

The scent of cooling moo shoo pork tickled her nose, reminding her that she hadn't had anything to eat that day except some stale cheese and crackers from the vending machine in the break room. Web Spinners had had a systems crash, and it had been all hands on deck all day long while the computers and their client files were resurrected from the dead.

Picking up her white bag that also had an order of roasted green beans, Faith headed for her kitchen. The room was currently a bright mango color that glowed an almost incandescent orange with the setting sun adding its heat to the vibrant walls. It was like standing in the middle of a forest fire. She really was going to have to paint again and had already chosen the color. The new paint can was sitting on a folded tarp just waiting for her to have some free time. The canister was labeled Island Sunrise. It was a bit darker, a shade more subdued than Mango Frost, and she had high hopes for it.

Her sister had accused her of using her home-improvement projects as an excuse for not dating, but a person's home had to be just right. It was one's retreat from the world, and no one could live with *that* color on their walls. By the time she finished making oatmeal in the morning she already had a headache. That was a lesson for her—no more choosing paint when she was feeling down. She had gotten away with the ripe apricot in the living room, but the bedroom was a bit overpowering in water-melon, and the bathroom was probably going to pall quickly. The paint was called Fuschia Garden but was really closer to Irishwoman's Sunburn once on the walls.

Her food heaped onto an aqua Fiestaware plate, and Ambrose's dinner with a side of green beans laid in his bowl, Faith headed for the living room, turning on the television. She liked The Movie Channel. That night they were playing *Royal Wedding* with Fred Astaire. She kicked off her shoes and wiggled contentedly into her yarn-cloaked sofa. She had at least found a use for the vivid, even violent-hued afghan that her grandmother had crocheted her for Christmas: It covered up her determinedly tan sofa, a gift from her sensible parents when she rented her first apartment. Eventually she would buy another couch, something more suited to her tastes, but for now she was content to keep what she had while saving up for a down payment on a seaside condo. Even the smallest of them were formidably expensive and she had a long way to go.

Faith ate quickly, forgetting to enjoy her meal. The shoes, so delicate and perfect, held her rapt. They were works of art, shoes that were made for Cinderella to wear to the ball where she would dance with her handsome prince and . . .

"The ball. Those shoes were made for dancing at a ball."

Faith put her fork down. Her breath caught. There it was: her omen, the sign from the gods. Hadn't she told her sister that she would go to the dance competition if she were sent a sign?

A part of her flinched, hearing her mother scold her for such magical thinking. The rest of her felt excited and breathless.

"But . . . I can't. Can I?"

The shoes didn't answer. They simply stood, radiant, beckoning.

"I know they aren't really mine, but it wouldn't hurt to try them on, would it?" she asked Ambrose, but the cat remained intent on knocking his roasted green bean around the floor. Prey had to be chased and then killed before being eaten.

Of course not. There was no harm in slipping into them and perhaps taking a walk across the thick pile of her carpet. That wouldn't leave any unsightly scuffs.

Moo shoo pork forgotten, Faith went over to the table where the faerie shoes were waiting. Again, she hesitated. But she heard Fred begin to croon "You're All the World to Me." Sighing, she leaned over and slipped on the beautiful pumps. Right foot, left foot. Her weight shifted forward, she stood up, tall and regal. Eyes closed, she could almost feel the satin of a beautiful ball gown sliding over her body as she was transformed into a cinema goddess.

Someone tapped her shoulder. Not surprised, Faith turned and looked into the eyes of a slender white man she had known from childhood. Fred smiled as he tossed his top hat and gloves aside. He slipped out of his tux coat and then removed the cuff links from his sleeves and rolled them back. Finally, holding out his hand to her, he leapt onto her desk and then onto the wall—and she was there beside him, dressed in a gown of virginal white as he pulled her into his arms. And they danced. Slow and then fast and then even faster.

Up onto the ceiling they went. Around the chandelier they fox-trotted, their feet moving so quickly that they were a blur when she looked at their reflection in the window. He spun her once, and then down the other wall they strutted. A small jump and they landed on her swathed sofa, collapsing into the cushions. Side by side they sat and laughed.

A commercial came on the television for a new

miracle mop. Fred reached for the controller and turned the television off. Then he leaned over and slipped off her shoes. Then he kissed her hand. Charmed speechless, Faith watched as he went to the table where he'd left his hat and coat. Shrugging back into his formal wear and stowing his gloves and cuff links in his pocket, he gave her a last lovely smile. Finally he spoke: "You'll do well, Faith Fleetwood. I'll see you at the dance. Just remember to stop at two times. Three is a tricky number, a playful and sometimes dangerous number. Take my word on this."

And then he was gone. So was her white gown.

"I'm dreaming. I must be," she said, but her voice was filled with lazy contentment. She had danced with Fred Astaire. Her sister was going to be so jealous when she told her.

Faith was still smiling when she fell sideways, her right hand just missing her plate of cold moo shoo pork balanced on the arm of the sofa. She never noticed Ambrose crouched in the corner of the wingback chair, fur standing on end, staring first at the door where the intruder had disappeared and then at Faith with large unblinking eyes.

After a moment, when no one reappeared and it was obvious that Faith was going to be sensible and sleep, the cat uncoiled his body and hopped up on the sofa. There was no point in letting those lovely green beans go to waste.

CHAPTER THREE

Sunrise seemed to have arrived early, and an unexplainably exhausted Faith stood gaping in the dawn's bright light, her toothbrush and breath stilled by the shock. There—right there above the sofa where she had fallen asleep, dreaming of dancing with Fred Astaire—were shadowy gray smudges on her apricot walls. Shoeprint-shaped smudges. Lots of them.

"Holy cow!" she gurgled. Not bothering to rinse away the minty foam, she raced for her computer. Faith opened her laptop with shaking hands and typed in *www.Hiheelia.com*. Never mind that those shoes were the most beautiful—well, second-most beautiful; Avel was still more attractive—things she'd ever seen. It was time to find out just where these slippers had come from.

The website was there, which was a bit of a relief, but nowhere did they actually offer her specific brand of shoes for sale. She looked diligently, clicking on page after page but not finding them. In fact, this site didn't seem focused on selling shoes so much as worshipping them. That wasn't the only peculiar thing, though. They gave no physical address or phone number where the company could be contacted. There was just a single button on the drop-down menu under *Help*. It said: Make a Wish.

"Ohmanohmanohman." Faith scrubbed at the toothpaste that had dried around her mouth in an itchy crust. "What is this? Who sent these things?"

She went to add the website to her favorites list so that she could find it again and discovered that it had already been flagged. Had she visited this site before? She couldn't recall ever going there. She had looked at shoes at some department store websites, but she was sure she'd never been to this site before. Still, there it was, bookmarked in her computer.

Make a Wish, the icon blinked.

Okay, maybe she had forgotten going to the site. She'd had the tiniest bit to drink that night and it didn't take much wine to be too much. But no way would she have ordered them. There wasn't enough wine in California to make her do that. The shoes had to be a gift. They had to be. But just to be sure, Faith pulled out her emergency numbers and called the credit card company to see if there had been any recent outrageous charges.

The electronic voice on the phone assured her that there had been no unauthorized purchases. So, she hadn't gotten drunk, lost her mind, and squandered her life's savings.

This didn't reassure her. More shaken than ever, she reached for her personal address book and picked up the phone.

Almost two hours later and in serious danger of being late for work, she had contacted every family member and friend for whom she had current phone numbers. No one had heard of this website and no one had sent her those beautiful but alarming shoes.

"Ambrose, I wish you could talk. You must have seen who delivered these," she said to the cat, who had hopped up on her desk and was watching her intently but unable to do anything useful. Her brain hurt from thinking about the conundrum. Who else could have sent her such a gift? Who else would think that she could want or need such an expensive and . . . well, magical, pair of shoes?

"Avel," she whispered suddenly. Her heart rolled over. Could that be it? Could he have sent her the shoes as a lure, knowing it would be impossible to resist such bait? Was Prince Charming trying to coax her into attending the ball?

Half convinced that she was right, Faith pulled open her desk drawer and started digging for the White Pages.

How did he spell his last name? *B-E-R-A-U-T*? Her mind was going blank. Probably it was the lack of oxygen. She needed to breathe.

Faith punched in the number and his phone began to ring. She eyed the box the shoes had come in. The tawny carton was nice, but a bit plain for being Pandora's Box. And surely that's what it was.

Of course, that thought lead to memories of other unhappy legends. Like the story of The Red Shoes. These shoes weren't red, but they were certainly magical. No normal shoes would let a person dance on the walls and ceiling. And if these were shoes out of some fairy tale, then weren't there some rules that went with them? She didn't recall all the details of the tragedy of the girl who wore the red shoes, but in most fairy tales things happened in threes. Aladdin got three wishes from the genie. The Princess got three chances to guess Rumpelstiltskin's name . . . and if you caught a faerie you had to ask it a question three times before it would answer. She'd dreamt something else about threes as well. Hadn't Fred said something—like three was a tricky number?

"Hello, this is Avel's electronic stenographer. Leave a name and a number and I'll let Avel know that you've phoned."

The voice wasn't Avel's. It wasn't even human. She had never called him at home before, and this strange but definitely female voice and message threw her off.

Faith blinked, breathed and waited for the buzz.

"Avel, it's Faith. Fleetwood. I wanted to ask you . . ." Ask him what? If he had sent her magic shoes that made her dance on walls? That sounded crazy. It *was* crazy. Bug-munching mad, but . . . She looked again at the ceiling. Okay, crazy or not, it had happened. But she didn't want Avel thinking she was nuts, so she had to say something else. "I . . . I wanted to ask you something about the dance tournament. When you have time, call me, okay?" She left her home number, though she had given it to him before. Twice, in fact.

"And now I have to fly," she said to Ambrose, but her eyes remained fixed on the box where the shoes rested. They lay on their sides, looking languid, post-orgiastic faeries resting under silken cabbage leaves until dark when they would rise up and dance again. On the bottom of the left shoe was a telltale smudge of bright orange paint. The sight shook her all over again. She wailed softly, piteously: "I'm going to be late and I don't even have time for a café mocha. It's not fair."

Ambrose looked unsympathetic as he stalked toward his cat door, thick tail swishing. If she didn't have time for a café mocha then there wouldn't be time for her to fix him a boiled egg for breakfast. It was Kattie Kibble city until dinner time, and that made him grumpy, even if he had had more than the lion's share of dinner last night. Being a cat, he didn't recall this last detail. Nor did he remember the strange apparition in top hat and tails.

CHAPTER FOUR

It was almost noon, and the sun had finally scrambled its way to the top of the coastal mountains and was resting there while gathering strength for the long swim over the Pacific Ocean. Faith barely noticed. Her thoughts were divided unequally between Avel, work, finding a dress to wear for the dance—assuming she went—and unease about her new shoes. Her most devout hope was that she would go home and discover that those shoeprints on the wall had been just shadows caused by pigeon droppings on the window. Because if those were really shoeprints . . .

"Hey, Faith!" The nasal voice interrupted her rumination. A large pink head appeared over the side of her cubicle. "Wanna grab a tamale at Donkey Hoties's place? We're heading out in about fifteen minutes." The voice belonged to Larry Truman, and he meant Don Quixote's Bar and Grill. You could always tell a recent transplant from the midwest. They didn't have the knack of Spanish pronunciation. Their *R*s didn't trill and the vowels were too long and too nasal.

Did she want to grab a tamale? A stomach rumble answered her.

"Sure, but I have to run home first. Can I meet you there?" Faith asked, already gathering her purse. Her answering machine was the highest of all tech and had detailed instructions for its use—but only in Chinese. She hadn't yet figured out how to retrieve messages remotely. She'd have to go home to find out if Avel had called.

Faith all but skipped home, feeling energized by trilling nerves that told her to hurry—hurry! She didn't notice the traffic or the unusual number of Rollerbladed pedestrians who were out early because of the sun's premature escape from the fog. She reached the cedars at the edge of the parking lot where she lived, and breathed deeply of the spicy air. Lying in a sunny patch of dirt was Ambrose, looking a bit dusty and cluttered with dry leaves, but content to be baking in the sun.

"Do you want to come in with me?" Faith asked. The cat opened one eye. "I'll feed you," she added. "Come on, Ambrose. I don't want to face that wall alone."

Ambrose chuffed and rolled to his feet. He stalked toward the door, tail twitching. Faith hurried after him.

She entered her apartment uneasily, half expecting to find the shoes dancing on their own, but all was normal, including the cat's loud demand for the snack he'd been promised. After a quick peep at the heels, which were still resting on the table in a halo of sunlight, she hurried to the kitchen to dish up Ambrose's bribe—tuna—mentioning that it wasn't wise to snack between meals if one wanted to keep a trim figure. The cat sneered.

The answering machine was blinking and showed a red *one* in the message box. Taking a bracing breath, Faith pushed what she had learned through trial and error was the *play message* button.

Avel's lightly accented baritone filled the room.

"Faith, it's Avel. I know this was short notice. Listen, if you don't want to do the Latin dance, I can use Sasha—" *Sasha of the long lean body and even longer blond hair.* "I mentioned it to her and she thought she'd be free to partner with me, even though she isn't as good at the Latin dances." *I'll just bet she's free,* Faith thought, scowling. She'd seen the way Sasha was eyeing Avel the last time they met up at the mailboxes. Sasha eyed a lot of men that way. She had a reputation for poaching anything another women wanted. Man-theft was her favorite sport. Not that Avel belonged to Faith. Not yet.

Ambrose jumped on the desk and stared at the machine. The cat seemed fascinated with Avel's voice: "—so don't feel bad if you can't do it. Competitive dancing, even for charity, can be stressful—especially with a TV crew filming everything—and I don't want you to feel pressured into doing something you won't enjoy. I'll be busy the next two days with rehearsals, but we can always get together after the tournament." *Unless Sasha has her acrylic red claws in him.* "Just let me know what you'd like to do. Bye."

"There'll be TV there, Ambrose. If I screw up, everyone will see."

Faith hated the idea of being filmed while dancing. But if she said no, then Sasha would do it. Sasha . . . The woman looked like a young Angelina Jolie who was in a perpetually petulant mood. Men didn't seem to notice the sulky expression that settled on her face anytime that she wasn't the center of attention, but Faith saw it and knew to be wary. She had an older sister who was also very beautiful and, like Sasha, unleavened with charm. Faith understood precisely how many kinds of hell a spoiled brat could raise when feeling thwarted. Beauty conferred certain privileges, or so her eldest sister thought. And though their parents had done their best to convince their eldest that if beauty carried privileges, it also brought certain obligations, they had never entirely succeeded. Sasha was another Brenda, strutting through life on her long legs, indifferent to the emotional damage she caused the opposite sex.

Or, Faith admitted, maybe she was just green with envy and inventing reasons to dislike the more beautiful woman.

"Dammit!" Faith felt trapped. She didn't want Avel dancing the sexy Latin dances with Sasha, but she didn't want him to dance with her and end up a laughingstock, especially not on television. If only she could be sure of not making spectacles of both of them. If only . . .

Faith's eyes went back to the shoes, peeping at her over the edge of their box.

Did she really *really* believe that the shoes were enchanted?

Her gaze traveled to the wall where the impossible shoeprints remained. Her brain said no, but her heart—filled with longing—said yes.

Okay, so she believed it. The shoes could make her dance like Jane Powell. Perhaps they were even haunted by the ghost of Fred Astaire. But did the fact that they were enchanted mean that something terrible really would happen if she wore them three times? She seemed to recall Fred being firm about three being a potentially dangerous number, but the details were hazy and he had never actually said not to wear the shoes three times, had he?

Faith was a cautious person. Most of her habits and impulsive acts came from her past, but this time she acted on hope of the future—one that would include Avel.

"And I don't have to wear them three times," she whispered, feeling relieved. "I just need to wear them once more, to dance with Avel at the tournament."

It was time to fish or cut bait. As though knowing she had reached a decision, Ambrose chuffed and jumped off of the table. He sauntered toward his swinging door, glancing back once or twice as if hoping she would stop him from leaving by offering him a food bribe.

She didn't notice. Taking another deep breath, Faith dialed Avel's office phone number. She was startled when the base began to ring. Somehow she had set the thing to speakerphone.

"By the Numbers, this is Trisha. How may I direct your call?" This was a silly question. Trisha and Avel were the only two people in the firm, but Faith went along with the efforts of professionalism.

"Avel Beraut, please. This is Faith Fleetwood calling." Her hands fluttered over the various buttons, trying to remember how to switch from speakerphone, but she decided not to touch anything in case she got disconnected.

"Hello, Faith. One moment please."

"Faith!" Avel picked up immediately. "How are you? I was so pleased that you called."

"I'm wonderful," she lied. "I've decided that I'd like to enter the tournament with you. I think it would be fun even if we never make it past the first round." *Liar, liar*, a voice in her head chanted. It would not be fun, and she most definitely cared that Avel made it into the finals.

"That's great!"

"I even have the perfect shoes for it," she added. Faith waited for him to say something.

"Yes?" The question was polite, expectant.

"They're Manolo Blahniks." She waited but there was no reaction. "Someone sent them to me as an early birthday gift."

"That's nice. Just make sure you can dance in them. We don't want you getting blisters."

Faith eyed her wall and the shoeprints that were still there. Blisters? She wasn't worried about blisters.

"Oh, I can dance in them all right. You might say these shoes were made for dancing."

"Excellent! I'm so happy you decided to give it a whirl." His voice was warm and sincere. "Will you be able to practice with me tonight? I'm afraid we'll only have an hour or two to run through the dances. I have to practice with Sasha as well. She and I are doing the ballroom dances and she is feeling insecure. You and I will be doing the Latin ones, all right?"

"Absolutely," Faith assured him, her heart beginning to jitterbug. She tried very hard not to mind that he would also be dancing with Sasha as well. Still, he would be dancing the sexy dances with her. She had had some definite fantasies about dancing the rumba with him. "What time should we meet?"

"Say, seven o'clock? At the studio? We can grab something to eat afterward. Maybe Sasha will want to come along." She liked to think that he sounded a bit dubious about this.

"Seven is fine." And Sasha wouldn't be joining them, not if Faith had to push her beautiful blond head under a passing bus. "I'll see you this evening."

" 'Til tonight. Bye."

"Bye." Faith hung up the phone and faced the disappointed cat, who had reconsidered going outside and was now pawing at the base speaker. "Well, Ambrose, that's that. I'm committed now."

She looked up at the clock. She still had forty minutes on her lunch break. Time enough to hit Classic Reruns, a vintage clothes shop that stocked some lovely dance frocks. The green of her shoes was unusual, but she had a strong suspicion that she wouldn't have any trouble finding a dress that matched them. Whatever force was at work in her life, it wanted her to be at this tournament and dancing with Avel.

Larry and the others would have to have lunch without her.

CHAPTER FIVE

As she predicted, the hand of God—or something else—was hovering over Faith and she found her outfit straight off. The slightly rubbed velvet Mexican circle skirt was tacked to the shop wall along with an enormous moth-eaten sombrero and a pair of maracas. The skirt was a black lush nap and painted over in vivid shades of green and hot pink and then appliquéd with tarnished sequins. It reminded Faith a bit of those tacky velvet paintings of bullfighters or dogs playing poker, but it was perfect for the competition. She had seen the room where the dance was being held and it made Louis's palace at Versailles seem modest and tasteful. Anything more subdued than a winning slot machine in a Las Vegas casino would be lost in the grandeur of the mirrored ballroom.

To finish the look off, she found two giant crinolines in lavender and celery green and she stripped a wire mannequin sitting on the glass display case of its jet-beaded bustier that gave her cleavage that almost reached her chin. The giant orange silk poppy at the waist was probably a bit much, but she could always cut it off later.

The grand total for this never-to-be-worn-again outfit was enough to make Faith blink, especially when they refused to break up the set and insisted that she buy the tatty sombrero and maracas, too, but she closed her eyes and thought of Avel. A seldom used Visa card did the rest.

"Good-bye, sofa," she whispered as she left the shop, but her sorrow didn't last long. She was going to look magnificent.

Sticker-shock should have inhibited her appetite, but it didn't manage to quell Faith's stomach once her nose caught wind of the hotdog vendor. A glance at her watch told Faith that she was right up to the deadline for her lunch hour and would possibly be late to the afternoon staff meeting, but she made a quick stop anyway. She had to keep up her strength and it would be a long time until dinner. Not bothering with mustard and relish, she gobbled her tubular lunch as she dashed toward the office, bags flapping gaily as she trotted down the sidewalk to the beat of her unwanted maracas rattling in her shopping bag.

As fate would have it, she nearly collided with her boss as she dashed through the door.

"Norton! I'm so sorry," Faith said, gulping the last of her hotdog as the shopping bag with the maracas fell to the floor. The handle had torn loose and was clutched in her hand. The bags at Classic Reruns, likes the clothes, were also vintage and not in the best of shape.

"Doing a bit of shopping?" he asked, bending to retrieve her sombrero. Faith accepted it quickly and clasped it to her chest.

"Yes. I've been asked to dance in the charity ballroom competition this weekend. It's all last minute and I had to find an outfit." Faith tried to inhale as she said this, not wanting to blow hotdog breath at her boss.

"I see." Norton looked interested rather than annoyed. "That's quite an honor. Dancers come from all over the state to compete."

Faith thought about explaining that the honor was Avel's and she was a third-string fill-in for a missing dance partner, but that was too complicated an explanation for her boss when she was late for a meeting. Instead, she just nodded her head and tried not to be embarrassed about standing in the lobby with a tacky sombrero.

"I'm a bit nervous about this," she confessed.

"We encourage our employees to do volunteer work. We even give them release time for charitable endeavors," Norton added. "If you need to take some time off to practice . . ."

"Thank you, but no. I'll be rehearsing tonight. I just had to shop on my lunch hour because the store closes at four o'clock."

"Okay, but if you do need time off, it's okay. You've been working hard, and we want our star employee to shine at this event. My wife and I will be there to cheer you on. We go every year."

"Really? That's neat." Great, now there was even more pressure. Faith made herself smile. Not sure how she was going to carry her torn bags, her purse, and the sombrero, she gave up and crammed the hat on her head.

And They Danced

"I have to dash. I have a meeting and I hate to be late. It's such bad manners."

Norton nodded solemnly, but she thought he was trying not to smile. In Santa Cruz, people tended to be more relaxed about time than she was, and her insistence on being on time or early often amused people.

Or maybe it was the stupid hat.

It was probably the hat.

Not bothering with the elevator, Faith dashed for the stairs, taking them two at a time and making a terrible clattering noise as the maracas slapped together. She was feeling breathless as she reached the third floor but didn't allow herself to slow. She would be working harder than this in just two days. She had to get into shape.

CHAPTER SIX

Off the dance floor, Avel reminded Faith of a friendly dog. On it, he became a stalking cat, his movements holding both grace and danger in equal parts. Faith hoped she looked more feline than canine as they danced but couldn't be sure. She hadn't made any horrendous mistakes and Avel smiled approvingly every time she met his eyes, but Faith couldn't help but notice that the beauteous Sasha looked increasingly more smug as she watched their performance from the sidelines. Faith had suggested that she go for coffee while they practiced, but sensing that her presence bothered Faith, the horrid witch had decided to "stay and observe your technique." Her presence was making Faith very tense and unable to relax in Avel's arms.

Just wait, Faith thought, *until I'm wearing my shoes. You've never seen such technique.*

"Relax," Avel breathed in her ear for about the tenth time. "Forget that there is anyone here except me."

"Avel?" she said as the music came to an end. They had already practiced a basic cha-cha, jive, and now a tango. Next was a rumba. Faith was both excited and also nervous about dancing the rumba with Avel. Of all the Latin dances, it was the most blatantly sensual. It might be as close as they ever came to making love.

"Yes?" His eyes were entrancing as he looked down at her.

"I just want you to know that I'll *bring it* tomorrow night."

"*Bring it?* Oh, you mean perform with verve?" His smile was entrancing, too. It made her stomach jitter pleasantly.

"Yes. I'll do well. You don't have to worry. I'll be ready."

"I know. I don't like to put too much into rehearsals, either," he said generously. "It dilutes the magic." Faith blinked at his choice of words. He went on: "And anyway, this competition is just for fun and to raise some money to help the children. We can't expect to win with so little time to practice, so there is no pressure."

Is he disappointed? she asked herself, trying to read his voice and expression. He didn't seem upset.

Of course he is, she admitted. Until his partner had deserted him, he had had every chance of making it to the finals. Even winning the amateur division.

Faith saw the eavesdropping Sasha smile even wider. It took effort, but Faith managed not to scowl at her. Avel might not be expecting her to be able to compete with the other dancers, but Faith was sure that she could do more than merely keep up. All she had to do was wear her shoes. She would have worn them tonight except . . .

Well, she wasn't superstitious—not really. But she hoped that she never had to find out what happened if she wore the shoes three times. She had done some reading online that afternoon and the stories varied, but with titles like *The Devil's Dancing Shoes* and *The Red-Hot Shoes of the Devil*, the vast majority seemed to agree that three times was the fatal number for unwary dancers. It had taken an effort to get one particular version of the shoe story out of her head before going to rehearsal. Caught up in a dance that would not end, the doomed girl had tried to enter a church. But one of the saints who guarded the doors of the sanctuary had passed a terrible judgment on her and the shoes: *"You shall dance until you are a ghost, until your skin hangs from your bones, and even when the skin is gone and only your entrails remain, they too shall dance."*

Faith hadn't blasphemed lately, so she didn't think she would be in quite that much trouble. Still . . .

"Let's skip the rumba," Avel said, interrupting her thoughts. He glanced once at Sasha. Faith couldn't be sure, but she thought that he wasn't happy with her silent taunting. "I know you'll be great at that, Faith. We are running out of time and I think it is more critical to rehearse the *paso doble*."

Faith wasn't certain if she was displeased or relieved to have the cup pass her by. On the one hand, she had had several fantasies about dancing the rumba with Avel. But by the same token, she had no desire to dance it with Sasha looking on. A large audience would be . . . well, just an audience. Sasha watching—critiquing—from five feet away would be like having a peeping tom looking in the bedroom window and commenting on one's sexual form and prowess.

"Okay," she said.

"And after I do a few turns with Sasha, we'll go to dinner. I made reservations at a new seafood place. Sasha, I know you can't join us because you're so terribly allergic to shellfish and they don't have anything else on the menu yet."

Sasha's lips parted, but before she could speak, Faith—who loathed seafood but could choke it down if she had to—smiled happily and said: "That's too bad. Maybe we can do something together some other time." Like, when rattlesnakes ice-skated in hell.

Avel's eyes twinkled—she was sure they twinkled. Had she sounded too enthusiastic about ditching her rival?

"I'm sorry you're disappointed. I hope that I can be entertainment enough for you." He was standing close. Maybe too close. She was feeling a bit dizzy.

"I'm sure we'll manage," she finally said.

From the corner of her eye, Faith noticed that Sasha was no longer smiling. It was an effort, but Faith managed not to stick her tongue out at her.

Though it made her feel a bit ill, Faith stayed to watch Avel and Sasha dance. She actually was watching their technique. It took some wrestling with her conscience, but she finally had to admit they made an excellent pair. They were almost matched in height and both of them were exquisitely beautiful. Hollywood couldn't have found a better pair in central casting. Sasha was also as graceful as Avel, so they seemed to float more than quick-step.

"You two look great," Faith admitted honestly when they paused after a Viennese waltz.

"Yes, I think we belong together," Sasha said, running her red-tipped claws down Avel's arm. Faith's desire for sportsmanship, harmony, and honesty disappeared, and she wondered where she might find a hose to turn on her rival who clearly needed to cool down.

"I think that's enough for this evening," Avel said, stepping away from Sasha. "We want to keep things fresh," he added when she began to protest. "Let's save it for tomorrow night."

The Catch was only a few blocks away, so Faith and Avel walked. Avel was concerned that her lightweight sweater was not offering enough protection now that the evening fog had rolled in, but Faith assured him that she was warm enough. In point of fact, she probably wouldn't have noticed a blizzard with Avel walking beside her a mere six inches from her side. Sometimes their hands accidentally brushed. At least, she thought it was accidental.

Avel knew the owners and they were seated immediately at a small table near the back that was quiet and as away from the wedding rehearsal dinner going on at the front as it was possible to get. On another occasion Faith would have enjoyed watching the unfolding nuptial Bacchanalia, but that night she had eyes only for Avel.

A glance at the menu showed her that The Catch actually offered many dishes not containing the allergy-provoking shellfish that Sasha feared. She pointed this out, but Avel only smiled that enigmatic smile she was coming to know.

"I must have misunderstood," he said. "I know you don't usually indulge, but shall we have wine?"

"That would be lovely." Faith rarely drank, and in fact hadn't touched a drop since the night she had cruised the Internet looking at luscious shoes she could never afford, but if Avel had suggested they try hemlock tea with their dinner, she would have agreed readily.

"What will you be having?" Avel asked, perusing the wine list. "Anything that a red can bully? Or shall we stay white with dinner and have some port after?"

Faith lowered her menu. "I'm torn between the eggplant and the '*Latest Greatest Grilled Cheese Sandwich*.' "

"Have the grilled cheese. It's fabulous."

It sounded fabulous: aged triple-crème cheese, apple-smoked bacon, and Livingston's White Queen heirloom tomatoes. Anyway, Faith didn't want to look at the menu anymore. Avel was much more appealing. Perspiration no longer made him gleam, but he was still slightly flushed and his hair damp with fog. Taken with his bedroom eyes, it wasn't hard to come up with a convincing fantasy about dining with a lover before returning to bed.

"And I will have the prawns bordelaise," Avel decided. "So, let's try something with a hint of fruit and a bit of flower. A pinot grigio, I think. Many think it a pedestrian wine, but this Gloria Ferrer is like golden silk."

Faith almost sighed.

Avel beckoned to a waiter and a man of about fifty approached. Faith, who was usually very good at remembering names, forgot Avel's introduction the moment it was made.

She sat, contentedly mute, while Avel ordered for them.

"It was generous of you to compliment Sasha on her dancing. I know that she annoys you," Avel said, taking Faith by surprise. He had given her an opening, but as much as she was dying to say catty things about her rival, she took a leaf from her mother's golden book of manners that went something like: If you have nothing nice to say, say nothing at all.

"It's mostly my own lack of confidence that annoys me," she answered. This was partly true. "I get clumsy around"—*handsome men*—"strangers. And I don't need anyone that perfect standing by as a reminder of my shortcomings while I am trying to get my groove on." Faith sighed. "I don't think that my being there while you two danced bothered Sasha at all. She never put a foot wrong."

"Sasha is very graceful and technically good. Nor is she shy," Avel said. "We'll do well enough."

Sasha was graceful and technically good—which Faith wasn't. And Sasha wasn't shy, which Faith was. It was enough to make a person spit—if they weren't indoors and a lady.

"Yes, you will be great." Faith was relieved when their wine arrived and they had to go through the ritual of sniffing and tasting and finally pouring. Saying nothing was proving harder than expected. A part of her just wanted to straight out ask Avel who he liked more.

"But, you have something that Sasha doesn't," Avel went on as soon as they had the table to themselves. "And that is a truly passionate nature."

Faith blinked. She had a passionate nature? A romantic one certainly. But passionate?

"I know you keep it bundled up under that prim and proper veneer," Avel went on. "But I know it's there. I've felt it when you've looked up into my eyes. If you can give in to it tomorrow night, if you can be joyous, it will give us a power that few of the others will have. I have been watching the other couples rehearse and they are all in such deadly earnest that they have forgotten how to have fun. In many cases, I suspect that they don't even like each other. We don't have that problem. If we are . . . *happy* in each other's company, that will make up for simpler dancing."

Happy? The word had other meanings when Avel said it. Faith dropped her eyes and took a swallow of wine. She didn't know what to say. Talking about hidden passion was like showing off your undies: You just didn't do it in a public place.

Besides, she had something better than a passionate nature so hidden that she wasn't sure she could find it; she had magic. She opened her mouth to tell Avel about her shoes, but then paused. She absolutely believed that the shoes had power, but to say so sounded insane. She didn't want Avel thinking she was a loony.

"What is it?" he asked.

"I swear that you won't be disappointed in me," she promised, instead of telling him about the shoes.

"I know. No matter what happens, Faith, I won't be disappointed," Avel promised back, making Faith feel quite a bit better. "Ah, here is the first course. The candied pecans are perfect with the Roquefort cheese. I think you will find that all the food is festive and open-minded."

Faith began to smile. Dancing should be joyous. Food was festive. She absolutely loved the way he talked about dinner and dancing.

CHAPTER SEVEN

Saturday eventually passed, going at once too fast and yet too slow. Faith was as ready—physically—as she could be when five o'clock rolled around. She had washed her hair that morning and then tied it up loosely in rags the way her grandmother taught her so that it would have soft waves when she brushed it out. She had thought briefly about putting it up, slicking it back with jars of hair product and then sprinkling it with glitter, but decided to leave it loose. It was unconventional if not unprofessional in the dance world, but her tresses whipping about helped her to feel *passionate*. And wasn't that what Avel wanted? He said that they should be *happy* in each other's company. Happy and passionate. That was her mantra, which she chanted to herself even after she had given up on actual meditation.

Every inch of her body had been creamed with an extravagant purchase of cherry-almond body butter, and all the bits that needed to be shaved had been so. And without a single nick! Makeup was carefully applied. She didn't usually wear eyeliner or mascara, but with proper care and a slow hand, she was able to transform herself from geek girl into a woman of mystery. The last step was red lipstick—bloodred, the shade of deepest love. Or at least deepest lust. Unable to resist, she blew a kiss at Ambrose, who was sitting on the bathroom counter, watching interestedly as the various tubes rolled around the beige tile.

Frowning at the plain counter that didn't go well with her hectic pink walls, Faith made a note to look into tile refinishing products.

An hour before she had to leave for the competition, Faith put on her outfit. Except for the shoes. Those she set on the floor in front of the mirror and, standing on tiptoes, she pretended they were on her feet. She took a few experimental steps, pleased with the way the rustling crinolines swayed when she moved and made the sequins on her skirt sparkle as they swished between light and shadow.

The corset was tight. She'd had to lay on the bed to get it fastened and then had trouble getting back upright when it was done, but the effect was startling enough to make her giggle. Her reflection was hardly recognizable, she thought, executing a slow, sweeping turn, glad when she didn't actually overflow the cups of her corset. The mysterious woman in the glass looked happy, expectant, passionate even. So what if she could barely breathe? She looked hot, a wanton woman capable of anything. Look out world—she was ready, willing, and able to take on all its Sashas, and any kind of dance.

Avel arrived on time, and with a tall vase of Stargazer lilies for her. Their scent was strong, floral but voluptuous enough to be sensual. He was dressed in a vintage tux coat from the Edwardian era and looked delectable.

The walk to the hotel from Faith's apartment was a short one, but she didn't want to get sweaty and ruin her hair and makeup before the competition began, so she had agreed last night to ride there with him. Faith had worried that he would have Sasha with him, but Avel told her that the blonde had decided to meet them at the Hotel Corazon where she had booked a room for the night. Faith was betting it was a bridal suite and Sasha was planning on dragging Avel up to her lair when the dance was over.

"You look . . . perfect." Avel's eye traveled Faith's body as she stood in the doorway, her skirts brushing either side of the frame. His expression was approving and something else as well. Under his heated gaze, Faith found it relatively easy to slip into the frightening shoes she had carried to the door. For Avel's sake, she would take any risk.

"Ah, the magic slippers," Avel said, causing Faith to start and teeter on her right heel. He took her arm in a steadying grip. "Careful. We really don't need you to begin the evening with a sprained ankle."

"Magic slippers?" she asked. "W-why do you say that?"

"Surely they are. Anything that beautiful must have some magic in them." Avel released her. His eyes were clear and guileless—well, not guileless, but innocent of any knowing. He hadn't meant anything by the expression. Faith wasn't certain if she was glad of this fact or not.

"You have no idea," Faith finally answered, wondering if it was her imagination, or did she truly feel a tingling in her feet as the shoes seemed to tighten over them, the silk snugging up as if pulled taut by laces?

"All set?" he asked.

Faith nodded. She had no purse. She had a credit card, lipstick, and her key in a tiny satin pouch attached to her garter belt.

"You're not bringing the sombrero? I have room in the backseat," Avel said, smiling at the giant hat she had tossed on the desk. Ambrose was lying upon the wide dish of the brim. He didn't look inclined to surrender his makeshift bed.

"Only if you want me to. I have some maracas, too. I'd be willing to loan them to you if you thought it would enhance your costume."

"Tempting," Avel said, offering his arm. "But I think it could only detract from your loveliness."

"That's a tactful way of putting it. I really don't know what I'm going to do with the things. Give them to the Salvation Army, I guess." Faith closed and locked her stubborn door, and then, whisking her skirt aside with daring bravado, dropped the key in the tiny reticule on her garter belt. She knew that Avel was watching, and barely hid a smile.

Avel drove an electric car around town. It was an experimental model designed by a friend at the college, and didn't have a lot of horsepower, but the ride was smooth and quiet. Faith's skirts took up more than her share of the small front seat, but

Avel didn't seem to mind her crinolines brushing his knee.

Five minutes later they were at the hotel. Faith behaved like a lady and waited for Avel to come around to let her out. Once she was extricated from the small seat, Avel turned over the car to the parking valet. Electric cars were common enough that none of the staff was surprised to see one.

"Ready?" he asked again.

This time Faith paused, looking through the glass doors at the lobby swelling with people in evening clothes. Framed by giant brass doors, they looked a bit like a Victorian painting. Most of the guests had restrained themselves to simple black ties and dinner jackets, but since costumes were being encouraged, a few men sported cravats and top hats. The women glittered like the contestants on the runway at the first round of a Miss America pageant.

"I'm as ready as I'll ever be," she finally answered, which was the truth.

Avel did a good job of using himself as a shield as they went through the door. With his arm around her, they were through the lobby and into an elevator before Faith had no more than half overdosed on perfume and aftershave. There were rooms set aside for the competitors to dress, and Avel guided them there without any delay. Large portable mirrors and folding tables that served as makeup counters had been brought in and now lined the walls. Neither she nor Avel needed any further titivation, but they stayed because the bustle offstage was comparatively calm to the milling crowds that surrounded the dance floor, held back from the stage itself by blue velvet ropes laced through the eyes of elaborate brass posts.

Faith stood behind a velvet drape and, parting it a mere inch, she watched the glittering crowd. The room mesmerized her as the tide of people shifted around the floor, always forming and then reforming new patterns, kissing cheeks, kissing air, laughing gaily. She barely noticed that the air-conditioning had been set to levels that her refrigerator could only aspire to.

The floorboards of the stage where they would be dancing were made of golden oak, but the wood was polished to a mirror brightness that reflected the walls gilded with gold leaf that also covered every pilaster, corbel, and Roman god in the pantheon who clung tenaciously to the walls and ceiling four stories overhead. Giant chandeliers on enormous gold chains shed crystalline light like fairy dust over the entire room. Tiny lights flashed all around, darting like fireflies as the television crew tested their spotlights.

If she didn't actually have to dance for a prize in front of all these people, Faith thought that the moment would be utterly perfect.

Faith's reverie was broken by Sasha's voice. Turning reluctantly, Faith saw exactly what she expected— Sasha standing too close to Avel and running her crimson claws down his arm. Her hair was up in an elaborate chignon and covered with translucent glitter. Faith was glad that she had resisted the impulse to do the same. The comparison would not have been in her favor.

The sight of Sasha was annoying, but Faith could hardly say anything since Sasha and Avel were partnered for the ballroom part of the competition, and they would be dancing first.

"Champagne?" a voice asked at her elbow.

Faith turned to find a waiter in pale blue livery that she thought she recognized from the local theater's last-season production of Cinderella. He held a large silver tray with a dozen tall flutes filled with pale gold bubbly.

Should she? On an empty stomach?

Sasha gave a trilling laugh, a sound that men probably found fascinating but that grated on Faith's nerves. She didn't have to dance for two hours yet; there was time to have some champagne and then sober up again. Maybe a little alcohol will dull the mix of terror and annoyance that was eating at her.

"Why, thank you," she said, taking a flute. She downed the contents in three large swallows and looked for a place to set her glass. There was no room on the tables so she tucked it under a folding chair, then returned to her place at the door to watch the crowds.

Out in the ballroom music began to play. It was a waltz, not her favorite music by any means, but still Faith's feet began to tap and she began to sway. She looked down at her feet, feeling both amused and dismayed. Was it starting already? What if she couldn't control her shoes? What if she ended up pirouetting out onto the dance floor while Avel and Sasha were waltzing?

"Cool it," she whispered at her feet, feeling a bit dizzy. Perhaps that champagne on an empty stomach had been a mistake. "We'll have more than enough opportunity to show them what we've got when the Latin dances start. Don't blow it now."

"Ladies and gentlemen, take your seats please," a smooth, amplified voice requested. A man had stepped onto the dance floor. He was short and a bit round and also wore his hair slicked back, though he had refrained from peppering it with glitter. "Our competition is about to begin. Please let me start by welcoming you all to our little soiree. Dancers, take your positions."

The crowd actually tittered at this, though Faith couldn't imagine why. She turned to ask Avel if he thought the emcee amusing but closed her mouth when she saw him attempting to pin the number twelve on Sasha's costume. He was having some difficulty because her white dress had a very low back. He finally gave up. At a gesture from Avel, some sort of official came over to confer, and it was decided that the number would be affixed to Sasha's hip instead of her entirely too perfect backside.

Dancers began filing past Faith, pushing through the parted drapes in dazzling two-by-twos as the emcee announced them. They smiled so widely that her face hurt for them.

Faith was barely able to wish Avel—and by default Sasha—good luck before they were out on the dance floor and lost in the sparkling horde of what had once been separate people but were now two-headed and four-footed competitors. TV cameras, mounted on cranes around the dance floor, hunched down. She thought they that looked rather a lot like robotic dinosaurs, hunting down their sparkling prey, dragging restraining cables behind them. Faith was sorry that image had ever entered her mind. She didn't need anything else to be nervous about. As it was, she was sorry that there had been no room in her garter after lipstick for a roll of antacid.

The emcee's voice grew distorted and Faith had to lay a hand on the wall as the room swayed wildly. She leaned her cheek against the cool plaster and took a deep breath.

She could do this. She *could*! She wouldn't be sick—and she really *would not* faint.

All at once Faith heard Fred Astaire's voice over the speakers. He began to croon about being in heaven while he was dancing cheek to cheek.

Knowing it was stupid, Faith nevertheless forced herself to stand straight and then peered through the crack in the heavy drapes, hoping to see her former dance partner out on the floor.

Of Fred there was no sign, but she did see Avel and Sasha as they whirled by. Of course, she was prejudiced, but she thought they were the most striking pair on the floor: The stage was crowded with dancers, since this was the first round, but they were both tall and moved smoothly when others were jostled or even involved in collisions. Dance transitioned into dance, and before she knew it the first round was over. Ten talented and beautiful couple were chosen to go on to the semifinals. It was not surprising that one of the pairs was Sasha and Avel.

And then the rotund emcee with greasy hair was announcing a break and urging people to visit next door where a silent auction was being held. Next up were the preliminaries for the Latin dances, and it was promising to be the hottest show they'd ever had at the beautiful Hotel Corazon located right on the beach in downtown Santa Cruz, California—a great place for a family vacation or a romantic getaway weekend.

The dinosaurs pulled back and the bright lights went out, returning the room to romantic shadows.

All at once, Faith felt coldly sober. Ice water replaced acid in her stomach. She shivered and laid her trembling hands flat against the cool plaster of the wall which held her upright.

"I can't do this. I really, really can't," she whispered, as Avel walked toward her. But her feet disagreed: The rest of her might have been freezing, but her feet were hot, tingling, sending surges of energy up her legs. If she had to, Faith was sure she could do the high jump. Without a pole. She might throw up while she flew over the bar, but over the top she would go. This thought began to panic her, and she had the strongest urge to rip the shoes off her feet, just to prove to herself that she could still remove them.

"I'll need five minutes to change—no more," Avel said as he passed her. He had shed his coat before the dance began and, unlike the other competitors, he looked calm and unflustered. One would never know that he had just placed in the top ten of the first round of a dance competition. This helped Faith reel back in some on the wild emotion that was unfurling in her stomach.

He glanced back as he reached the door to the men's changing room. "Are you ready? You look a bit pale. You aren't nervous, are you? We'll be great."

Knowing it was a flat-out lie, Faith nevertheless nodded her head.

"I'm good," she answered, forcing her face into what she hoped would pass for a smile.

All the while her feet kept tapping, dancing away to some music that only they could hear.

CHAPTER EIGHT

Faith needn't have feared for her performance. Her shoes were in top form from the moment they glided onto the dance floor. She knew that Avel was surprised but also pleased that she was dancing so well. She didn't blame him for the wonderment; a last glance in one of the mirrors on the makeup table had told her that her face was pale beneath the two circles of rouge on her cheeks, and her eyes as wide as a bunny rabbit facing down a fox. She thought of lines from a song from childhood, a disturbing ditty her grandma used to sing about a fox and a rabbit who didn't want to end up as its dinner.

He is running for his dinner.
I am running for my life.

Only, she wasn't running. She was dancing.

Other couples had traffic accidents on the dance floor, elbows flew and feathers and beads scattered wildly as costumes failed, but Avel and her shoes danced Faith past all danger and she was able to spend her time gazing into Avel's eyes. Eventually her nervousness faded. It came as no particular surprise that, when the music stopped and the winners were announced, they had been chosen to go on to the next round.

As they left the dance floor, each lady was asked to draw a slip of paper from a giant brandy snifter. Faith reached in and removed a slip without so much as a pause in her strut. She couldn't have lingered if she wanted to; her shoes had decided that it was time to leave the dance floor, and so leave it she did.

"You have moved like a pro all evening," Avel whispered, as he squeezed her hand. "I guess when you *bring it*, it stays brought."

Faith unfolded the paper as soon as they were out of the spotlight. It was no revelation to her that they had drawn the rumba for their first solo dance. After all, magic was all around her, in her. The magic wanted her to win, perhaps not for her own sake, but it demanded a triumph.

She showed the paper to Avel.

"Good," Avel said softly. "This will be perfect. We will be perfect."

"Perfect? We didn't rehearse this one." She swallowed, nerves coming out of their stupor and beginning to thrash about now that they were out of the spotlight. It was half fear and half anticipation that made her heart beat erratically. Wasn't this what she had wished for? Hadn't she said a small prayer that someday she would have the chance to dance the rumba with Avel? Well, her prayers had been answered.

"Yes, perfect. Remember, the rumba is . . ." He

paused. "It's a pantomime of sex done slowly, sensually. The male is the aggressor. It's my job to seduce you. Your job is to at first tease, flirt, and cajole."

"Okay. I can do that," she said, staring into his dark eyes, her shoes temporarily forgotten.

"I will attempt to . . . contact you sexually. You will . . ." Again a pause. If Faith didn't know better, she would say that he was embarrassed and searching for more subtle language to instruct her. Had they been in a bedroom, meeting as lovers, he might simply have taken her hands and guided her to what he wanted. As it was, they were surrounded by dancers and forced to rely on words.

"I will . . . ?" She would . . . what? Her mind was suddenly a blank. What was she supposed to do? Her feet were zapped with another surge of impatient energy. Her shoes were saying that she needn't concern herself with this. They knew exactly what to do.

"You will use your skirt to fling my sexual overtures away." He smiled suddenly. "Try to throw it at the judges, if you can. Some of them are looking stern. They are annoyed at all the costume failures and jostling."

Right. That's what she was supposed to do. She'd whip her hips around and fling all that sexual energy away with her velvet skirts.

"Take a breather and get something to drink. I have to change back into my ballroom shirt." Avel touched her cheek. Then, for the first time, he frowned. "Sasha and I drew Viennese waltz for our solo. I know they want to keep the audience interested and that is why they are bouncing back and forth between the different divisions, but it makes for a lot of costume changes for those of us dancing both categories. I wish that they had set this up like a normal competition."

"Good luck anyway," Faith said, and meant it. She could feel the lingering touch of his fingers caressing her face even after he was gone, and she was left with only the faint scent of his aftershave, a lovely musky scent that seemed part of Avel.

Faith forced herself to turn away. She didn't want to be seen staring pathetically at the door where Avel had disappeared. She found a table laid out with bottles of water and helped herself. There were also several flutes of champagne, but this time wisdom prevailed. She found a spare chair and sat down, resting her feet and legs. She thought about taking her shoes off, but froze the moment her heel cleared the back of the shoe. It was a relief to know that they would come off, but if she removed them now, even one at a time, would putting them on again count as a third wearing?

Not willing to risk it, Faith left the shoes in place. She would be content with knowing that she could escape them if she wanted to. The shoes might be magical, even tricky, but they weren't like the ones in the story where the poor girl had to have her feet cut off to make her stop dancing. Feeling better about things, Faith gave the footwear a gentle pat.

Avel and Sasha returned to the dance floor. There were fewer couples backstage now, those who had failed to make the make the cut preferring to be out in the ballroom where they could watch the dancing and drink at any of the four bars.

Faith didn't go to the curtain this time to watch Avel dance. Instead, she closed her eyes and practiced her meditation and breathing.

In what seemed only a moment, the second round of the ballroom finals were over and only three couples remained. Again, Sasha and Avel were among them. There would be one final solo dance before the cumulative scores were tallied and the winner was decided, it was announced—and there was still plenty of time to bid on the fabulous prizes at the silent auction.

Faith watched as Avel walked Sasha offstage and then strode for the men's changing room, looking slightly harassed by whatever she was saying to him. He had the excuse of needing to get back into his red satin shirt for the Latin dance, but Faith believed he was actually escaping Sasha's claws. The abandoned blonde sauntered for the ladies' changing room, smirking as she passed Faith. It was a hollow gesture though. Faith knew that she was nervous and angry because Faith and Avel were doing well, too. She might have to share the winner's circle with her rival, and that would disrupt her plans for the evening.

"Ready?" Avel asked, appearing a moment later. Unlike the one he wore for the ballroom dances, this shirt had very few buttons and showed off a good deal of delightful chest.

"Very." And she was. This was her moment—their

moment. They would finally dance the rumba. Nothing—not Sasha, not shoes, not even robotic dinosaurs—was going to spoil this dance.

They walked quickly to the velvet curtain and paused while the emcee requested everyone resume their seats. Lights dimmed in the ballroom. Chairs scraped noisily and people stopped chatting. The mechanical dinosaurs pulled in tight again and the emcee began to blather into the microphone. He looked like someone begging for his life as the predatory booms and mikes swayed overhead, descending on their prey.

Avel waited for their names and their dance to be announced and then walked Faith onto the floor. She felt his hand, warm and firm against her back. Just before the spotlight hit them she was able to take a last look at the room. To either side of the dance floor extra tables had blossomed, a formal border of pastel rounds with eight chair petals at each, where the colorful butterflies that made up the audience alighted. Unlike the preliminary rounds, excitement now rode the air, thicker even than the scent of the tuberose bouquets donated by the Forget-Me-Not Florist.

The spotlight slapped them and Faith barely stifled a flinch. The music began. The beat was staccato, changing the rhythms of her heart, her pulse. A slow wave of sexual energy traveled up Faith's body, beginning at her toes and not stopping when it reached the ends of her hair. She was sure that she must be leaving a trail of passionate red in the air behind them.

Avel drew Faith close and then spun her away with a look of disdain.

They began. This was the play, the highest of drama with a musical score, and they had the stage to themselves while they acted out their assigned roles. Lit with a spotlight, they could feel the audience around them, waiting with stilled breath and fixed gaze to see their dance of passion. Would hearts be broken? Would love triumph? They had paid twenty bucks for a ticket—for charity yes, but still hard-earned money—and they wanted to see madness and obsession and insane lust. Faith was ready to give this to them.

Then she noticed Sasha, standing at the edge of the dance floor, watching them—watching Avel—with eyes that might have been plucked from a territorial Doberman. Her perfume was clear and bitter, and as bracing as smelling salts. In that moment Faith knew for certain that Sasha didn't want Avel because she was attracted to him; this was simply about winning the prize she had set her mind on achieving. Faith knew that she would rather die, shot through and through with poisoned arrows, than let Sasha have him. She would win this competition even if she had to dance herself to death to do it.

As though hearing her thought, her shoe sent a shot of energy into her legs. Almost in unison, Sasha's gaze flashed downward to Faith's feet and there it stayed, fixed on her slippers. Her face was hard, her lips pinched.

She knows, Faith thought. *She's guessed about the shoes.*

There wasn't time to worry.

For the opening of their routine, she did as Avel asked. She pouted and teased and flicked her skirts enough to show off the tops of her stockings. The shoes guided her; no thought about the steps was required. But as the dance went on she failed completely to fling away any of that sexual tension that was building in the room. Instead she netted it, held it, letting the heat gather between them. She wanted them to become one flesh, and it showed in the movements of her body. She knew the judges were captivated, because they were leaning forward in their chairs, their eyes wide and fixed as she turned into a seductress.

Then the room did one of those disconcerting shifts and reality fell away. The music changed tempo and then Faith and Avel were running over a castle wall on a moonlit night, a Spanish maiden pursued through the darkness by an enemy that wished to be her lover, an enemy that she had secretly always desired but to whom she would not easily surrender. Down in the courtyard her people cheered . . .

And then even the castle was gone. They ran through a moonlit meadow, but not far. In a moment, he had her in his strong arms. The lovers sank into the velvet field where they were showered with apple blossoms that fell from quaking trees disturbed by a night wind from the north. Her back was arched over her lover's bended knee as his head bowed toward her bosom. His long black hair fell over her like a veil. She moaned softly, happily. They would at last consummate their love and they—

The music stopped and bright light again hit Faith's eyes and she heard wild cheering. Her lids snapped open and Faith found that she was no longer bathed in moonlight under a sky of a million diamond stars, but rather staring at a crystal chandelier that shed hard bits of fractured light. The cheering multitude was not the distant crowd of villagers screaming for the triumph of their hero subduing the beautiful but haughty maiden; it was her friends and neighbors and even total strangers applauding because the dance was over and partly because her skirt was hiked up and she was showing a lot of thigh and her black lace garter belt.

Faith reached for her skirt and was pulling it down when Avel rose, easily pulling her to her feet. Still dazed and disoriented, she barely remembered to bow as they had practiced and leaned against him as he led her from the floor. She felt both hot with exertion and desire, and yet also chilled.

The first time, when she had danced with Fred Astaire, hadn't been a hallucination. The shoes had done it again, removed her from reality and transported her to another place. She had danced like one possessed out there on the floor, and probably won them a first place in the competition, but was that a good thing? Had she perhaps made a deal with the devil? What would happen when she finally took her shoes off? Would she and Avel ever be able to dance like this again?

Her body still throbbed, deprived of its lover, and maybe a bit with fear. Her mind was in chaos, unable to think.

Avel's movement remained graceful but he was breathing hard, and not all of it was due to the aerobic workout they'd just had. They pushed through the crowd that was still applauding and cheering and made for the dressing room.

"We . . ." He cleared his throat. His cheeks were dark. "I think we're in the finals. That was . . ." He stopped, clearly at a loss for adequate vocabulary.

Faith stumbled and he caught her against him. Heat flared immediately. Avel felt it, too. She saw his eyes dilate and she heard him catch his breath. If she hadn't been wearing double crinolines, she was certain that she would have felt other physical reactions as well.

"You need to rest," he said suddenly, becoming aware that she was flushed and still weak of knee.

Avel lead her to a vacant chair by a window that someone had pried open. From the expanse of leaded glass on the third floor they could hear the sea, muted and melancholic behind a curtain of fog that netted the moonlight and made the night glow silver.

Avel knelt before her. His eyes were bright. His full lips were compressed as though trying to restrain an impulse to speak about inappropriate things.

"Let me help you relax," he murmured, and reached a long-fingered hand for her knee. He massaged the leg gently. Slowly his hand slid down her leg, delicate and almost tickling. He gently squeezed her calf and then cautiously circled her ankle. One finger tucked into the edge of her shoe.

Before she realized his intention, he had taken off her slipper.

"Oh no!" Faith exclaimed as she swooned back in her chair, all strength leaving her body along with her shoe. "What have you done?"

CHAPTER NINE

"Faith? What's wrong? Are you ill?"

"I . . ." She stared at the shoe lying on its side with its smudge of orange paint on the sole, and panic set in. Had the spell really been broken? If not, could she maybe go on wearing only one shoe? She could borrow one shoe from someone else—surely there was another size six somewhere in the room! Or should she just do a Cinderella and run away into the night wearing only one slipper and pray that Avel eventually forgave her for deserting him?

Avel's arm was around her, urging her to sit up.

"Faith?" His voice was low but filled with concern. "You've gone white. What is it?"

Faith forced her eyes to meet his. She had to answer, but what could she possibly say that wouldn't make her sound insane or as stupid as a booger-eating moron?

"I don't know what to do. I don't know if it's safe to put the shoe back on," she finally confessed.

Avel blinked.

"The shoes aren't safe? Are your feet swollen? Have they blistered?" he asked with renewed concern. His hands again reached for her stocking-clad leg. "You were dancing like one possessed. I feared that you might injure yourself."

She shuddered. Yes, she had danced exactly like one possessed. But possessed by what?

"No. It's . . . Avel, it's stupid." She felt herself blushing and hoped he wouldn't notice with all the makeup she was wearing.

"What?" He looked back up from her feet. "My dear, just tell me what's wrong. It can't be that bad."

Faith swallowed hard.

"These shoes are . . . like a good luck charm. But I can only wear them once. Well, twice. But if I put that shoe back on it will be three times, or at least two and a half, and something bad will happen," she finished in a rush. Horrified, she could feel tears gathering in her eyes. She tried not to blink because her mascara wasn't waterproof and she hadn't brought any makeup with her. "If I don't put it back on then we won't win. But if I do put it back on then we might not win either because I'm not really sure what bad thing might happen."

Avel exhaled and looked relieved.

"If that's all. I didn't know you were superstitious. I never would have suspected. You are so very level-headed in every other respect."

"I'm serious, not crazy. Didn't you feel that—that *whatever* out on the dance floor? That wasn't normal. You said I was dancing like one possessed. Well, I was, at least for a while."

"Yes, I certainly did feel it." His smile was wry. Suddenly she was aware of how close his lips were to her own. "But that had nothing to do with your shoes. I often feel this way when I'm around you. It's adrenaline and desire."

"Really?" she asked, surprised out of her incipient panic. The threatened tears receded before they precipitated a cosmetic crisis. "You've never let on that you liked me."

Avel shrugged. The gesture was very French.

"I have been taking my time. Nevertheless, it's true. I *like* you, and we don't need the shoes to win. Let me prove this to you." With a gentle but firm hand, he reached down and lifted her foot. He pulled off her other slipper.

Faith all but moaned, but she didn't stop him. Now she really was in trouble. What was she going to do? Without the shoes she was just her old clumsy self. They could never win. And then he'd be in the winners circle with Sasha—and then maybe he'd fall for the blonde, not realizing that she was just hunting him as some sort of trophy for—

"Leave them," Avel said, standing up. "Walk away with me onto the balcony and get some fresh air. The door is right over here. Come now. You can do this."

"You need to change clothes. Sasha is probably waiting," Faith objected halfheartedly as she took his hand and let him lead her to the French doors. It felt wonderful to have her hand tucked into his. And it might be the last time it would happen, if she really messed up their last dance. He might like her, but would that be enough to compensate for being caught on television dancing with a spaz?

"I can dance in this shirt," Avel said firmly. "I'm

tired of changing clothes. I'll do the last two dances in this costume."

"What did we draw for our last dance?" she asked fearfully. This time the men had chosen papers from the giant brandy snifter. The fact that Avel hadn't shown it to her made Faith nervous.

"Jive."

Jive. That was the highest energy dance, the most physically demanding. She couldn't do it on her own. She was drained, empty. She'd dance like a dachshund, a rabbit, while he went on being a graceful cat.

"Look—I'll wear the shoes again. How bad can it be?" She knew she sounded a bit like a junkie after a fix and tried to rein in her voice.

"Faith—"

"It's okay. I'll gladly do this for you. We can still win it."

"But I don't want you to do it for me," he said gently. "How could you think that I would want you to do anything that would frighten you? Winning isn't as important as your happiness."

"But . . . Look, I'll just try them on. If things feel . . . bad, then I'll take them off again." Faith turned back to the French doors. The chair she had sat in was still there but her shoes were gone.

"Oh no!" she breathed, now truly horrified.

"What?"

"My shoes are gone!"

"Gone?" Avel stepped around her and looked back into the room. His brows drew together. "Wait here and stay calm. I'll ask around. Someone might have just picked them up and taken them to the dressing room by mistake."

Faith felt too weak to move, and so she waited and stayed calm, at least calm in the sense that she wasn't crying or screaming, but her heart sank when Avel returned without her shoes. He was looking rather grim.

"I don't know if it's true, but it sounds like Sasha may have taken your shoes. She isn't in the dressing room, though. Maybe she went to the bathroom."

"Oh." *Sasha. Of course.*

"There must be a reason for this, but I can't find her. No one has seen her since she left the ladies' dressing room."

"It's the shoes. She knows about them," Faith whispered.

"Sasha isn't superstitious," Avel began.

"Neither am I. Well, I wasn't. But those shoes are . . ." *What? Cursed? Blessed?* Faith changed her mind about saying anything mystical. "She doesn't want us to win the competition. This is sabotage."

"Nonsense. She wouldn't do that." But he looked uneasy. "Faith, listen to me. They are a lucky talisman—I understand. But you don't need them to win. At most, this is a petty annoyance. You can't let this affect you."

A voice came over the speakers asking the audience to resume their seats, and for the final three dancers to come to the floor.

"Damn Sasha. Where the devil is she?" Avel demanded. "We are about to miss our cue."

Faith tried to feel cheerful that Avel was finally

annoyed with her rival, but couldn't shake off the feeling of approaching doom. Her stomach told her that something bad was about to happen.

"Avel!" Sasha's voice called from the doorway that led into the woman's bathroom. She sounded triumphant.

"Dammit, Sasha!" Faith had never heard Avel swear at anyone, and had to stare at him. He saw her glance and apologized.

"I'm ready now. I'm—" The voice turned into a squeak and then a full-throated screech. Dancers at the far side of the room began diving out the way as Sasha whirled toward Faith and Avel, doing something that looked like a cancan but was completely out of control. Her arms flapped and she was squawking like a chicken.

Faith felt horrified laughter welling in her throat. It was the shoes! It had to be! And this could have happened to her if she'd put them back on? Thank all the gods and goddesses that Sasha had stolen them before she could step back into them!

"Sasha!" Avel reached for her, but her size-eight left foot—somehow clad in Faith's size-six shoe—kicked his hand away. Before he could snatch at her again, she was out the French door and racing for the railing. Avel swore again, but this time in melodious French.

There were several gasps and screams then, but the loudest by far was Sasha's as she leapt into the air, executed a perfect pirouette, and then fell over the wrought-iron railing. Everyone in the dressing room stood frozen with shock and horror—or, in the case of one couple demoralized by their failure to make the finals, alcohol.

Avel and Faith were the first to move, but before they could reach the balcony, they heard the sound of a splash and then angry thrashing and cursing. Everyone surged for the balcony then, but Avel and Faith got there first.

"The pool," Faith breathed as they reached the railing and looked down. A few smokers exiled to the outdoors for their nicotine fixes were already dropping their butts and moving to assist the thrashing Sasha out of the water. Their efforts were impeded by her flailing legs, which continued to dance the cancan.

"Get them off!" Sasha gurgled. "Get the damn things off me! They're cursed! Ginger Rogers pushed me into the pool!"

"She jumped into the pool!" Avel sounded astounded. "But why? That's just crazy. And what is she talking about? No one pushed her into the pool."

The crowd muttered agreement. Faith thought about insisting that it had been her shoes that caused the accident, but decided not to bother. Avel wasn't going to believe her, and she wasn't sure that she wanted him to.

"Who knows? She may just have cracked under the pressure. It's happened before," Faith lied in a soothing voice, urging him away from the railing. She had to get Avel's mind back on the dance or they wouldn't just lose, they'd be utterly humiliated.

At least one of them had to know what they were doing if they were to turn in even the barest of face-saving performances.

"I'll have to notify the judges, withdraw from the contest, call security . . ."

"I think it's been done," Faith said, looking over at the dressing room, which was now full of uniformed security people who were advancing on the balcony. The other dancers in the finals were gone, called to the dance floor. She wondered if the audience had heard anything, and whether any of Sasha's wild dance had been caught on film. That was one video she wouldn't mind having in her collection.

"Okay." Avel gave himself a shake as the security guards pushed by them. "I'm out of the ballroom competition, but we can still win the Latin division. I will not allow her antics to ruin your evening. You deserve this win. No one has danced better."

Win? He still thought they could win?

"But . . . how can we?" Faith asked, feeling the rough plaster of the balcony snag her stockings. She could maybe dance without magic shoes, but she needed shoes of some kind, didn't she? "I haven't any extra shoes. And even if we got them back from her . . ." She wouldn't wear them for love or money. Well, not for money. Faith finished by saying: "They'd be sopping wet."

"You're right." Avel turned to stare at her. His new expression was what Faith could only call mulish. "Take off your stockings," he said finally.

"Wh-what?"

"Your stockings. They'll just catch on things. Take them off. They're ruined anyway." Avel took a seat in the chair Faith had been using and began to untie his own shoes.

"What are you doing?" she demanded with trepidation.

"We're dancing barefoot." Avel looked grim and full of purpose. This obviously wasn't a joke.

"Can we? Is it allowed?" she asked.

"There's no rule against it," Avel said. "Some of the cabaret dancers do it. I can't imagine they'll try and stop us. After what happened with Sasha, it would look like they were deliberately trying to keep me out of the competition."

Faith again thought about arguing with her partner, but again chose discretion. Obviously Avel wanted this and she didn't have the will to say no to him. He'd be disappointed soon enough. "Okay. We'll dance barefoot."

It took a bit of maneuvering to escape her garter belt with her modesty intact, but a minute later she had peeled her hose off her legs and draped them over the back of the chair. She was feeling very grateful that she had shaved, and that the television would not be immortalizing their last competitive dance with her sporting hairy legs.

Faith was only aware that there had been music playing when the ballroom competition ended. Two names were announced and there was loud applause.

"Doris and Rowan won," Avel said, glancing toward the stage. The curtains parted and a happy couple pushed through. "Congratulations," he called to them. Then to Faith: "We're up first. Are you ready to jive?"

He is running for his dinner.

I am running for my life.

"As ready as I'll ever be," Faith said, echoing her earlier words, but not entirely sure she meant it. In her heart of hearts, she thought she might be more ready in about April of 2009.

"Then smile, my dear. By joyous. This one is for the record books. We've made the finals. Win or lose, this is the part of the evening where we get to have some fun." Avel's own smile was genuine as he offered her his hand. His eyes sparkled, daring her to be happy with him.

Unable to help herself, Faith smiled back as she took it. He might have been shaken by Sasha's leap into the pool but he had recovered his aplomb. She would do the same. That much she could give him.

"Let's go make history," she said.

CHAPTER TEN

Without her shoes, Faith would have to rely on her own resources. She smiled blindly as they walked onto the cool dance floor and rapidly reviewed what she knew of the jive. Most jive was danced at thirty-two beats-per-minute, but in competition it was revved up to forty-four bpm. The steps of the basic dance were simple enough. They were a fast syncopated chasse that went side-close-side-left then side-close-side to the right. She also had to remember to keep her weight on the balls of her feet. That was what made the dance appear springy and weightless. In some ways, this would be easier to do without shoes, though she'd have to watch the landings. Avel had trained in the Ceroc style while her method might best be described as Jumpin' Jive. The two styles were very close, though, and they shouldn't have any problems if they didn't get too fancy.

The opening notes of "Boogie Woogie Bugle Boy" began to play, and Faith allowed herself to feel a moment of hope. She had danced this many times with her father when she was small and was used to doing all the traditional lifts, dips, drops, and seducers. Of course, she'd been a lot younger the last time she'd danced this song, but she was sure that she could handle anything Avel threw at her. She let some extra bounce move into her hips, telling him that she was ready to go.

Avel's hand felt warm in hers. In fact it was more than that. It was almost as if she could feel his energy sinking into her muscles. In fact, it seemed an awful lot like what had happened when she was wearing her shoes, though this time she felt no fear. The dance seemed effortless as they began, as though they were of one mind that controlled both bodies.

They made their first show move, a double-assisted spin drop. Faith had only tried this once, but as Avel's hand tucked in at the back of her head, she allowed herself to trust that he would keep her safe and shifted her balance as required to follow his lead. Grateful that she didn't sprain an ankle or bounce her head off the floor, Faith was only dimly aware that the audience began clapping.

Then they were flying over the golden floor. Hip rolls moved into a Lady Lean. Then they did a New York Sweep, a double-return head-chopper, a seducer sweep, and then a rotating tango lunge. Faith's skirt snapped audibly like a flag on a windy day, and sparks of light scattered over the audience. The crowd roared its wholehearted approval of their favorite couple.

And then it was over. A last drop, a last pose, and they were done. The judges made a show of conferring, but the decision was made in seconds. A paper was passed to the emcee. Their names were announced to further cheers and applause. Flowers were stuffed into her arms and Avel was handed a trophy. The audience, ignoring the velvet ropes, swarmed the dance floor, and the TV cameras crowded in trying to get a look at Faith's tonsils—or perhaps to peer up her skirts now that she was missing her stockings. She and Avel were separated before she could thank him or hug him or kiss him, or even just say a good-bye.

Faith looked about quickly, feeling suddenly naked and depressed. She saw Avel being herded toward the judges' table where the sponsors were gathered, and she started in his direction, but before she could follow, her boss was there, shaking her hand and introducing his wife, Sharon. Retaining just enough sense to know that it would be unwise to blow him off, Faith made herself stay and smile politely.

"I never imagined you had so many talents," Norton told her.

"Thank you. I never imagined it, either," Faith said. And then she went on saying some version of this to every person who rushed in to congratulate her as she fought her way toward the place she had last seen Avel. The muscles in her face began to cramp and her teeth got dry, but aware of the cameras and that her family would eventually see this, she forced her smile to remain in place.

At the moment when she felt she had reached the very end of her fraying rope, Avel again appeared at her side. He took her arm in a firm grip and pulled her toward the dressing room. His smile no longer looked sincere.

"I don't care what the camera crew wants, we're leaving before the conga line," he said as they passed through the velvet curtains. He didn't stop to retrieve his clothing, and Faith didn't suggest they linger. Avel headed for the stairwell, and though her legs were suddenly tired and her feet had begun to ache, Faith followed after him, wanting nothing so much as to have a moment alone in which to savor their impossible victory.

Though Faith thought Avel would immediately dash down the stairs and out to the parking lot, he paused the moment the door closed behind them, shutting them into relative quiet.

"I've been wanting to do this for weeks," he said, and then cupped her head as though getting ready to perform another dangerous spin drop. But instead of moving them toward the concrete floor, he pulled her body close and finally—finally—he kissed her.

The feel of his body against hers was stunning, a shock to the nervous system. First kisses left her feeling more nervous than aroused, a part of her hanging back, analyzing. But not this time. His flesh seemed to burn against her skin even through two layers of clothing. His arms, which had been around her much of the evening, were now bands of steel, holding her close. They touched chest to chest and thigh to thigh. His breath tickled her lips and his eyes glittered.

The first touch of their mouths was light, soft as a whisper, a small hint that tantalized the nerve endings. His lips were firm, warm, tender. But they lingered teasingly, and she could once again feel the heat building between them. The air around them seemed to shimmer. She closed her eyes and waited to be taken away. Shyly, heat unfurled inside her, urging her closer.

Lured in, in spite of the fact that she knew there was every chance that they would be discovered by others hoping to avoid the crowds, she threw caution to the wind and parted her lips.

A feeling of rightness or perfection spread through her, an antidote for all the tension and the worry of the night. She wanted him in other ways—of course she did—but the here and now was perfect. She would be content to share this kiss for the rest of her life.

A fire started in her belly and rushed through her blood, a brush fire in dry emotional timber that was quickly out of her control. She willingly burned, giving herself to the greedy desire that consumed everything, even the air in her lungs. His lips left her mouth, moved to ear and then her throat. Had he said something? She couldn't tell; blood was roaring in her ears, louder even than her heart. A quick gasped breath and then she turned her head, her lips again seeking his.

Avel obliged her. His left hand found her waist. The heat in his fingers scorched her even through the beading of her bustier, which was tight, strangling. She might even die from lack of air, but didn't care.

He finally, reluctantly broke the kiss. The separation was wrenching, disorienting, and it took a moment for the floor and ceiling to right themselves.

Faith realized that she was clutching the banister. Both of them were breathing too hard and this time she felt his body's arousal even through two crinolines and a heavy velvet skirt. It was all she could do not to press herself back into him.

"Just for the record," Avel said. His voice was rougher than usual and his expression bemused. "This thing between us is not, and has never been, caused by shoes. I've wanted you until I'm all but cross-eyed, but not because you are wearing high heels. Hell, I even wanted you when you were wearing those hideous brown, flat-footed sandals that no attractive woman should wear. And I am begging you now to burn them."

"Of course it wasn't the shoes that made me want you," Faith agreed. Her desire for Avel had always been there. That wasn't what the shoes had given her. Scary as they were, the slippers had lent her the courage to believe that she could actually pursue him in the way that he loved best. Without them, she might never have found the fortitude to accept his invitation to dance, and seduced him on the dance floor.

"Okay. Just so that we're clear about this. It's you—and it's always been you that I want."

"It's crystal clear," she agreed, taking his offered hand and allowing him to lead her down the stairs and into the night.

AUTHOR NOTE

As you may have guessed, I love to dance. I don't do it particularly well, but I do it often and fantasize like crazy whenever I watch *Dancing With The Stars*. Any errors about the technical side of the dances or competition are my fault and I will say my mea culpas now.

The Santa Cruz in *And They Danced* is not completely accurate in every detail, though the general outlines of the state of mind are correct. There is no Hotel Corazon on the beach and I sincerely hope that no one named Faith Fleetwood or Avel Berault live there. Otherwise, I think you'll find the town much as I describe it.

I hope you'll visit *www.Hiheelia.com*, and please don't worry about killer dancing shoes. Those are a figment of my overheated imagination.

As ever, I hope you will write if you have comments, questions, or want to gush profusely about the story. You can find me at either *melaniejaxn@hotmail.com*, *www.melaniejackson.com*, or PO Box 574, Sonora, CA 95370-0574.

Be well. Be happy. And if you can't be good, be careful.

Melanie Jackson

☐ **YES!**

Sign me up for the Love Spell Book Club and send my
FREE BOOKS! If I choose to stay in the club, I will pay only
$8.50* each month, a savings of $6.48!

NAME: _____

ADDRESS: _____

TELEPHONE: _____

EMAIL: _____

☐ I want to pay by credit card.

☐ **VISA**   ☐ **MasterCard**   ☐ **DISCOVER**

ACCOUNT #: _____

EXPIRATION DATE: _____

SIGNATURE: _____

Mail this page along with $2.00 shipping and handling to:
Love Spell Book Club
PO Box 6640
Wayne, PA 19087
Or fax (must include credit card information) to:
610-995-9274

You can also sign up online at **www.dorchesterpub.com**.
*Plus $2.00 for shipping. Offer open to residents of the U.S. and Canada only. Canadian
residents please call 1-800-481-9191 for pricing information.
If under 18, a parent or guardian must sign. Terms, prices and conditions subject to
change. Subscription subject to acceptance. Dorchester Publishing reserves the right to
reject any order or cancel any subscription.